Gillian dropped her jacket on the floor.

She sank to the bed, trying not to think about the long-term consequences of what she had in mind. Eyes steadily on his, she raised her arms.

She might have wanted him to say something. But the sound of the light switch plunging the room into darkness was all she got from Mitch Valetti.

His silence would have bothered her if he hadn't undressed her with such reverence and touched her so tenderly that a lack of words didn't matter. Tonight it was enough to know they were safe. To know that Mitch was one of the good guys. To know she was powerless to change how she felt about him and equally powerless to change their circumstances.

Mitch represented the very best of the good guys in Gillian's estimation. If this short week was all the time she would be granted to love him, then so be it.

And if, by some miracle, she was already carrying his child…she would deem it a gift.

Available in May 2004 from Silhouette Superromance

Lost But Not Forgotten

ROZ DENNY FOX

SILHOUETTE® SUPERROMANCE™

*Silhouette, Silhouette Superromance and Colophon are
registered trademarks of Harlequin Books S.A., used under licence.*

*First published in Great Britain 2004
Silhouette Books, Eton House, 18-24 Paradise Road,
Richmond, Surrey TW9 1SR*

© Rosaline Fox 2001

ISBN 0 373 71013 5

38-0504

*Printed and bound in Spain
by Litografia Rosés S.A., Barcelona*

Dear Reader,

In writing *The Baby Cop*, I found Ethan Knight's partner, Mitch Valetti, to be a character worthy of his own story. In the first book, Ethan and Regan were married in Mitch's hospital room while he recovered from multiple bullet wounds. His love interest, Amy Knight, had begun seriously dating someone else and later eloped with her newest love. Few writers would be able to walk away and leave a nice guy hurting in body and heart the way Mitch hurt. Especially if that man indicates by word and deed that he would like to have a family of his own. So I promptly went in search of the perfect partner for Mitch, and found a woman who has lost the most important thing in her life—a baby. Gillian Noelle McGrath (or sometimes Gillian Stevens, her alias) is also on the run from a difficult situation. What better lap to land in than that of an ex-policeman who hasn't quite let go of his profession?

I hope you enjoy reading about Mitch and Gillian's rocky path to love!

Roz Denny Fox

Readers can contact me by post or e-mail. My address is PO Box 17480-101, Tucson, Arizona 85731, USA, and you can reach me by e-mail at: rdfox@worldnet.att.net.

CHAPTER ONE

"YOUR HUSBAND got himself into trouble, Mrs. Mc-Grath. Dirty as sin, and big from the sound of it."

The woman glanced uneasily around the empty precinct parking lot before letting her gaze settle on the kindly old cop Daryl had instructed her to meet in Flagstaff, Arizona. Fall was definitely in the air. Leaves from the cottonwoods skipped across the asphalt in the brisk wind. She pulled her jacket tighter. "Daryl and I…were divorced, Sergeant Malone," she blurted. "Now he's dead." Her voice thinned. She raked a nervous hand through pale-blond hair that brushed her collar each time she moved. Tears welled in her pleading blue eyes. "I'm trying to say I don't understand any of this."

"Neither do I. But I watched Daryl grow up. I'd stake my life on him being a straight arrow, Noelle."

"Shouldn't you call me Gillian? Gillian Stevens is the name on the driver's license and Mississippi car registration Daryl insisted I use…even though we live in New Orleans. Oh, nothing makes sense. How—*why* did he phony up a social security card and driver's license?" She blotted away tears and braced her hip against the car Malone had just finished searching.

The portly cop, who'd been a second dad to her exhusband, shook his gray head. "Daryl was scared, I can tell you that. His one e-mail to me is proof. I only wish I'd had the chance to explain I'm two weeks away from retirement. This is the type of case for a young cop. On the other hand, missy, you've gotta be careful who you trust. A money-laundering operation the size of the one Daryl hinted at isn't anything to mess with.''

''There must be some mistake. Daryl wouldn't—'' The prediction falling from her lips was cut short by squealing tires. Breaking off, she straightened. A sinking sun struck the windshield of a car bearing down on them. Splintered rays blinded Gillian.

Malone moved fast for an old man. Hooking a beefy arm around her waist, he spun her out of the path of the onrushing vehicle even as it clipped him hard.

She felt the impact separate their two bodies, and gazed in horror as the policeman flew up and was dragged twenty yards or so by a wildly careening blue car. She scrambled to the curb, not daring to breathe. Finally Malone was dislodged, and Gillian ran to where he lay crumpled on the pavement.

''Help!'' she shouted at two uniformed cops who'd been heading up the steps into the station. They had either heard the blue car's acceleration, or had seen the hit-and-run, and were already in motion.

Gillian's limbs shook so violently she didn't know how she'd managed to keep from fainting. Clearly Malone's left arm and leg had suffered fractures. Blood trickled from his nose and mouth. ''It was them,'' she whispered. ''The men who've been following me. I thought I lost them in El Paso.''

Malone had great difficulty breathing, yet he wheezed out instructions. ''Get…the hell…out of here. Now. Go south. Hide.''

''No! I can't. You need help.'' Clutching his hand in both of hers, she kept shaking her head.

He coughed raspily. Gillian cried out again to the two

cops darting between parked cars. Both had drawn their weapons, but they seemed bent on chasing after the blue car instead of assisting Malone.

"Don't be a damn fool," Patrick choked out. "Run, but watch your step."

His hand went limp in hers. Gillian laid her ear against his chest. She wasn't sure whether the rattle she heard was good news or bad.

Stay or run? Torn, she made a split-second decision that he, being a cop, knew best. It was a miracle her shaking legs actually carried her back to her car. After executing a wobbly U-turn, Gillian did her best to blend with the parked cars until she worked her way to the opposite side of the police station and merged with street traffic.

Less than a mile from the precinct, she came to a clover leaf and followed signs directing her south on the interstate. She spotted the blue car on an overpass. At least, it *looked* like the vehicle used in the attempt on her life. *She would be dead if not for Malone's bravery.* The thought gave her chills.

Gillian fought the panic threatening to overwhelm her. Daylight was fading. Oncoming cars had begun to turn on their lights. She checked her rearview mirror for the umpteenth time before she realized it was impossible to tell the color of the cars spread out behind her. Sweat ran down her spine, welding her T-shirt to her vinyl seat cushion. She drove aimlessly, constantly peering over her shoulder.

Minutes ticked into a quarter hour, then to half an hour. Odd things registered. For instance, how flat the land was and how long it took for the sun to actually set. And it was warmer here than it'd been in Flagstaff.

Dusk gradually deepened, but she still didn't know

where to hide. Fearful of being overtaken, she eventually left the interstate. So did several other cars. The blue car—she felt it drawing closer. After driving miles on the perimeter road, she saw a graveled road angling off to the south. Blindly, she turned. A series of bumps and pings made her flinch as gravel struck the car's undercarriage. Her headlights illuminated a split-rail fence lining both sides.

The road's condition required her to reduce her speed. She prayed that this obscure byway led to a small Western town, where she could find an innocuous, run-down motel. She needed to grab a nap and think out her next steps.

Provided *they* didn't catch her first.

Of all the things crowding her mind, she suddenly remembered one—that today was her thirtieth birthday. What a way to spend it. Using an assumed name, running from thugs she didn't know, for reasons not fully clear. Reasons involving her ex-husband's CPA firm.

One thing that *was* clear—the thugs wanted her dead. They'd already killed Daryl. Suddenly. Violently. And then poor Officer Malone...

A stab of raw fear chased goose bumps along Gillian's skin underneath the sweat. *She didn't want to die!* The discovery itself surprised her. For the last ten months, she hadn't cared one way or the other.

Once again her eyes strayed to the rearview mirror. There was blackness in her wake. She rolled her shoulders, wishing her mind would be still, wishing she could focus on her dilemma. Had she managed to elude the blue car? If so, good. Except...where was she? This road stretched into nothingness. "You were stupid, stupid, stupid not to stay on a better-marked highway," she muttered to herself.

Bam! The car fishtailed all over the bumpy road.

Gillian screamed. At first she thought she'd been shot at and she lost her grip on the steering wheel. When she reassessed the situation, jamming her foot on the brake, the car stopped inches from the fence. The way it lurched told her she'd blown a front tire. That was a relief, and yet it wasn't.

Here she sat in the middle of God-knew-where. The landscape had gradually begun to change. What was desert had evolved into brush and trees along the fence. The minute she stepped from the car, she'd be vulnerable, a target for anyone hidden in among those trees. Dropping her forehead to the steering wheel, Gillian listened to her hammering heart.

She couldn't drive on a flat. Nor could she sit there all night hoping for a white knight to ride up and save her.

Slowly, with shaking hands, she switched off the engine. Leaving only her parking lights on, she slid from the car on unsteady legs and quietly opened the trunk, using the penlight attached to her keychain for illumination. All the while, she prayed for a decent spare tire. Not for the first time since she'd been drawn into this insane ordeal did she long for the safe world she'd left behind. This was a nightmare. "Oh, Daryl, what did you get us into?"

She dug through the trunk and took out a satchel filled with emergency supplies—a lantern, a first-aid kit, bottled water and a box of granola bars. Some of her panic faded as she removed the two suitcases Daryl had packed for her. Even in haste, his attention to detail was reassuring.

Except now he was dead.

Refusing to allow useless tears, Gillian muscled out the spare tire. She tripped and almost fell over the smaller of the two suitcases. Scooting it aside, she retrieved the jack and the tire iron. Thankfully, her father—rest his soul—had taught her to change a tire years ago. She hoped the skill came back easily.

Never one to procrastinate, Gillian bent right to the task. She'd just finished tightening the last lug when she felt, more than heard, a low rumble—a vibration in the gravel road under her feet. Glancing in both directions, she saw car lights on high beam coming toward her, along the section of roadway she'd already traveled. Gray shapes danced eerily along the fence row. Gillian's pulse leaped wildly.

"Oh, no," she sobbed. "They've found me!"

Her hands slick from sweat as well as grease, Gillian struggled to shove the blown tire into its rightful place in the wheel well. She'd have to stop at the next service station and get it fixed; the way things were going, she'd probably need it again. It landed crooked, hiked higher on one side so she couldn't put back the carpet. There seemed to be far less room in the once spacious trunk.

Fear made her clumsy. She was all thumbs trying to force the large suitcase in beside the satchel. At last, the case slid inside. Dousing her penlight, she slammed the trunk lid closed.

The oncoming lights grew larger, like an angry cat's eyes piercing the black night. Gillian fought the bile rising in her throat. She jumped into her car. Her hand shook so hard it took three tries to fit the key into the ignition. The approaching headlights were mere yards away when finally her engine caught and the car shot forward.

At the last minute, Gillian remembered her parking lights. She knew it was reckless to travel an unknown road without proper illumination. But the thought of what would happen if the thugs caught her drove her to do unwise things.

Without warning, the lane narrowed further. Too late, Gillian realized this must be someone's private drive. Maybe it led to a farmhouse, and she could throw herself on the owner's mercy.

And ask them to phone the police? "OhGodOh-GodOhGod!" If Officer Malone had died, she had, in effect, fled the scene of a hit-and-run murder.

The lane came to an abrupt end. Or rather, it became a keyhole-shaped area in front of a single-story ranch house. A house devoid of light.

Frantic, Gillian braked and let the car idle. "Think," she commanded. "What to do?" Massaging her temples, she willed her terror to subside. She dared not go back the way she'd come.

Her gaze swept the moonlit landscape. Her addled brain registered a barn and scattered outbuildings. Both the house and barn were flanked by pastures. Off to her left, about a mile as the crow flies, ghostly car lights bobbed, passing one another. This ranch apparently sat between the perimeter road she'd left and another highway that paralleled the mountains. All that stood between her and escape was a spindly fence and a few acres of raw desert.

Closing her eyes, she gunned the motor and smashed through the rails. Restoring her headlights, she prayed there was nothing on the flat expanse of land that would blow another tire. Bumping across the uneven ground, Gillian tried to keep an eye on the headlights rounding the bend of the lane she'd left. As she drew even, the other car seemed to slow down. Once again her heart climbed into her throat. She couldn't bear to look. What if they'd recognized her? Pressing hard on the gas, Gillian focused on escape.

MITCH VALETTI, former Desert City, Arizona detective, cruised along the private lane leading to his ranch. It'd been three months since he'd driven this route. Three endless months he'd spent recovering from bullet wounds at the home of his best friend and former partner, Ethan Knight. Mitch felt he shouldn't have intruded as long as he had. Ethan and Regan were newlyweds. They already had their hands full caring for the quadruplets Ethan had rescued from an abusive home. The bastard who'd knocked those defenseless babies around was also responsible for firing three slugs into Mitch. Three slugs that had caused nerve damage in his leg and left him with a limp.

That wasn't why he'd stuck around longer than he should have, all the while allowing a neighbor to care for his stock. It had just seemed easier than coming home, facing a life that was in shambles.

His odd melancholy tonight had little to do with his injury—which wasn't his first. He'd survived being knifed in the stomach a few years back when he'd gone in alone on a domestic dispute call. His staying at Ethan's wasn't connected to the doc's news that he'd be left with a permanent disability. Mitch had dealt with that early on. Almost immediately after waking from the extensive surgery, he'd made up his mind to resign from the force. To expand his horse herd. Although he'd told Ethan he might take a few private investigative jobs on the side. Just until his ranch stood on its own.

When Ethan and Regan tied the knot in his hospital room, Mitch thought his own future looked, if not bright, okay. He owned and leased enough land to raise horses, had a serviceable home and loyal friends—including a woman he was pretty crazy about. Amy Knight, Ethan's youngest sister.

Hell, he knew Amy didn't feel the same about him. She flaunted the fact that she'd been dating Desert City's prissy-faced, wonder-boy district attorney. Deep down, though, Mitch had assumed Amy would come to her senses. She hadn't. Instead, she'd eloped with the jerk D.A. while Mitch was recovering. He'd never admit to anyone on the force how much Amy's defection hurt. Especially not to Ethan. To Ethan and their fellow cops, Mitch represented the consummate swinging bachelor. In truth, Amy's marriage had ripped the heart out of him. For the first time in his thirty-five years, Mitch questioned life's purpose.

Oh, he knew his friends had seen a change in him and were worried about his moodiness. Because of that the Knights had insisted he stay on, and he'd hung around several weeks beyond when he probably should've bid the newlyweds farewell. Ethan had gone back to work right away, and Regan's at-home social work private practice was taking off. The quads, two boys and two girls, cute little tykes, would probably miss him the most. Already he missed them. Darn, but those rascals had gotten under his skin. Wouldn't the cops who gathered at Flo's Café to eat and shoot the breeze get a walloping laugh if they ever found out he envied them their families?

Mitch snorted inelegantly and contemplated how that image contrasted with his life. Man, maybe he should've stopped at Flo's before coming home tonight. Guys and gals from the precinct tended to hang out there between shifts. He probably just needed to get back in the swing of things.

The very thought lifted his spirits. ''Shoot, how can a man feel down when he's lucky enough to be behind the steering wheel of a sweet baby-blue fully restored '68 Corvette?'' Grinning foolishly, Mitch caressed the steering wheel. He nearly missed the flash of his headlights off metal ahead.

Chrome. Damned if there wasn't a car without running lights parked in his lane. He'd worked too many drug busts to shrug off the significance of a car traveling without lights after dark. And this one was moving. Mitch could hear the sound of the other car's engine, too. It was plain the driver didn't have a hankering to stick around.

Mitch's headlights barely pierced the swirl of dust kicked up by the fast-departing car. Mitch tried to make out its type, but as he peered out his windshield, he plunged into a curve in the lane.

Pressing on his gas pedal, Mitch was determined to read the license plate before the car reached his turnaround and came back at him with lights on bright. Only reactions long-honed by his police training saved him from plowing into something sitting in the road—a small suitcase. He braked and swerved.

Once he'd squealed to a stop, Mitch sat there a moment, sweat beading on his brow, his teeth clamped tight to stave off the pain he'd brought to his bad leg. Fighting off a wave of dizziness, he backed the hell up fast and scrambled to locate his cell phone.

Cursing, he watched the other car disappear and decided to relinquish the chase. Instead, he punched in the number of the precinct's bomb squad. Why else would someone drop a suitcase on a private rural road at night? Especially as the drop coincided with an ex-cop's arrival... If Mitch didn't know for certain that the crazy who'd shot him was locked up tight, he might think Tony DeSalvo had come back to finish the job.

DeSalvo wasn't the only creep he'd ticked off in his career, though. Just the latest. Tony was still safely put away—Mitch verified that first. He had no clue who'd left him a hot calling card, but he would damn sure find out as soon as the sucker discovered this road dead-ended.

"What the hell?" Mitch saw headlights bobbing across his west pasture. He slid out of the Vette, wincing at the stabbing pain in his left leg. Hands on hips, he watched the fleeing car slow midway in its run to intercept the 181 cutoff. Probably waiting to see him blown to smithereens.

"Sorry to disappoint you," he muttered darkly as the distant vehicle sped up again. He ought to notify the county sheriff, whose territory was intersected by Highway 181, but Mitch knew they couldn't respond in time. The perpetrator could turn north and lose himself in Tucson's winter-visitor traffic, or turn south and cross the border into Mexico at Agua Prieta. Either way, they'd shake a tail. So rather than give futile chase, he'd be better off seeing if his old department's bomb squad could lift any prints from the suitcase. It shouldn't be hard with the new computer system to cross-match prints to any of the bad guys he'd helped put away during his six years on the force.

It took fifteen minutes for his former co-workers to show up. Mack Rich and Pete Haslett wore gear that made them look as if they were headed to the moon. They seemed particularly eerie in the hazy spotlights they trained on the item in the lane.

"Wow, cowboy," quipped a third member of the team. "You really know how to throw a homecoming.

Since it could get hotter than your standard college bon-fire around here, I suggest you move that classic car before it gets torched, ruining your day and mine.''

Mitch, long used to being tagged "the Italian cowboy" by his comrades at the station, complied without taking issue with their friendly taunts.

"No audible ticking," shouted the dough boy closest to the suitcase. "Could be she's set to explode the minute anyone lifts her. Let's give the case a shot with the X-ray camera to see the setup inside." He turned to Mitch. "You said you saw a car drop the suitcase and leave the scene? Did you get a plate and a make?"

Mitch stood well back from the others while they readied a boom attached to a portable X-ray unit in the bomb van. "I saw a car," he said with a grimace. "It was already in motion. I swerved to avoid the bag and missed getting details. I figured something was fishy. The car ran without lights and didn't turn around at my ranch where the road ends. The driver took out across the field. Had to have torn out a section of my fence."

"Doesn't sound good, buddy. On the other hand, the X ray doesn't show any wiring in the case. One metal object, and it's not in the center as I'd expect to see with a bomb device. See, it's off to the right. Looks like some kind of…vase."

"A *vase?*" Mitch's breath whooshed out in disgust. "Damn, who would've believed that? Sorry I called you out on a wild-goose chase. Shall I go ahead and open it?"

"Not yet." Pete dragged him away. "Mack will pick it up with a grapple, drop it in a padded container and I'll douse it with cryogenic foam. A layer of supercold compound will freeze any components if they're assembled in that pretty little bottle just to throw us off," he added by way of explanation. "The vase could be made of lead."

Mitch nodded. He leaned against his car to ease the pain radiating from his left hip while he watched the process unfold.

"Now!" one of the squad members called. "Pop the lock and see what we have. You want the honor, Valetti?"

"Sure." Mitch limped forward and accepted the tool they handed him to pick the lock. The suitcase lid sprang open, revealing a stiff quilt. The officers' flashlights glinted off ice crystals beaded on appliqués of yellow ducks, pink cats, green elephants and blue dogs. A frilly, tiny pink dress and bonnet lay folded neatly next to the quilt. Tucked in one corner was a silver bottle with an ornate stopper.

"It's an urn," murmured Lori Peck, the only female member of team.

"What?" Mitch raised his eyes and squinted at her through the ring of bright floodlights.

"Ashes," she said more clearly, as if the men were dense. "What we've attacked and put through the wringer is nothing more than a suitcase filled with somebody's memories."

Mitch knelt, ignoring what it cost him in added pain. "Sad memories," he said, hesitantly using the tongs he'd been handed to lift the urn.

Light from Pete's torch reflected off a raised teddy bear on one side of the vessel.

Mitch felt his heart lurch. "It says Our Beloved Katie," he whispered, his voice unsteady. "Below that is a single date, 11-18-00." He set the silver vase almost reverently back on the quilt. Rising awkwardly, he cleared his throat. "A baby girl. She must have died at birth."

Mitch fought against his heart turning inside out over a kid he'd never even known.

"Odd thing to leave sitting in the middle of a country road," Mack said. Turning away, he began to stow their gear.

The female cop retrieved an evidence bag from the front of the truck. After donning plastic gloves, she started to close the suitcase and slide it into the bag.

"Hey, what are you doing?" Mitch demanded.

"Bagging the evidence," she returned shortly. "It's creepy. A crime that goes beyond malicious mischief."

"Uh-uh." He shook his head vigorously. "What crime has been committed? Whoever packed that case *cared* about these things. I'm not going to let you toss them into the evidence room like so much garbage."

Mack shot out a hand and gripped Mitch's arm. "You said the car took off like a bat out of hell, no lights. Granted, that's not a criminal act in itself. But you've got to admit it's suspicious."

"Did you ever think the owner meant for someone to find this stuff? What if baby Katie's mother is being dragged around in that car against her will?"

"You mean, like kidnapped?" Lori asked.

"Maybe. I don't know. I'll grant you it sounds off the wall." Mitch brushed a thumb back and forth over his lower lip. "All I know is these are...they aren't... Hell, it's clear Katie is *somebody's* baby."

"Well, duh!" was Pete's helpful response.

Ignoring him, Mitch didn't budge. "Leave the case, please. I've got time to look into this. I'll do my level best to find out who left it here and why."

His friends from the force glanced from one to the other until at last all had shrugged. Lori shoved a clipboard with an evidence release form into Mitch's hands.

"Sign for it here. If the chief has a problem with this after we file our report, he'll let you know."

Pete tried again to dissuade Mitch. "If it was me, Valetti, I'd forget the whole deal. What kind of person carries stuff like this around in a suitcase?"

"Somebody off their rocker," Mack supplied.

"Or someone in big trouble." Mitch scrawled his name on the form. "I'll place an ad in tomorrow's paper. I had my phone turned off, but I've got my cellular. That's probably the most I'll have to do to solve this mystery."

The others just shook their heads. After telling Mitch not to be a stranger around the station, they said goodbye and backed out to the perimeter highway.

Mitch stowed the suitcase in his trunk. When he arrived home, he saw he'd been right about the section of fence being knocked down. Clearly someone had seen his car coming down the road, panicked and hightailed it off his property.

As he unlocked the front door, juggling his odd collection of objects, he worried that maybe Pete was right. Maybe he should hand the suitcase over as evidence and forget the whole thing.

But when he set the small valise on his coffee table and examined its heart-stopping contents, the haunting connection he'd felt earlier only grew stronger. Placing the urn on his mantel, he gazed at it for a long time. In the end, he renewed his vow to find its owner.

Before retiring, Mitch sat and chewed on the end of a pencil while he composed an ad to run in the local paper. Tomorrow was Thursday. He'd run it through Sunday, he decided, and when he shed his clothing and climbed into bed, his life again seemed to have purpose.

GILLIAN DROVE onto the asphalt highway with a bump and thump. She turned south without hesitation. An hour later, faced with showing false ID to cross the border, or hunting up a passable motel in the dusty border town on U.S. soil, she chose to stop short of Mexico. She had to hold on to some scruples.

Seeking the least accessible motel, she rented an end unit, the one farthest from the cobbled motel entry. It was a relief to find the room clean. Hidden parking in the rear was a big plus. The rent, cheaper by the week, fit her budget, too. It occurred to Gillian as she went out to get her bags that she'd already begun to think like a fugitive.

In a week she ought to be able to alter her appearance enough to fool the men chasing her. She'd have to dump this car. With luck, she might be able to sell it to a private party and buy another in a different town. That's what crooks in movies did.

Tonight she was too exhausted to plan beyond that. The money Daryl had left in the glove box along with her phony ID wouldn't last forever. Eventually she'd have to find a job. She'd face that ordeal later—if she made it through the week she'd paid for in advance.

Gillian refused to dwell on the fact she was probably a wanted person in New Orleans and Flagstaff. Before she ditched this car, she'd go over it inch by inch, searching every nook and cranny again. Daryl had e-mailed Patrick Malone, saying that when Gillian arrived she'd have in her possession a key. To open what, Daryl hadn't said. He hinted that he'd hidden a notebook with enough lethal information to expose a huge money-laundering operation. He also indicated to Malone that he suspected they were on to him. Daryl had promised to contact Patrick later via a different source. He'd never had the opportunity.

She and Malone had failed to turn up a key. Now Daryl was dead, and probably Patrick, too. She would be next if she didn't unearth what Daryl had put in safekeeping. Gillian knew him too well to think he'd forgotten to put the key in her belongings. *But where?* Could it be so small it'd fallen out in the police parking lot and they'd missed it?

Her brain numb, Gillian pawed through the car's trunk looking for the smaller of her two cases. Had it slipped behind the tire? "It's not here!" she cried. "Where is it?" In spite of the late hour, and her questionable surroundings, Gillian removed everything from the trunk. The small case wasn't there.

Her stomach heaved. Tears coursed down her cheeks. That case contained all she had left in the world that was dear to her.

Last Monday, she'd been nothing but confused when Daryl awakened her, babbling. She'd watched as, in a frenzy, he packed the small case and a larger one. The night was still blurred in her mind. For too long, she'd been an emotional wreck—a decline that had begun when she'd first broached the idea of starting a family. Daryl resisted. Said he wanted to wait. Until his CPA firm was more secure. Until they had more money in the bank. Until she could sell her flower shop and stay home full-time. Silly reasons, she'd thought.

So she had defied Daryl, stopped her birth control pills and gotten pregnant almost overnight. That definitely strained an already strained relationship. In hindsight, she wished she could go back and change everything.

Especially the part where something went horribly wrong in the last month of her pregnancy, resulting in the stillbirth of her long-awaited daughter. The rift widened between her and Daryl because after the autopsy, while she was heavily sedated in the hospital, he'd unilaterally arranged for baby Katie's cremation. Oh, he attempted to explain. Families who'd lived in New Orleans for generations had access to above-ground burial vaults. Others, like them, had limited choices. He'd done what he believed was best, he'd told her.

For weeks, Gillian had wept. Weeks turned into months during which she couldn't eat, sleep or work. Daryl did the opposite. He rarely came home from the office. And so after six months of that, they'd split, bound only by their joint partnership in Daryl's firm. Maybe if she'd been a more active partner…if she hadn't sunk into emotional oblivion, perhaps she wouldn't be here four months after their separation, with both Daryl and Katie gone. Gone!

Suddenly she knew exactly what had happened—where she'd lost the suitcase. The place where she'd changed the tire. She entertained the idea of going back. What if the thugs were, even now, waiting in the trees? As desperately as she longed to retrieve the case, self-preservation dictated she wait.

Exhausted, Gillian dragged herself inside, stripped off her dirty clothes and fell into bed. Her agenda had just taken a new turn. She wouldn't rest until the thugs who'd killed Daryl were brought to justice. And they'd better know she would go to any lengths to rescue Katie's ashes.

CHAPTER TWO

GILLIAN STOOD in the cramped office off the kitchen of Flo's Café. She'd come to speak with the café's owner, Florence Carter, about a waitress position listed in a current edition of the *Desert City News*. It was the first newspaper Gillian had bought since departing New Orleans, although she'd followed the TV news and was relieved there'd been no mention of Daryl's or Officer Malone's murders. Her objective in buying this paper had been for the employment ads. Desert City was the closest town of any size to the back road where she'd lost her suitcase.

This morning, when she dressed to go on interviews, Gillian had barely recognized herself in the mirror. Little by little over an extra week spent in her border hideout, she'd pulled together a disguise of sorts. The most dramatic change in her appearance came about after she'd ruthlessly cropped and colored her shoulder-length blond hair, leaving a bob of coppery red curls.

As well, she'd transacted a satisfactory car exchange, buying another used car. However, because the new car had taken most of her cash reserves, she was now almost broke.

Flo Carter, a cheery, round woman, studied Gillian with curious hazel eyes. "Why did you answer my ad? There were at least two other waitress jobs posted yesterday for yuppie-style restaurants where you'd earn higher tips."

Gillian didn't want to say those places all had bars where creeps from New Orleans might go to drink and eat. She'd checked them first. It would be self-defeating to admit Flo's Café was last on her list. Or that the one other place she'd applied had demanded references she couldn't produce.

"According to your ad, you provide uniforms and you pay weekly. Did I mention I was divorced? The truth is—" she hesitated marginally while deliberating how much to reveal "—I left home and this is where my money ran out." Best to stick as close to her real story as possible, Gillian decided.

"I'm sorry, honey. Enough said." Flo patted Gillian's arm. "Frankly, you look like you could use a few good meals, too. The job's yours. Minimum wage plus tips, a uniform and two meals a day if you work two shifts. Tracy, my brother's niece, left me high and dry. Kid up and moved to San Diego with her boyfriend. I nearly killed myself over the weekend. I'm flat getting too old to wait tables from opening to closing. When can you start?"

"Anytime. Today, if you'd like." A weight lifted from Gillian's shoulders. "I have a small apartment three blocks east of here." She waved a hand in the general direction of the furnished place she'd moved into yesterday. It wasn't much.

"Saguaro Arms, right? A brick building behind the police station?"

"That describes it." Gillian didn't know if she'd made a wise choice or not. On one hand, she figured the men who were after her wouldn't want to be noticed by the local police. On the other, she didn't know how vigorously the police in Flagstaff and New Orleans were trying to find her. Surely she was wanted for questioning, at least.

"I hope you're comfortable around cops," Flo said. "They make up half our clientele. A great bunch, but demanding customers. They want coffee on the table the minute they sit down. They need their orders quick in case they get a call."

Flo opened a cupboard and took out a pink uniform still in its plastic laundry bag. "You're skinnier than Tracy, but this has an adjustable belt. The bathroom's down the hall. How fast can you change? First crew from the precinct breaks at ten." She glanced down at Gillian's feet. "I'm glad to see you're wearing sensible shoes. Next time we catch our breath is nigh on 2:00 p.m."

"I'm stronger than you might think," Gillian said, reaching for the door knob. She hoped that was true. Normally she'd be in great shape from handling crates of flowers at the shop she'd once owned. That had been a while ago.

"You'll get a complete workout before the end of the day. I'll spell you for breaks and meals. Otherwise, I sling hash onto plates while my husband, Bert, cooks. You okay with working a shift before we fill out employment papers?"

"Sure. Okay." Gillian looked over her shoulder. "Is there someplace I can leave my street clothes and purse?"

Flo scooped things out of a drawer in the bottom of her cluttered desk. "Tracy left all this junk. She was big on running in to apply makeup every ten minutes."

Gillian uttered a genuine laugh. "I won't do that, Mrs. Carter. What you see right here is what you get."

"Call me Flo." She examined Gillian again. "Cops flirt a lot. They'll like what they see in you. You sure you've waited tables before? I'd have pegged you for one of them fashion models.''

''No way. I prefer anonymity.'' This time Gillian's laughter held a nervous edge. She'd waited tables during high school and college. And she'd never been comfortable with the way a lot of male customers felt they had every right to flirt with women servers. She used to have a knack for discouraging that sort, and hoped she still did.

When she'd donned her uniform, Flo introduced her to Bert. Unlike most cooks Gillian had ever met, Bert was rail-thin. He was also bald as a cucumber.

''Bert learned to cook in the Air Force,'' Flo said after introductions were complete. ''As we moved around, I began waiting tables for the NCO clubs on base. Buying this café once Bert retired seemed a logical way to pool our talents and get our kids through college.''

''How many children do you have?'' Gillian asked.

''Two of our own. Off and on we've raised a slug of foster kids. One of the cops who comes in here convinced us to open our home to teens who need a healthier environment than what they have.''

''How can you bear to let them go again? Doesn't it tear your heart out?''

Flo shrugged. ''We provide a clean bed, good meals and a shoulder to cry on. Or in some cases an open ear. Sometimes that's all they require to get them through a rough patch. You obviously don't have kids, or you'd have requested to work shifts around school or daycare hours.''

Swallowing hard, Gillian gave a shake of her head. She couldn't bring herself to talk about Katie. Twice yesterday she'd driven past the lane where she'd left the suitcase. Once, a vehicle directly in front of her entered it first. Not the blue car she was trying to avoid, but a big pickup. During a second pass-by, she noticed a man herding cattle in a nearby field. Tonight, after work, Gillian intended to go back under the cover of darkness.

Flo gave Gillian's hand a sympathetic squeeze. "Now, don't go fretting over your divorce. You're still young enough to make plenty of babies. You have to concentrate on finding a good man to father them."

"A man of any kind is the last thing I want. Shouldn't I concentrate on hitting the floor running? Do I have everything? Pencil." Gillian pulled two out of her uniform pocket. "Order pad? A smile." She hauled in a deep breath. "Well, here goes." Waving, she disappeared through the swinging doors.

Within two hours, Gillian discovered how out of shape she was. Luckily the technique for keeping orders straight came back to her before the large lunch crowd arrived. Good thing she'd had that experience, even if it was ten years ago, she mused, plopping down ketchup and mustard at a table of boisterous men.

Three at the table wore police uniforms; a fourth had on street clothing but was undoubtedly a cop. He indicated that they were waiting for someone who'd just entered. Gillian had already noticed that man the minute he walked in. *Sauntered* was more like it, in spite of a pronounced limp. Gosh, she hoped he wasn't offended by her lengthy stare. It wasn't his limp that drew her attention but his attire. He wore dusty cowboy boots, worn blue jeans, a body-hugging denim shirt and a Stetson set rakishly on his head.

Gillian had never seen a real cowboy in her life, and he was an eyeful. He seemed to be friendly with all the cops in the room. It took him a long time to reach his table because he stopped to talk with occupants at practically every booth along the way. So many people piped up to yell, "Hey there, Mitch, how you doing?" Gillian couldn't help but learn his first name. Especially as she waited impatiently to add his order to those of his pals.

The name suited him. Mitch was a strong moniker. He certainly appeared commanding in spite of his limp. What had caused it? she wondered. Probably a fall from a horse.

Gillian felt herself blush as he turned, caught her still staring and tipped his hat. Hastily averting her gaze, she sorted menus to pass around at an adjacent table full of men wearing business suits. "I'll be right back," she told the group awaiting the cowboy, and dashed off to draw glasses of water for the businessmen.

The cowboy needed a haircut, Gillian decided after he finally removed his hat and reached for a chair. A haircut was pretty much all he lacked, though. He had dark-lashed coffee-colored eyes and a ready grin that creased lean, tanned cheeks. In her estimation, he possessed more sex appeal than all the other men at his table put together. Except, perhaps for the other man not wearing a uniform. Mitch greeted him effusively, calling him Ethan, as he spun a chair around across from the plainclothes cop and straddled it. So did that mean the cowboy was a cop, too?

At first Gillian thought they were brothers who hadn't seen each other for a while. She nixed that idea based on snatches of conversation overheard on various trips past their table. Ethan, she saw, sported a shiny gold wedding band. Brand-new, she'd bet, mostly because he mumbled thanks but didn't so much as lift his eyes whenever she brought something to the table. By contrast, his cowboy pal tracked her every move—to the point that Gillian found herself fumbling dishes. It occurred to her with a

sudden start that maybe he'd seen her picture on a handbill. The fear galloping through her nearly made her drop
a full tray.

"Ma'am," said a gravelly voice at her elbow. "You're
obviously new to Flo's. But I'm pretty sure she wouldn't
want you to be totin' more than you can carry."

How he—Mitch—managed to check out her every
curve while he steadied her tray, Gillian didn't know. She
just knew there wasn't a wrinkle in her uniform he
missed with those lancing brown eyes.

"This is my first day here," she said quietly. "While
I appreciate your concern, if you don't let go and sit
down, you'll make it look like I'm incapable of managing
the job I was hired for."

Cops seated around the room watched the byplay
openly. Few tried to mask their amused expressions. Finally, one round-faced rookie, whose wire-rimmed
glasses constantly slipped down his nose, chortled.
"Wouldn't you know it, Flo gets a pretty new waitress
to replace Tracy, and it just happens to be the first day
Valetti shows up in town. I swear, he has radar when it
comes to sniffing out gorgeous, single babes."

Gillian jerked away quickly and finished unloading the
tray. She smacked one of the noon-time specials down in
front of the loudmouthed kid. "Married or single, I'm
not on the menu here."

Turning to reclaim her tray, she realized Mitch's interested gaze had slipped to her ring finger.

"Order up," yelled Flo, pausing to slide several plates
under the warming light. "Jeez, fellas, meet Gillian Stevens, okay? She's new in town as well as on the job.
Show a few manners. You're Desert City's finest. I'll be
in a *very* bad mood if you macho lamebrains scare her
off."

The young cop immediately bent to his food. Mitch rolled his eyes, but he immediately released her tray and backed off—although not so far that Gillian didn't have to brush against him as she squeezed between the tables.

Mitch felt the waitress's annoyance. Smiling to himself, he sat across from Ethan again.

Ethan Knight leaned back in his chair. His narrowed gaze rose to the exact level of Gillian's swishing hips. ''Down, boy,'' he muttered.

''Wha-a-at?'' Mitch drawled, pretending interest in blowing on his hot coffee. ''So what if I have a weakness for sassy redheads?''

The uniformed cop seated opposite Mitch broke into the conversation. ''Redheads. Blondes. Brunettes and every shade in between. Isn't that why Amy threw you over for the D.A.? I heard she didn't like the odds.''

Mitch bunched his napkin, his expression shutting down.

Leaning close, Ethan murmured, ''Regan said you took my sister's elopement hard. I'm sorry. Guess I missed how you really felt. So, if you're ready to be fixed up with somebody nice, I'll tell Regan. No reason to take chances on a perfect stranger.''

''Listen, Buttinski, I can still rustle up my own dates. And I believe I'll have my second cup of java at the counter.'' Mitch stood up. Carrying his cup, he limped to the counter, where he reached for the pot and helped himself to a refill.

Ethan made it a point from then on to study the new waitress. Until his contingent of friends came over and one of them nudged him out of his stupor. Trailing after his pals, Ethan paused behind Mitch's stool. ''Regan's planning to make sour cream enchiladas Friday night. Why not come on over? We'll invite a fourth, and after we eat and get the kids to bed, we'll play a few hands of poker.''

''You're being a little obvious, Ethan. Thanks, but no. You and your bride saw too much of my ugly face over the past three months.'' Mitch realized both he and Ethan had zeroed in on Gillian Stevens as she lifted three hot plates off the warming counter. ''Two bits says, with that long lean body, she's a jogger,'' Mitch said thoughtfully. ''You know, the doc recommended I stretch the muscles in my injured leg.''

Ethan scowled. ''So make an appointment with Gil Peterson, the precinct's physical therapist.''

Mitch flashed Ethan a wicked grin. ''Gil puts me in mind of a sumo wrestler. Besides, my man, if I remember right, you hauled your ass out of bed at the crack of dawn to chase Regan around a few tracks. And you don't even *like* exercise.''

Mitch had him there. Ethan said something indistinct and undoubtedly rude. Before stomping off, he announced that there were plenty of single women in town who were dying to go out with Mitch. Wearing a thunderous expression, Ethan joined the men waiting for him outside the café.

Gillian watched the drama with half an eye. She wished the plainclothes cop, Ethan, had succeeded in talking his pal at the counter into leaving. Her heart did a funny jig once it became evident that Mitch Valetti wasn't going to budge. She told herself it was first-day job jitters. She wasn't attractive enough to draw more than a passing glance from a man like Mitch Valetti. She was too tall. Too thin. Her chin was too pointy and her mouth too wide. Her eyes weren't even an exciting color. Blue was blue was blue. So what gave her the idea he'd stuck around because of her?

Gillian managed to stay convinced that he hadn't until the lunch traffic waned enough to slow her hectic pace. He was still there. And he snagged her arm as she darted past.

"Hey, Flo," Mitch called, hunching to peer into the kitchen via the pass-through. "Isn't there a state rule requiring employees to take regular breaks? Appears to me that Gillian, here, is overdue."

Flo stuck her head out around the kitchen door. "Gilly-girl. Climb up there on the stool next to Mitch and take a load off. I said earlier you've got to eat. What'll it be? Bert's special is chicken-fried steak. But, shoot, you'd know that. You've served a gazillion plates of the stuff so far."

Gillian would have rather sat anywhere than beside Mitch Valetti. Unfortunately, a mob of high schoolers bounded in at that moment, filling the remaining empty seats at the counter. "Uh, Flo. I'll just take these kids' orders first. I can eat later. A dinner salad will do me, if you want to set one aside. The house dressing looked good."

Flo came all the way out of the kitchen. She fanned a ruddy face with the tail of her apron. "All that bunch of twerps ever order are french fries and Cokes. I'll handle 'em. You eat."

"Skinny as you are," Mitch observed, "you ought to eat something more substantial than a damned salad." He rounded on Gillian. "You're not anorexic or anything, are you?"

She felt her jaw slacken and snapped her mouth closed. "Are you always so free and personal with someone you haven't even met?"

"We met. Flo introduced you earlier." Mitch stuck out his hand and grasped hers gently. "I'm Mitch Valetti.

Detective. Er...former detective.'' He acted flustered, quickly releasing her hand to curl his wide palms around his coffee mug instead. ''Guess you could say I'm a rancher now.''

''I'm sure there's a story somewhere in that statement.'' Allowing a reluctant smile along with a small sigh of capitulation, Gillian slid onto the end stool. ''A detective turned rancher has the makings of an intriguing book.''

''Are you a starving writer, then?''

She shook her head. ''Gee, I thought I was a bona fide waitress.''

Grinning, Mitch took another swig before setting his mug back on the counter. ''Touché. I deserved that. You're a good waitress. At least, you managed Flo's lunch crowd better than her niece, Tracy, ever did. Say, I didn't mean to offend you.''

''You didn't,'' Gillian said, glancing up as Flo placed a huge taco salad in front of her. ''Hey, this isn't what I ordered.'' Frowning, she dragged her fork through the mountain of lettuce, black beans, olives, avocado, chicken and grated cheese heaped inside a crisp tortilla shell. She'd never be able to eat even a quarter of this.

''Are you allergic to any of that stuff?'' Mitch enquired.

Gillian's frown deepened. ''No. Not that I know of.''

''Then stop complaining and chow down. I guarantee Bert makes the tastiest taco salads in town. Add a generous splash of his homemade salsa and you've got a lip-smacking meal.''

''So now you're a detective turned rancher turned restaurant reviewer?'' As she spoke, Gillian brought a forkful of the concoction to her mouth.

''You gotta forgive this guy,'' Flo said, scooting past

them again, hands laden with steaming platters of french fries. "He's still recovering from an on-the-job injury. Must be the medicine making him act so smart-aleck. He's never been shy, but usually his mouth is connected to his brain."

"Oh? A head injury, was it?" Gillian didn't know what had gotten into her. She rarely teased people she knew well; being sarcastic to a *stranger* was unthinkable. Especially since she was trying to keep a low profile.

Mitch and Flo found her remark amusing. Flo broke off laughing first. "At last, Valetti. A woman who can toss back all the baloney you dish out. I hope you cultivate her acquaintance. I've always said you flit from date to date because the ladies you ask out bore you to death within a week."

Tilting his head, Mitch stared at Gillian so long she choked on a slice of olive. An infusion of heat seeped up her neck and across her cool cheeks. "I shouldn't have said anything. It was rude of me. I don't know you well enough to crack jokes about your injury."

"I'd like to get to know you better," he said, gazing directly into her eyes.

Excitement fluttered in her stomach before tightening into a coil of apprehension. Gillian hadn't fielded a pass in so long she'd forgotten how to extricate herself gracefully. She wasn't sure what words to use. "Look," she said at last. "I'm, uh, sure you're sincere. And nice. But I, ah, have been married before." It was lame, but the first thing that popped into her head.

Mitch stiffened visibly. "Bitter divorce?"

"No. A relief." Gillian responded more honestly than she'd intended.

"Then what's the problem? I'm more than willing to keep things simple."

As Gillian scrabbled for a comeback that would end his pursuit, the door opened and a petite blonde dressed in a police uniform walked in. "Mitch. Hi!" Beaming, she waved and looked as pleased as a cat who'd found a fat goldfish. "Ethan said I'd probably catch you here. He told me you might be taking on some private investigative work. I have something that may strike your fancy if you've got some free time. My sister Lori said you could be busy—that you had a strange case fall right in your lap."

"It's not really a case," Mitch admitted, casting Gillian a quick apology with his eyes. "I posted an ad in the paper for a week, but only one person responded. A sicko, at that. So, what've you got, and what does it pay? My pension covers my bills. But if I want to increase my herd, I need extra cash."

The woman took Gillian's measure. "You're involved at the moment," she said to Mitch. "My case is confidential. I'll be at the station if you want to swing by later. Or come to Lori's house tonight. I'll fix dinner and we can talk. Lori has a class at the college, so we won't be disturbed."

Mitch rubbed his neck. Christy Peck-Jones was a good cop. She was also separated, not divorced, from a bad-tempered husband. Tangling with Royce Jones was the last thing Mitch needed or wanted. While Christy had indicated her interest in him more than once, she didn't ring any bells for Mitch. Even if he was attracted to her, he'd never act on it unless she was free. Some guys on the force didn't have much integrity when it came to honoring their wedding vows or those of women cops they worked with. They found it easy to blame their betrayals on an excess of adrenaline from being thrown together in life-and-death situations. Mitch had met death face-to-face, twice. Both experiences had only served to solidify his values. This last time, he really thought he'd bought the farm.

Which could be why he felt an uncustomary urgency to meet the right woman. He'd been given a new lease on life. Now he'd like kids and even grandkids. The next time he met his maker, he wanted to look back and see that he'd accomplished something worthwhile. Men ought to have a legacy to leave behind.

''My lunch break is over. I'm going to the kitchen to box this to take home. Please, don't let me keep you from exploring a potential job offer.'' Sliding off the stool, Gillian whisked away her plate and utensils.

She flat-out disappeared before Mitch could press harder for a first date. Not altogether surprising. She'd made her reservations clear. And with all the crime against women he'd seen while working the streets, he couldn't really blame her. What did she know about him? Nothing. But if she stuck around town, he'd have a chance to ask her out again. If she moved on— Oh, well, she wasn't what he was looking for anyway.

Exactly what is that, Valetti? And when did you start picking up strangers? Confused by the questions, Mitch attempted to push her out of his mind.

He crossed slowly to Christy's table. As he settled in the chair farthest from her, Mitch recalled Ethan experiencing a similar bewilderment the day he met Regan, whom he later married. Mitch couldn't say why, but when he exchanged banter with Gillian Stevens, he felt a lot like his former partner had looked back then—like an alley-cat standing hip-deep in fresh cream.

Gillian walked back into the room. From the erratic way Mitch's heart flip-flopped, he knew he'd definitely be making a second trip to town. Possibly even a third and fourth…

CHAPTER THREE

PREPARED TO RESUME her duties, Gillian noticed that Flo had delivered the last plates of french fries to the kids, and stopped on her way back to take the order from Mitch's lady friend. Uncertain why she didn't want to wait on them, Gillian nevertheless recognized her reaction as one of profound relief.

Late lunch-goers from the police station and other area businesses converged on the café. The flurry of activity served to take Gillian's mind off the couple in the corner, whose pale and dark heads drew closer together as time wore on. The fact that she kept an eye on them at all annoyed her. The very last complication she needed, considering her own plight, would be to develop a *thing* for a cop.

"Ex-cop," she muttered under her breath as she tore three order sheets off her pad and tucked them under clips that she spun toward Bert. He glanced up and grinned.

"Your first day and already you're talking to yourself? Bad sign, Gillian."

"Sorry. Talking to myself is an old habit. I'm enjoying the job. Truly."

"Hey, I believe you." Still smiling, he handed her two steaming platters.

Her need to define Mitch as an *ex*-cop irritated Gillian even more than being caught talking to herself. Why couldn't she forget him altogether?

Apparently putting him out of her mind wasn't going to be simple, she realized, all the while deriving immense satisfaction from watching him walk out some twenty minutes later, leaving the lady cop to finish her lunch alone.

It fell to Gillian to collect Christy Jones's plate, though, and ask if she wanted anything else.

"I want Mitch Valetti," the blonde stated boldly, drilling Gillian with arctic-blue eyes.

Maybe blue *wasn't* blue wasn't blue, Gillian thought, recoiling from the hostility aimed her way. In marked contrast, she tried for a guileless expression. "Sorry, ma'am, he's not on our menu." She made a joke of the same phrase she'd used earlier, that time referring to herself. When it became apparent that her joke had only irritated the other woman, she fervently wished she'd kept her comment to herself.

"Don't play naive," the cop snapped, pausing to count out exact change for her meal. "I know every officer on this beat. Any one of them could make it tough on you in a million small ways. For instance, someone whispers a word in the ear of a restaurant inspector. Maybe you don't wash your hands after trips to the john. There are dozens of possible infractions—even leaving plates under the warming light too long. A few reprimands, and Bert and Flo can't afford to keep you on."

Climbing nimbly to her feet, the speaker shifted her heavy leather belt in a manner calculated to draw Gillian's attention to the tools of her trade. She obviously thought they gave her stature above a mere waitress, even though Gillian stood head and shoulders above her.

A chill not caused by the lazily churning overhead fan marched rows of goose bumps up Gillian's bare arms. She reined in her temper and said nothing at all in response to the policewoman's veiled threats. After all, the woman had no idea how much trouble she could cause Gillian. Because if Christy Jones had the slightest inkling, Gillian didn't doubt for one minute that she'd be hauled in for questioning wearing those impressive silver hand-cuffs.

Using more force than necessary, Gillian scrubbed the table clean. Twice she fumbled and dropped the coins she tried to sweep off the table onto a tray.

Flo motioned her to the pass-through. "Was Christy complaining about her sandwich?"

"No. Nothing like that." Gillian wrinkled her nose as she turned to dump the money in the till. "Actually, she issued a personal warning for me to stay away from Mitch Valetti. I take it they are or were an item?" Gillian hadn't meant that to come out as a question; it did of its own accord.

The older woman laughed, then said in a more subdued voice, "See the brawniest of the three motorcycle cops walking in right now? That's Christy's husband, Royce Jones."

Gillian whirled. "Her *husband?* She's married?"

"Well," Flo muttered, "a few months ago I heard she'd moved in with her sister again. It's happened be-fore. The other times she's gone back to Royce. I dunno, maybe this time she won't." Raising her voice, Flo greeted the trio who stood inside the door surveying the dining area. "There's space at the counter. Or if you wait a minute, Gilly's about ready to reset a table that was just vacated."

"Has Christy been here for lunch?" the man in the middle asked. He stripped off his goggles and gloves and tossed them into a helmet he held hooked under one arm.

Shivering at the mere size of him, Gillian ducked past

the trio. She wouldn't want to meet any of them in a back alley, or out in broad daylight for that matter. Let Flo field the man's query. Better she avoid any personal contact with cops.

"Just missed her, Royce," Flo noted cheerfully. "Christy left here no more than five…ten minutes ago."

"Damn." The big man, who'd followed Gillian to the table, threw his helmet down on one of the chairs. She jumped a foot straight up at the noise.

"Easy does it." The shorter of the two men with Royce threw an apologetic glance at Gillian. He elaborated for her benefit. "I called the dispatcher myself to see when Royce's wife was scheduled to go to lunch. If he's testy, it's because Christy's department thinks it's clever to play mind games with us. Next time she comes in, tell her he only wants to talk. A man has a right to see his own wife, doesn't he?"

"I guess that depends." Gillian pulled her order pad out of her pocket. "Coffee or sodas?" Her voice squeaked. Clearing her throat, she asked if the men knew what they wanted to eat, or if they needed a minute to decide. No one responded. She handed them menus and walked away.

"Hey, Royce," hollered a uniformed cop getting up from a back booth. "Christy and Valetti sat at that same table while she ate. Cozy as two peas in a pod."

"Mitch Valetti? Come on, Billings, quit lying. You think I don't know Valetti got his balls shot off and left the force a couple months ago?"

"No kidding? His balls? Well, he was stove up some. But I'm not lying. If you don't believe me, ask Red there. She was chatting with him when Christy walked in. Valetti dropped Red like a hot potato and made a beeline for Christy."

Royce pinned Gillian with angry eyes. "Tell me. Is Don having me on or not?"

Gillian slopped coffee onto the clean table from a pot she'd gone to fetch while the men talked. "I believe, ah, they were discussing business. Are you three ready to order yet?" she asked, nervously sponging away the spill.

"Like hell they were discussing business," Royce roared, slamming a hamlike fist down on the table. "If Valetti didn't lose his balls in that shoot-out, he will when I finish with him. Come on, Jeff. Chico. Let's ride out to Valetti's place and show him what's what. I always said he was too free with his pretty-boy smiles."

The other two men each grabbed one of Royce's massive arms. "Mitch lives in the county, dude. We don't have jurisdiction there. You want his balls, you'll have to wait till the next time he comes to town. Settle down, Royce. Tell the lady what you want to eat."

Gillian noticed Bert had left the kitchen to stand at the end of the counter. As she scribbled the men's orders on her pad, she saw him replace the telephone receiver. The notion that he'd been about to call the cops struck her as funny, since at least a dozen from the nearby station sat in the café. Or were they off duty during lunch? She didn't know that much about how police operated.

A new thought replaced the previous one. Perhaps Bert had intended to notify Valetti. For no reason at all, Gillian felt a stab of sympathy for the injured ex-cop. She hoped he had enough sense to stay put on his ranch. Though whatever happened wouldn't have anything to do with her. *Sheesh.* She had troubles of her own. Perhaps that was why she empathized. It was a frightening experience to have brutish men wanting to hurt you.

Except…when push came to shove, how did she know he *wasn't* deserving of Royce's accusations? After all,

Mitch had certainly come on to her. Somehow, though, she believed Mitch was blameless. Gillian found herself wondering about him off and on the remainder of the afternoon. Had he really lost his reproductive organs in a senseless shooting? He certainly came across as virile. But she knew men went to great lengths to hide their weaknesses. They hid most of their emotions. As Daryl had when they'd lost Katie.

He gave her no hint that he'd suffered, too. Not until he'd packed the quilt and baby dress she'd sewn, along with Katie's urn, that night he'd arrived at her apartment. If only he hadn't waited so long to show some understanding. Maybe they could have talked out their problems. Maybe their marriage wouldn't have disintegrated.

Gillian dropped a set of silverware she was rolling into napkins to get ready for the dinner crowd. Her fingers shook when she bent to retrieve the utensils for rewashing. Odd that only now did she remember certain details about that night. Portions of the scene flooded back. There'd been urgency in Daryl's voice and, she thought, a plea for forgiveness. His hands weren't steady as he packed the smallest case. Yet he'd grown cross when she couldn't seem to emerge from her mental fog. The sleeping pills left her confused and only half-awake.

Oh, how she wished she could recall every word Daryl had uttered that night. Eventually he'd recognized he wasn't getting through to her. He'd thrown up his hands and instead of continuing to explain, he wrote down instructions telling her the location of a hidden car.

If he hadn't stormed out then with the cases and gone straight to place them in the trunk of the hidden vehicle, she wouldn't have a stitch to her name. Scarcely two hours later, one of his next-door neighbors had phoned to say he was dead. Without the written instructions, she might not have run. It wasn't hard to imagine how she'd have ended up then.

Another memory appeared. Gillian realized she hadn't destroyed Daryl's message. No wonder the thugs were on her trail so fast. She'd left them an engraved invitation. The note gave the location, color, model and make of her getaway car.

Daryl had finally demonstrated that he did care about the baby they'd lost, and Gillian had failed him. Or felt she had. She hadn't asked the right questions, and worse, she'd lost all that was dear. Tonight, after work, no matter how tired she was, she would search that lane. The worst of the devil's disciples. That was how she thought of the men who'd killed Daryl and Pat Malone. Surely not even they would be so heartless as to destroy the contents of that suitcase. Those men only wanted a key, and there was no key. Of that Gillian was sure. So what in heaven's name had Daryl—meticulous, methodical Daryl—done with the blasted thing?

Too exhausted after ending her shift to do more than drag up the stairs to her apartment, Gillian escaped from the issues plaguing her into the pain caused by aching feet.

She'd rented a third-floor apartment for security reasons. Now, having trudged up three flights of stairs leading from the parking garage, she might have considered trading safety for the convenience of living quarters on the first floor. Or an elevator, she thought, falling fully clothed across her bed. There was an ancient elevator at the front entrance, but because the building sat between two streets, it would have taken more energy to walk a block to go in through the front door than it did to climb the back stairs.

A shower turned out to have amazing recuperative

powers. Afterward Gillian felt rejuvenated enough to eat one of the three pieces of chicken Flo had insisted she take home along with her leftover taco salad. The chicken looked good. Not a bit greasy, and yet she must not be hungry, after all, she decided, rewrapping it.

In the hour between when she'd left work and when she returned the food to her refrigerator, the sun had almost finished setting. It was merely a glow on the horizon, now. Calculating the distance to the side road where she'd had the flat tire, she figured darkness would arrive before she could drive out there. A perfect time to search the area without being seen.

Well, the owners of the ranch might see her light. But even if they were home, they might not investigate. Gillian remembered entering an S curve to reach the point where the lane dead-ended in front of the house.

Donning black jeans and a charcoal, long-sleeved knit top, Gillian slid her driver's license into her back pocket. Bless Daryl for packing a pair of sturdy, ankle-high boots. She dug them out of her closet and slipped them on. Next, she purposely left everything but her keys behind. The last concession she made to a disguise was to stuff her short curls under a dark-blue baseball cap.

The trip took just under thirty minutes.

"Darn." In the gathering darkness, she missed the lane on the first drive by. She had to go an extra mile before she found a spot where she could turn around.

On her second approach, moments before she touched her left-turn blinker, a big blue sedan shot out of a road on her right side. The car careered across the highway, nearly clipping Gillian's front fender. She slammed on her brakes and watched in horror as the heavier car swayed and almost lost control. The driver gunned his motor, straightened the lumbering vehicle and entered the lane that had been Gillian's destination.

Her headlights illuminated the reckless driver's back license plate. *Louisiana.* "My God, it's them," she sobbed aloud. It had to be the thugs who wanted to kill her. They were obviously still hoping to locate her in this area, where they'd lost her three weeks ago.

Her mouth went dry and her muscles tightened. *They wouldn't know this car.*

Or would they? Had they tracked her to the border? Was it only a matter of time before they caught her?

Gillian was aware of the exact moment determination edged out her fear. Time was now her enemy. If she had to disappear again, she didn't intend to run and leave Katie's ashes to the likes of them.

Coldly she reasoned that if they were still searching these side roads, they probably hadn't found her suitcase. Shaking, she pulled onto a fire road and parked behind an outcrop of boulders, dousing her lights. If the men were inspecting each byway intersecting the perimeter road, they'd have already searched this one.

Leaving her car, Gillian crouched low and zigzagged across the main road. She counted on blending with the underbrush. It was quite a hike on legs already weary from hustling food orders all day, and now spongy from fear. She stumbled frequently, but dared not risk using her flashlight. Once her eyes adjusted, a bright three-quarter moon allowed her to distinguish solid form from shadows.

Creeping along the fence row, Gillian expected at any minute to come upon the men rifling her suitcase. At each bend, when the lane remained vacant, she released a little more of the breath she'd been holding. *Where were they?*

Somehow, she hadn't thought she'd driven this far before her tire blew out.

Of course, it would seem longer on foot.

As she inched along the fence, taking care to keep out of sight, a cloud of dust rolled across her brush cover, obscuring her view of the starry sky. She dived toward a thicket and flattened herself against the rough bark of a squat desert tree. Forced to eat grit, Gillian spat it out as quietly as possible. She needn't have worried about being seen. The heavy sedan thundered by, traveling at far too great a speed.

Gillian, who'd shut her eyes to avoid the dust, almost left her hideaway too early. Thinking it'd be easier to walk in the lane, she was about to vault the fence. Bobbing headlights from a second car sent her scurrying back into hiding. Auto number two also moved toward the highway, although compared to the first, it crawled like a snail.

During its approach, Gillian noticed that the driver had some type of searchlight he or she was shining into the brush flanking the fence.

Her heart slammed inside her chest. As before, she molded herself to the tree. Just before the light could flash over her face, she dropped to the ground. What she saw from that vantage point, through a tangle of weeds and grass, shocked her. Not the car itself, which was a well-preserved baby-blue Corvette, but the driver. He was someone she recognized. New fear spiraled through her veins. The Vette's driver was none other than the cowboy ex-cop she'd flirted with at Flo's Café.

"Mitch Valetti." Her lips formed his name, letting it spill happily from her lips before she had an opportunity to add things up. When she did, and the pieces fell into place—like the fact that he was combing the underbrush for something or someone—she clambered to her feet, then ran away as fast as her quaking legs would carry her.

Gillian didn't look back. Throughout her mad retreat, her brain shut down. Her throat constricted, making breathing next to impossible. Still, she didn't stop until she fumbled open her door, started her engine and roared out of the fire road onto the main highway.

She'd wrongly assumed the men who were chasing her had discovered the lane by chance. Instead, they were obviously in cahoots with Valetti. "Think," she ordered herself. Did the thugs have enough of a head start to make a meeting with Valetti possible? During lucid moments, she'd have said probably not. Sergeant Malone had warned her the men might have local contacts. It was the only thing that made sense. In the café Valetti had admitted to Christy Jones that he needed money. Gillian had heard Christy allude to a case that—how did she put it? *It had dropped in his lap.* Why else would Valetti have made a concerted effort to get to know her—a total stranger? If he wasn't working with the bastards doing their level best to find her, why would he be spotlighting a country lane at this hour?

Her cover was blown. That was Gillian's first and last conclusion. The big question now was: did she have what it took to dig in her heels and face them all?

MITCH GLIDED to a halt. He held the powerful spotlight aloft and went back over a section of trees where he thought he'd seen an outline of something. A person.

"Damn, Trooper," he said aloud to a big-footed Alsatian pup Ethan had presented him with that very day at suppertime. "Instead of chasing phantom shadows, we ought to be tailing the car that left squirrel marks so close to my corral it scared the living daylights out of my best broodmare.''

Mitch, alerted to trouble outside by his new dog, hadn't been quick enough to record the dark sedan's license plate. ''Just as well,'' he grumbled sourly. ''I'd wring their bloody necks if Pretty Baby foals early. Then I'd be viewing the county's big jail from the inside out rather than the other way around.''

The pup had begun to whine and lick his hand. Mitch tugged absently at the dog's soft, gold-brown ears. All but smiling, the puppy flopped down on the passenger seat and laid his chin on his new master's knee.

''Good boy,'' Mitch murmured automatically. Off and on during his recovery at Ethan and Regan's home, he had mentioned maybe purchasing a trained police dog like Ethan's Taz. It had been the type of remark one made off the cuff. Mitch was stunned when Ethan showed up at his door tonight—with the pup, a month's worth of food and a bloodline certificate from a Dutch breeder.

Although he had to admit his friend's timing had been suspect. Not that Ethan had come right out and said a dog would give Mitch something to think about other than the woman—the stranger—who'd caught his interest today at Flo's. Mitch doubted Ethan had any idea how transparent he was. His old partner probably had to twist arms to take delivery of a pup so fast. The gift was a thoughtful gesture, as Mitch had been restless and at loose ends since the accident.

He'd never owned a dog, so he couldn't help wondering if he'd be good at caring for one. Taz went everywhere with Ethan. A dog would be great company.

''Shoot.'' Snapping off the spotlight, he heaved a sigh. ''There's nothing out there, fella. I'll run on out to the highway, but I'm afraid I lost any chance of catching our joyriders. I'd hazard a guess it was kids out for a spin in daddy's wheels. That how you see it, Trooper?''

Raising his head a fraction, the pup yipped sharply.

Mitch chuckled and tossed the spotlight into the back seat. ''I see definite benefits to having a pal who always agrees with me.'' As his smile faded, Mitch eased off the emergency brake. ''If we'd been together a little longer, buddy, I might've sent you out to check those bushes. I can't shake the notion that what I saw was a person hiding there.'' Mitch gnawed his upper lip and released it as he peered hard into the deepening shadows. Ethan had told him he was obsessed with the idea that the owner of the suitcase would show up one day to claim its sad contents. Mitch supposed he was. He sighed again as he pulled up to the highway and sat with the car idling.

Not detecting any sign of headlights in either direction, Mitch shut off the Corvette's lights and rummaged under his seat for a regular flashlight. Climbing from the car, he attached Trooper's leash. Together, they sauntered back along the lane. When they reached the place where Mitch thought he'd seen a silhouette, he went over the fence. Sure enough, the dog picked up on a scent that had him going crazy. The pup growled so loudly, Mitch knelt down beneath the old mesquite tree to get a clearer look. Thanks to recent rains, the ground shaded by the branches was still soft.

Footprints.

As far as Mitch could tell, considering the less-than-perfect conditions for gathering evidence, what they had here was a single set of prints. Made by a small boot. And the person had stuck around for a while. Unlike in the dusty lane, the soil remained moist enough to show that the wearer of those boots had probably climbed the fence and secluded himself for a time. Several sets of the same tracks crisscrossed, indicating the person had been jumpy, too.

Standing there, Mitch had a strong sense that if he'd explored the area when he'd first stopped he might have solved the mystery of the abandoned suitcase.

He felt a sensation he couldn't identify. An unnerving impression that somehow time was running out. Whether for him or the person who'd been hiding here, he wasn't sure.

The uneasy feeling plagued him throughout the night. For that reason, he decided to stay home for a few days. With Trooper, he'd patrol the lane at sporadic intervals.

BACK AT HER APARTMENT, Gillian shucked off her black clothing. The bottoms of her jeans were filthy. Her shirt was littered with twigs and cactus quills, and the soles of her boots were caked with sand. The mess she left didn't stop her from pacing around her bedroom while she mulled over her options.

In truth they were few. Suppose she decided to pull up stakes and flee, which good sense begged her to do? Money was her biggest stumbling block.

She had not one solid reason to doubt that Mitch Valetti was tied to the men in the blue car. Yet, throughout the return to her apartment, doubts invaded her head and lodged there. It was a huge stretch of the imagination to think that a group of men who did their dirty work in New Orleans would have a Desert City, Arizona, cop in their pocket. How could they *possibly* have known that this town was where she'd accidentally run out of funds? They couldn't, she told herself.

On the other hand, Gillian would be first to admit that nothing in this entire debacle made sense. At first, while hiding in the dingy border town, she hadn't been able to fathom how Daryl—shy, bookish, slightly out of step with the world Daryl—had hooked up with crooks in the first place. Eventually she'd decided he probably hadn't been the one to make contact. More than likely they'd found him. The fact that Daryl was a conscientious, hard-working CPA would have targeted him as the perfect patsy for men walking on the wrong side of the law.

Gillian flopped down on her bed. None of this rambling provided solutions to her dilemma. However, she continued to believe that the men who'd taken advantage of Daryl weren't the type to buddy up to an honest cop. Now the question of the hour—was Mitch Valetti an honest cop? Correction—an honest *ex-cop?* Everything in her screamed *yes.* The God's truth—she didn't know.

So, was she willing to take a chance on her intuition?

Before the night erupted into a bright, sunny day, Gillian resorted to playing *eenie, meenie, miney, mo.* In choosing *mo,* she elected to stay where she was in the vicinity of an active, bustling police station.

Two could play the game of snoop. It should be easy to subtly pump Mitch's friends who ate at the café. Plus, he might keep trying to get her to go out with him. That didn't mean she had to see him outside the café. If he had something up his sleeve, sooner or later he'd have to show his hand.

Feeling better for having come to a decision, Gillian arrived for the early shift at work exhausted but with a plan in mind.

Too bad Mitch Valetti didn't cooperate. Not only didn't he come in to eat that day, neither did he appear the next day. Or the day after that.

Christy Jones came in every noon hour for lunch, acting as if Gillian were personally responsible for Mitch's truancy. Gillian thought it more likely that Christy's husband, Royce, was the one deterring Mitch. Royce and company stopped in for food and coffee at varying hours, clearly hoping to catch Christy with Mitch.

"Where's Mitch been keeping himself?" Flo asked Ethan Knight on the fourth day of Mitch's absence.

Gillian slowed her pace and perked up her ears. It almost seemed as if Ethan aimed his reply at her, along with a triumphant smirk. "Regan and I bought him a pup from the same breeder who sold me Taz. Pups are a lot like kids. You can't just take off on a whim and leave them home alone."

Flo grunted. "You tie Taz to one of the trees out front while you eat. Can't Mitch do the same?"

"Gee, Flo. Does Bert know you're hankering after another man?"

As Gillian worked at a nearby table, she recognized Ethan's attempt to subvert Flo's line of questioning. She jumped to the older woman's defense. "Flo only wants to warn Mitch to stay away or risk being torn limb from limb by Royce Jones."

Ethan slanted a frown at Gillian. "Royce has a beef against Mitch?"

Bert carried two plates of food out of the kitchen instead of placing them under the warming light for Gillian to collect. "I thought you must've put a bug in Mitch's ear, Ethan. We're all on the lookout for him. I tried phoning him that first day when Royce was in here blowing off steam. I got a recording saying Valetti's phone's out of service. Royce has a screwy notion that Mitch is making moves on Christy. He'll cool off by and by, I expect. Until he does, it's better if Mitch keeps his distance."

"Hmm. Royce has a history of letting his temper get away from him." Ethan rubbed his jaw. "Thanks for alerting me, Bert. I'll raise Mitch on his cell phone. I don't think he's had his house phone reconnected since his surgery. Flo, I owe you an apology…even though you know I was only teasing you about Mitch. All the same, I had you pegged as trying to do a little matchmaking.''

"And so I was." Flo kept one eye on Gillian as she ran off to deliver the meals Bert had brought out. "Mitch is a good man, Ethan. Right now he's lonely and at loose ends. He lost Amy and his best friend at the same time. I happen to think a good woman might be what he needs. Gillian's sort of in the same boat. She has so much time on her hands she's volunteered to work double shifts, for pity's sake. Why not get two needy souls together?''

"What do you mean Mitch lost his best friend? *I'm* his best friend," Ethan stated flatly.

"Yeah. Used to be you and Mitch were joined at the hip. Now you've got a wife and four kids to take up your free time. I'm not saying you aren't still his friend, Ethan. But you've got to admit the dynamics of your friendship are different.''

"Why *that* woman?" Ethan glared across the room at Gillian's slender back.

"Why not her?" Flo challenged.

"I got bad vibes that first day she waited on me. Like she's trouble disguised in an attractive body. Well, okay…for example, that's not even her real hair color.''

Flo laughed. "If *that's* what you're basing your suspicions on, Ethan, you've got some nerve. If it's a crime for a woman to color her hair, you'd better jail half the females in town. Me included.''

"It's more than that, Flo. Darn it, I can't put my finger on anything specific. Except I ran a make on her. Nothing showed for a Gillian Stevens.''

"See there." Flo did her own smirking.

Ethan shook his head. "You don't understand. I mean *nothing* showed. It's like the woman doesn't exist."

Bert snorted and headed for the kitchen. Before reaching the door, he turned and shook a finger at Ethan. "Anyone tell you that cops are naturally paranoid? Lay off the poor kid, Knight. She's the best damned waitress Flo and I have hired in five years. And if you've got nothing concrete, you'd better think twice before dumping this on Mitch. Flo and I figure Amy's elopement shook him way more than he lets on."

Ethan's mouth opened as if he meant to say more. Then not only did the object of their discussion return to their midst, but the front door opened and Mitch himself strolled in, wearing a wide grin. It became patently obvious to everyone watching that his welcoming smile was for the sole benefit of Gillian Stevens.

"Hey, gorgeous," he teased. "You miss me?"

Gillian's stomach did handsprings before settling again. Oddly enough, she *had* missed him. But she wasn't nearly ready to admit any such weakness. "Dream on, cowboy," she mocked as she sailed past on her way to pour coffee for a table of customers. "Anyway," she said, making a face at him over her shoulder, "your friend there—" she indicated Ethan "—said there's someone new in your life." Sliding a pencil behind her ear, Gillian continued to walk.

Mitch spun on his former partner. "What lies are you spreading?" Though his tone remained light, there was an aggressive undercurrent.

"I meant the dog," Gillian exclaimed, stopping mid-stride. For a minute there, she thought Mitch was ready to scrap with his best friend over her. Daryl rarely if ever came to her defense, regardless of provocation. She considered what it would be like to have a protector. She couldn't deny that Mitch's action lit a sexual fire deep inside her.

Her suspicions of him made it a foolish reaction. However, at that moment, if Mitch Valetti asked her out again, Gillian knew she'd live dangerously and accept. After all, her life couldn't be any more on the line than it was now, with people chasing her, wanting her dead. If by some bizarre coincidence Valetti was connected to their efforts, at least she'd be taking charge of her fate.

As long as she remained careful. As long as she never dropped her guard.

CHAPTER FOUR

ETHAN KNIGHT tossed his tip on the counter. He told his new partner to go on back to the station, that he'd catch up. "Got a minute, Mitch?"

"Sure, Big E. Time's a plentiful commodity with me right now. What can I do you for?"

"I see you haven't lost your sense of humor." Ethan smiled with his mouth, not his eyes. "Walk out with me to where I left Taz? What I have to say is private. I want to, ah, discuss a case." His gaze slid from Mitch to Flo's new waitress, who'd leaned around the counter to give Bert special instructions on an order.

Mitch's stance showed resistance to Ethan's suggestion. Staring at his friend, he capitulated with a shrug, his limp more pronounced during their exit.

Gillian sent a glance at them as they left. *What case?* She'd felt Ethan's eyes boring into her back. Did his need for secrecy involve her? A current of fear rattled Gillian's equilibrium. The fear was accompanied by a vague disappointment that Mitch wasn't staying around to order lunch.

What was there about the man that caused such conflicting emotions? She snatched up the coffeepot and hurried to refill patrons' cups, mentally cautioning herself against any loss of objectivity.

Outside, Mitch sauntered over to Taz, who was straining against his leash. "Hi there, sport." Hunkering down, he rubbed the dog's head and patted his wriggling backside. "Next time I come to town, I'll bring Trooper. Bet you'd like company, wouldn't you?"

Ethan untied the dog and gave him a couple of treats he pulled from his jacket. Propping a shoulder against the tree, he methodically coiled the leash.

"What's the problem, Ethan?" Mitch asked. "Do we play twenty questions or you gonna spit out what's bugging you? You need my input on a case? Which one?"

"I lied about wanting to discuss a case. This probably won't win me any points, but here goes. *You're* what's bugging me, Mitch."

"Me?" After his initial start, Mitch laughed on seeing Ethan's grim expression. He relaxed enough so that Taz almost knocked him over. "Jeez! And here I moved out of your house so I wouldn't get on your nerves."

"Knock it off. I'm trying to be serious and you're clowning around."

Mitch straightened, dusting dog hair from his hands. "You're so transparent, Ethan." He puckered his lips. "I can take care of myself, so save the lecture. We're not blood kin, and you're no longer my senior partner." Mitch let it stand at that, even though he wanted to say more.

"I *am* your friend." Ethan's sudden, tense stillness dared Mitch to disagree. "What's more, I wouldn't be standing here if it wasn't for you. You took bullets meant for me. I had no defense against DeSalvo when you drew his fire. That damn well bonds us, whether you like it or not, Valetti."

"Quit it, Ethan. You're the closest thing I have to a brother. You'd have done the same for me if our roles were reversed. But dammit, man, that still doesn't give you the right to mess in my personal life."

"It does if you insist on acting like a fool."

"Give me a break. Half the department thought you were crazy to get involved with Regan Grant. Did I ever stick my nose in and try to warn you off?"

"No. You tried to steal her away from me right in front of my house. Remember how thick you laid on the Italian charm?"

"Hell, Ethan, if you couldn't see that I was trying to help you make up your mind…"

"So, is that why you're flirting with Christy Jones? If it is, her husband isn't buying your act. She *is* still married, you know."

"Christy? Dammit, you oughta know that's strictly business. And she said you told her I was open to doing contract investigative work."

"Okay, okay. I did. It was a mistake, okay? Maybe you should think twice about accepting her offer. Bert says Royce is on a tear. We've both seen good cops go bad. Royce has never been rational when it comes to Christy." He squinted at Mitch. "Sort of like how you aren't firing on all cylinders where Bert's new waitress is concerned."

"Ah. Finally we're getting to the crux of this conversation."

A guilty expression flashed across Ethan's face.

"Oh, don't tighten the reins now, Ethan. Let's take this at a gallop. What's your problem with Gillian Stevens?"

Ethan released a pent-up breath. His gaze didn't waver. "It's a gut feeling. How often in the years we worked together did we go with one of my gut reactions and been glad we did?"

Breaking the eye lock Ethan had on him, Mitch massaged the back of his neck. "A lot. I never kept track. There were a couple of times you were wrong, though."

"A couple out of six years?" Ethan sounded scornful.

"Closer to seven," Mitch mumbled. "Dammit, Ethan. I haven't asked the woman to marry me, I only asked her for a date. She turned me down," he admitted quietly, ramming his hands in his back pockets while he scuffed the pointed toe of his boot in the dirt.

"She did? What the hell's wrong with her?"

His head snapped up at Ethan's outburst. Laughing, Mitch reached over and slapped Ethan's shoulder. "Thanks for the vote of confidence."

"Yeah, well…" Ethan glanced away. "Maybe we should trust my gut this time. A couple of uniforms from the day shift said the Stevens woman asked some not-so-subtle questions about you. Her being down-and-out, I figure she has her eye on your ranch and your police retirement."

"Who said she's down-and-out?"

Ethan rubbed his chin. "I don't know. Why else would a woman with her looks be content working for Bert and Flo? Not that they're not great people—they are. But you know as well as I do that there are other restaurants in town where a pretty waitress can make a whole lot more in tips."

The grunt Mitch gave signaled his satisfaction. "So we agree she's pretty. Do you think we can start there and work up? I'm going to ask her out again, Ethan. Until she says yes, as a matter of fact."

Ethan called Taz to heel. The dog had strayed to sniff a parking meter a few feet away. "Regan and I ended up not asking anyone over to play cards this weekend. I admit, the offer I made was a ploy to set you up with a hometown girl. If you're not afraid to get Regan's assessment of Gillian Stevens, I'm off next Saturday. I'm willing to reschedule dinner and let you bring your own date.''

Mitch glanced thoughtfully at the café. ''She might be more comfortable going to someone's house.'' Turning back, he crossed his arms. ''You've got to promise me Regan won't launch one of her all-out psychology evaluations.''

''Aw, man. Regan tells everyone you're her adopted brother. Maybe we'd better forget the whole thing if you're gonna hold me responsible for any nosy questions my wife asks. Regan's her own woman.''

''I know.'' Mitch hooted. ''It's refreshing to know there's a lady who doesn't slaver like Taz every time you flash the famous Knight smile.''

''Now you've gone too far, Valetti. I never dated a woman who slavered.''

Mitch thumped Ethan's chest with one finger. ''Nor have I. Remember that, please.'' Leaving his former partner, he ambled toward the café. At the curb he stopped and glanced back. ''I'll call tonight and let you know if she agrees. If she does, I want another concession. No shop talk. I'm not an officer anymore, and sometimes women bail when they're forced to dwell on the bad stuff that can happen to a cop.''

''Okay. Sure. You have my permission to kick me under the table if I start talking about a case. But I have a feeling that old habits die hard....''

''I understand. It's just...cop talk can get intense. And Ethan—talk about gut feelings. I can't put it into words, but this lady...uh, darn.''

Ethan said nothing for a heartbeat. Then he feigned interest in what his dog was doing. ''It's no mystery to me, Valetti. You always had a weakness for a nice ass.''

Fighting a smile, Mitch returned to the café. That was point two he and Ethan agreed on concerning Gillian Stevens.

Embarrassed by the direction of his thoughts and afraid Gillian might read his mind, Mitch turned instead to plotting what he'd say to her when she came to take his order.

Good, the back booth was available. Easier to make a play without an audience.

Even if he no longer worked at the precinct, he had friends there and the place was a hotbed of gossip. If Gillian rejected him again, he could do without Amy getting wind of it. Why didn't Gillian come and take his order? Maybe he was all wrong in thinking they felt a mutual attraction.

The crowd had thinned. But a full house wouldn't have stopped Gillian from being aware of Mitch's return. She found it odd that he'd passed several clean booths to hide in the corner. Or was someone joining him? She hated to think it might be Christy Jones. That would explain why he'd plant his back to the wall near a ready escape if Royce happened to stop by.

Heavens, she could be guessing all wrong. Maybe Ethan Knight went to collect materials on the case they'd disappeared outside to discuss. Again her heart did a flip. What if a handbill with her picture on it had come across his desk? What if they wanted to compare an old picture of Noelle McGrath with the waitress they knew as Gillian Stevens?

Pacing nervously, she tried to figure out if there was any likelihood of New Orleans or Flagstaff police finding out that Noelle McGrath's birth name was really Gillian Noelle? It could all depend on what Daryl's neighbor, the one who'd relayed his dying request, had told Daryl's brother, Conrad. Conrad was his only sibling—his only living relative. He'd never liked her much. No telling how he'd react once he discovered Daryl had kept her on as joint owner of McGrath CPA.

"Hey, what does it take to get service around here?" Mitch's voice held a teasing quality. If not for that, Gillian might have been tempted to ask Flo to wait on him. No, she wasn't a coward. Besides, Flo would demand an explanation if she tried too obviously to avoid Mitch.

Gillian plopped a glass of water and a menu down in front of him. "Sorry. I wasn't ignoring you. You made such a point of wanting privacy, I assumed you were waiting for someone to join you."

"I am." He turned up the wattage of his smile. "This is about when you took a lunch break the other day. Truth is, I'm sick of my own company, and was hoping you'd consent to join me."

"Oh, I…think there's a rule about not fraternizing with customers." Gillian hoped she sounded normal, even though she was dealing with a rising panic. She fumbled the napkin-wrapped silverware before dropping a set near his right hand.

Mitch steadied her elbow in time to keep the whole pack from spilling onto the floor. "Give me one good reason anyone would make such a stupid rule. You're entitled to lunch. In fact, it comes with the job."

Suddenly pulling back, Mitch inspected his hands. "I forgot I petted Taz. I probably smell like dog. Excuse me while I go wash. When I pass the kitchen, I'll stick my head in and tell Bert I want a burger. Tell me what you want, and I'll pass it on."

Her sigh was probably more exasperation than capitulation. Mitch chose to misunderstand. Keeping his smile in place, he slid out of the booth and brushed against her, murmuring, "My mother would tell you I've always known all the angles to get my own way."

Gillian smiled in spite of herself. "Does your mother live in Desert City?"

He wasn't fast enough to cover his guarded expression. "My parents winter in Palm Springs and summer in Vermont. Right now they're somewhere in the Mediterranean finishing a world cruise. At least, that's what their housekeeper told Ethan when he tried to notify them I'd been shot." She was aware that he watched her closely as he spoke, as if to garner a reaction.

Gillian couldn't hide her shock at his parents' absence. "They didn't come to see you?"

"No big deal." His shrug matched his proclamation. Gillian noted a deeper pain in his eyes. Clearly he was hurt by his parents' indifference—a revelation at odds with his tough-guy image.

She'd rather not think about the inner man. Her purpose in furthering their acquaintance had only one reason—to find out whether Mitch Valetti was connected to the criminals she'd seen him rendezvous with a few nights ago. *Keep all contact superficial.*

Gillian McGrath had changed into a person no decent man would ask to lunch if he knew all the things she'd done these past few weeks.

That's different, insisted a little voice. And yet, long-ingrained values continued to increase her guilt.

"I've lost you again," Mitch observed. "Oh, if you're worried some fruitcake will walk in off the street and open fire on me, rest easy. I'm a simple rancher now, remember? My days of dealing with the bad guys are over."

Gillian hoped she didn't look as skeptical as she felt. His statement was pretty ironic; if the men from the blue car walked in, *she'd* be the one shot at. "You go wash your hands. I'll order your burger. You want coffee or a soft drink to go with it?"

"A pitcher of lemonade and two glasses. Even if you won't sit down and eat with me, take time for a cool drink."

"That sounds good. I'm not really hungry."

Mitch took stock of the entire package that was Gillian Stevens. She was slender for her height. Too slender. From her remarks, she didn't strike him as the type to be on a perpetual diet. "Bert fixes great homemade soup. A bowl of that would see you through the rest of your shift."

"Soup. Did Flo put you up to this? She's been talking about Bert's potato-cheese soup as if it were some magic potion."

Mitch clapped a hand across his heart. "I thought this up all on my lonesome. And *lonesome* is the operative word. Take pity on me, woman. I've spent the last three days and nights in the company of horses and a lop-eared pup. I'm wondering if I'm cut out for the solitary life of ranching."

Gillian rolled her eyes. "Time to cowboy up. That's a new term I learned the other day. It means—"

"I know. It means suck it up and quit whining. Join me for lunch and I'll be on my best behavior. I promise." A smile brought deep, appealing creases to his cheeks.

"You never give up, do you?"

"Nope. That's a trait needed by every good cop."

"Hmm." The bell over the door sounded, saving Gillian from getting embroiled in a discussion about what traits made *good* cops. Was he still one, and lying to her about having quit?

"We've talked so long I have customers," she murmured, pulling the order pad from her apron pocket.

"We've talked five minutes. You get a lunch *hour*. Let Flo take their order."

As if she heard her name, Flo appeared in the kitchen doorway, menus under her arm and three glasses of water in her hand. "I'll catch that table, Gilly. Bert's already dished you up a nice bowl of soup. He's putting the finishing touches on Mitch's burger. All you have to do is pour whatever you want to drink, sit and take a load off your feet."

"Tell me again this isn't a conspiracy," Gillian muttered, half to herself and half to Mitch.

"She must be psychic. Honestly," he said, "I didn't prearrange anything."

"Bert just happened to know you wanted a burger?"

"I hate admitting how predictable I am about food. Ask him. He'll tell you I ate here an average of three days a week for six or so years. Rain or shine, I ordered a burger."

"I don't know why I believe you, but I do. It's too bizarre to be a lie. You win. Go wash. I'll join you for lunch."

Mitch felt like clicking his heels together. He was careful not to act too triumphant. On the way to the men's room and back, he tried to figure out arguments that might convince her to go with him to Ethan's on Saturday night.

"You're right about this soup," she said, flashing a smile as he returned and slid into the booth. "It's delicious."

"Now that you know I'm so wise, we'll save time if you trust everything I say."

She paused, her spoon halfway to her lips. "Do I have *gullible* stamped on my forehead? I don't think so."

Mitch grinned around a bite of hamburger. After he'd chewed and swallowed, he changed the subject. "Flo calls you Gilly. I like that. It fits you. Can anyone call you that?"

It was on the tip of her tongue to tell him she went by her middle name of Noelle. She hadn't realized how hard it would be to watch her words in personal conversations. Shrugging, she focused her attention on opening a packet of crackers. "Suit yourself. I answer to a broad range of names." She gave him a brief smile.

His brows drew together quizzically. "Oh. I guess you mean customers yell, hey you, miss or waitress—things like that. Before I became a detective, when I still wore a uniform every day, I got called a lot of other things, too," he said wryly.

"You mention your old job a lot. Maybe you shouldn't have quit."

Unconsciously, he rubbed his thigh. "Cats may have nine lives. People don't. I woke up in the hospital positive that if I made it through surgery, I'd leave there living on borrowed time. So I quit the force."

Gillian considered the damage bullets did. Daryl, killed on his doorstep. Mitch had probably hung on by a thread. She didn't realize she was crumbling her crackers until Mitch reached across the table and took her hand.

"I made Ethan promise no cop-speak if I managed to talk you into going to his house for dinner with me on Saturday night. And here I'm guilty of doing the same thing. Really, that part of my life is behind me. The most dangerous thing I'll be doing in the future is breaking a green horse or two. Not for a while, either." He smoothed his thumb over the soft skin on the back of her hand. "I'm sorry if I frightened you, Gilly. I'm a normal, everyday Joe now."

She pulled her hand loose, unable to decide if he was trying too hard to convince her. Was he attempting to lure her into his web of deceit? No matter. At the moment he represented the only tie she had to the men in the blue car. The men who most likely had her small suitcase. Gillian shoved the mangled packet of crackers under the edge of her plate and picked up her spoon again. "Sorry. I may not be keen on eating while talking about bullet wounds, but there are aspects of detective work I find fascinating."

"Such as?"

"Oh, I don't know." She rolled one shoulder. "Methods used to find stuff that's lost or stolen." Realizing she might be sticking her neck out too far, Gillian ignored the escalated pounding of her heart and plunged on. "I'm reading a mystery that opens with hidden documents," she improvised. "The character who hid them dies suddenly, but not before sending a garbled note to a friend saying his, uh, girlfriend had the key to wherever he'd hidden the papers. No one can find the key. So, ex-detective Valetti, where do you suppose he put those documents?"

Mitch polished off his hamburger, took a sip of lemonade and wiped his mouth with his napkin. "Skip ahead to the last chapter and find out."

"Thanks a lot. Somehow I doubt you did that on your cases."

He laughed. "You like mysteries, huh? Police procedurals? Well, well, I guess that means you'll enjoy spending the evening with me, Ethan and his wife, Regan. Dinner's at six this coming Saturday. Where shall I pick you up?"

Gillian had walked into that one with her eyes wide-open. This was where he'd been headed all along. She felt the control she wanted to maintain slipping out of her hands. "Tell me where the Knights live. I'll meet you there."

"Huh? What kind of date is that?"

"No date." Rising, she stacked their dirty dishes. "Take it or leave it."

"Sheesh, woman. Okay." He heaved a sigh. "Hand over a pencil and tear off an order form. I'll write down their address and draw you a map. Starting from where? Where do you live?"

"If I wanted you to know that," she said, "I'd have agreed to let you come by for me. Start at the café. I'll find my way from here."

Mitch fiddled with the pencil. "You really aren't very trusting. Makes me wonder about your ex. I know you said your divorce wasn't bitter, but I've seen abuse before. If he knocked you around, it's better to admit it. Getting all that out helps heal the wounds."

Hit hard by his unexpected strike at Daryl, Gillian felt a sudden welling of tears. With her hands full of dishes, she couldn't brush them away. Mitch, of course, saw her blinking frantically. "You've jumped to the wrong conclusion about my marriage," she finally managed to say. "My ex-husband's only mistake was that he married the wrong woman." She paused. "On second thought, I'm not ready to participate in a couples thing."

"Sure you are," Mitch insisted, stuffing the address he'd written into her apron pocket. "An evening playing cards and having a few laughs has gotta beat sitting home alone reading a bad mystery."

"No, Mitch. Look, I was wrong to think—"

He touched a finger to her lips. "Don't think. Please."

Before Gillian could answer one way or the other, the front door banged open and Royce Jones stomped in. He had a wild look in his eyes as he made straight for her and Mitch. This time, his sidekicks were missing, Gillian noted. Which probably meant he was more likely than not to start a brawl.

Mitch, his gait always slow and uneven after he'd sat a while, remembered Ethan's warning. The last thing he wanted was to bring trouble down on Bert and Flo. Nor did he want an unpleasant scene in front of Gillian. Especially after he'd been so quick to tell her that trouble didn't follow him anymore.

"Royce." Mitch stuck out his hand in greeting and worked to keep his voice level. "Long time no see. I talked to your wife a week or so ago. She asked if I'd be interested in a possible contract job. Never got back to me. I guess her department wouldn't kick loose with the funds. You know how that goes. Say, have you met Flo and Bert's new waitress?" He eased far enough to one side to reveal Gillian, who still clutched their empty dishes.

"We haven't actually met." Royce grudgingly transferred his attention from Mitch to Gillian. The ploy worked to defuse some of his bluster.

"Gillian, Royce Jones. Royce, Gillian Stevens," Mitch segued right into formal introductions. Unleashing a chuckle, he lightly tapped the man in uniform on the shoulder. "Frankly, buddy, your timing stinks. You interrupted me in the middle of asking this lady for a date. Now, maybe being an old married man and all, you might've forgotten how long it takes a guy to get up the courage to ask out somebody new. I'm here to tell you it hasn't gotten any easier. Since you did interrupt, the least you can do is vouch for my character."

Gillian shifted the dishes, almost dropping them. Mitch Valetti had amazing nerve. Apparently Royce Jones thought so too, judging by the way his jaw went slack.

Mitch waited, his face carefully masked.

The charade dragged on for several minutes; Gillian regained her poise and sense of humor. Donning a properly cynical smile, she let her gaze travel between the two men. "If you have to work that hard on an endorsement," she told Royce, "it's probably just as well if I turn him down now and give him time to ask someone else to be his date at the Knights' dinner party."

"What? I thought you'd agreed to go." It was obvious from Mitch's face that he hadn't expected his machinations to backfire.

Royce suddenly found the whole situation amusing. He laughed, lording it over Mitch and his predicament. "Well, Valetti, 'pears to me your reign as Desert City's stud has come to an end."

"Come on, Jones. Fun is fun. I'm trying to be serious here. Ethan said you think I made a pass at Christy. I didn't. Never have. Never would."

Royce tucked his hands under his bulging biceps and scowled. "Don Billings said he saw you two right here, tight as termites. Said you were coming on to the waitress, but the minute Christy walked in, things changed."

"Excuse me." Gillian regained their attention. "Mitch was drinking coffee at the counter. I was eating lunch. Two separate entities. Christy asked to talk to him about a job. Mitch carried his cup over and sat at her table. In the center of a packed room. There was nothing private about their meeting. You asked me that day to clarify what happened. I said the same thing then. It was strictly business."

Muttering, Royce backed down. "She did stick up for

you, Valetti.'' The beefy man rocked from foot to foot. ''Christy makes me crazy. She's moved in with her sister again. Sorry, Mitch. I should know Don Billings gets sadistic pleasure out of causing trouble in the ranks.'' He growled a bit more, cleared his throat and edged closer to Gillian. ''You're probably safe enough going out with this guy.''

She barely avoided a smile as Mitch muttered, ''Thanks a heap, Royce. Remind me never to ask for your backing if I ever decide to run for public office. It'd be like handing my opponent the victory.''

''That's the best you're gonna get from me, man. If you want more, don't be doing side work for Christy, even if she finds the funding.''

At a stalemate, the men continued to posture and glare at one another.

''Stop it, you two. I'll go with you on Saturday night, Mitch. Tell Mrs. Knight I'll bring dessert,'' she said more softly. By then, though, Royce was on his way out the door.

''Regan. Ethan's wife is Regan. I'll tell her.'' Mitch touched Gillian's cheek lightly with one finger. He let his hand drop when she raised her eyes to meet his. ''This is for real, right? You're not saying you'll go just to get rid of me?'' he asked.

His obviously shaky confidence chased away the last remnants of her doubt. ''Have you ever been stood up in your life?''

''Yeah, I have. And Ethan's never let me live it down.''

There was a vulnerability in his admission that touched Gillian. Maybe because it had crossed her mind not to show up... ''I'll be there. Six o'clock, you said.'' She turned and all but ran to the kitchen, never looking back.

Mitch, although slower to gather his wits, remembered to drop money on the table for his meal and a tip before he left. He even made eye contact with the remaining lunch-goers. He didn't know any of the men, so if they'd overheard his exchange with Royce, who would they tell?

All the way home, he felt like a man who'd pulled off a big coup. Dammit, he couldn't remember the last time he'd been so desperate to make a woman like him. There was something in the shadowy blue of Gillian Stevens's eyes that sent his hormones spinning and his mind into chaos. Not a good combination. If he were counseling a friend in a similar case, he'd suggest running like hell in the opposite direction.

Maybe she'd screw up really badly on Saturday night. Then he'd have to heed Ethan's warning. Or Regan's, if the women didn't hit it off. That meant any chance for a relationship with Gilly would be finished. Mitch hadn't owned up to it before, but the real reason he'd hung out at Ethan's as long as he had was to wallow in a sense of family and home. His mother and father had been too involved in Wall Street to act like parents with Mitch and his two sisters, who were both school-age when he was born. He'd decided he'd either been a pure accident or a product of his father's egotistical desire for a male to carry on the Valetti name. In any event, Mitch had been partially raised by his dad's mother. Following her death, his guidance had come from a housekeeper, a cook and a nanny, respectively. Ethan's folks were the total opposite of *his* parents, and they were genuine role models, to boot.

In marrying Regan and requesting to adopt quadruplets, Ethan had landed for himself everything his parents enjoyed and more. Mitch envied the love his friends shared—that sense of family. Hell, he even envied their sleepy exchanges when they got up to console wakeful babies in the small hours of the night.

Maybe he wouldn't feel so footloose if he went back to coaching the kids' basketball team at St. Margaret's. His job, coaching, part-time ranching—before Ethan got married, it had all seemed enough. Why was he suddenly spending so much time wondering what it would be like to teach a kid of his own how to play ball? Wondering who might mother that child?

He sat in the car outside his home for a minute and surveyed his domain, trying to see it through a woman's eyes. Amy had called it a typical bachelor pad, he remembered as he climbed from the car and unlocked his front door. Trooper bounced all over him, barking and licking Mitch's face. "Whoa. Hey," he said, kneeling to rub the pup's belly. "Are you trying to tell me all I really need is a dog?"

Once, Mitch might have bought into that philosophy. Not now. After he'd fed Trooper and seen to the horses in the barn, a long empty evening stretched ahead of him. That was followed by a hard time falling asleep. Dreams just didn't cut a man's loneliness, even if these nights Gilly Stevens invaded most of his.

CHAPTER FIVE

ANXIOUS TO BEGIN his eagerly awaited night out, Mitch sped through the tasks of mucking out stalls and spreading fresh hay. He showered, shaved and put on slacks and a sport shirt rather than jeans. Ready to walk out the door, he recalled that he hadn't discussed what to wear with Gillian. According to an article in a men's magazine someone had brought him at the hospital, first dates went better if the woman showed up dressier than the man. The author warned that, the other way around, women tended to feel awkward and embarrassed. Mitch didn't know how seriously to take this, but why risk it?

Back to his bedroom. He rummaged through his closet, hoping to find a pair of laundry-pressed jeans. Ah, good, one pair left. The shirt he had on looked dorky with jeans. He pawed through drawers until he found a navy-blue T-shirt Regan had washed before he moved home. He'd fussed at her for doing his wash. Now, seeing how full his hamper had gotten, Mitch was grateful for Regan's insistence.

And it was a good thing he'd gone back to change clothes, even though Trooper yipped and loped back and forth to the door as if to question his master's sanity. Mitch had nearly forgotten to call his neighbor, Dave D'Angelo, to ask if Dave would check on Pretty Baby a couple of times over the course of the evening. Her due date was still two weeks away. Since this was her first foal, Mitch would feel more comfortable knowing she was looked after.

"Hi, Dave. Mitch. I'm going out for a while tonight. Could I impose on you to keep an eye on my pregnant mare while I'm gone?" He listened a moment. "You will? Thanks, Dave. You can reach me at Ethan's if Pretty Baby goes into labor. Oh, and I'm taking Trooper with me."

The men exchanged a few more comments, and then Mitch heard a woman's voice in the background. "Tell Barb I heard that," he said. "It's sort of a date. I mean, there'll be an unmarried woman there." Mitch listened again. "No way. Dave, tell Barb I'll know who to blame if Father Costanza calls to ask when I'm posting banns. This is a *first* date, for crying out loud. Not even a real date. Yeah, I'll let Barb know if it gets serious. Bye. Thanks again. What? No. Those two incidents seemed to be the extent of it. No more strange happenings. The last creep scared my horses. Didn't destroy anything, though. You bet, phone our vet if you think Pretty Baby's in distress. Don't wait."

After hanging up, Mitch turned on a light in the living room. He paused at the fireplace, as had become habit, and ran a finger lightly over the lettering on Katie's urn. Stupid, he told himself. Except it made him feel that, somehow or other, he *would* connect with her family. Although he didn't seem to be making any headway, he admitted as he also touched Gran Valetti's rosary beads.

She'd left the world before her time, too. Mitch had fallen away from her church and her beliefs after the day he'd come home from elementary school and found her bludgeoned to death in the kitchen. A robbery, the police declared. All that was missing from the house was a fifty-dollar emergency fund she'd kept in a cookie jar. The person responsible was never brought to justice. The incident changed Mitch's life. In spite of his parents' objections to his being a cop, Gran's death led him to police work. He made one concession to her faith: for every rotten crook and killer he'd jailed, Mitch lit a candle at church and gave a donation in Gran's name.

As he looped her rosary around the pewter urn, he whispered an old prayer she'd taught him. It ended with, "May the Saints protect you wherever you are." Though he felt foolish, he asked Gran to watch out for baby Katie.

Backing away from the fireplace, he called Trooper. The pup responded with a bark and bounced toward him.

EVEN FACTORING IN all the delays, Mitch still arrived at Ethan's twenty minutes early. Looking harried, Regan Knight answered his knock. She held a crying child under one arm. A cheese grater dangled from the opposite hand. Two more babies crawled down the hall behind her, while a third scooted on his butt, propelled by a hand and a foot.

Mitch had Trooper on a leash, but it tangled around his ankles when the babies and the puppy tried to connect.

"Mitch, thank heavens you're early. I was so afraid you were—what's her name?" Regan looked blank.

"Gillian? Gilly. Oof." Mitch momentarily lost his wind as Regan shoved the wriggling, crying ten-month-old girl at him. Trooper threatened to knock him off his feet now that juggling a child placed him farther off balance.

"Yeah, that's the name Ethan gave me. Gillian Stevens. It has a nice ring," Regan said. "I don't know why it's so hard to remember. Would you change Cara while

I finish grating cheese to go over the green corn tamales? Don't ask me why I suddenly felt domestic and decided to concoct tamales from scratch.''

''Where's Ethan? Loafing again?''

Regan shook her head. ''He's out on a call. He took Taz. Last month a little girl his sister Elizabeth had in foster care was returned to her natural parents. Ethan got a call from a neighbor who claims they're abusing Brittany again. He's gone to get a court order to pick her up. I haven't seen her case file. Based on what Ethan and Lizzie have told me about her situation, I think we have grounds to remove her permanently this time. The good news is Lizzie would love to adopt Brittany.''

''Like you and Ethan are doing with these guys?'' Mitch said, bending to tweak Rick's nose before he unhooked Trooper's leash. ''Can I put Trooper in the backyard? He's only paper trained.'' Mitch wrinkled his nose. ''Not well-trained at that.''

''I'll let him out through the kitchen.'' Regan called to the dog, maneuvering carefully through three of the four quadruplets.

Mitch, having spent a long time in this house recovering, didn't have to ask where the nursery was.

''Hey, when did you put the kids in separate rooms?'' he asked when he returned to the large, welcoming kitchen, toting a much happier Cara. Already the aroma of the corn tamales filled the air and whetted his appetite. Mitch grabbed a squeaky toy from the floor and examined it to make sure it belonged to the babies and not Taz before he put it in the drooling child's hand. Cara, the smallest of the quads, was the one most damaged by Tony DeSalvo. No longer in casts, she wore Velcro braces now to help with damaged nerves that restricted the movement of one arm and a leg. And her development was slower than that of her siblings.

"We rearranged the cribs last weekend. Mark and Rick are light sleepers. Angela and Cara still wake up several times a night. Moving the boys means they aren't bothered when the girls fuss. Put Cara in her walker, Mitch. The doctor said it'll strengthen her muscles. I'll pour you a glass of vino. Then I want to hear all about this new woman in your life before she arrives." Regan had things in the kitchen under better control. She seemed ready to devote time to grilling Mitch.

He set the child in her walker and hoisted her sister, tickling Angela to make her giggle. "What has Ethan told you about Gilly?" He placed Angela on the floor again.

"Not much." Regan pulled the cork and poured a robust red wine into two glasses.

"You can't lie worth a damn. I know she rubs Ethan the wrong way."

Regan tasted from her glass before handing Mitch his. "Don't swear around the kids. And I should've asked if you'd rather have a beer."

"Isn't wine more civilized? I want to make a good impression on Gillian. I wonder where she is," he muttered, stepping around Regan to peer out the window that faced the street.

"Goodness, Mitch. It's not quite six. She isn't late."

"I know, but…"

"If she worked today, she could be running late. I've never seen you so antsy, Mitch. Why don't we talk about something else? Then maybe you'll quit clock watching."

Mitch watched Angela crawl over to the boys, who played with a small wagon filled with blocks. As if he hadn't heard Regan, he turned away and pressed his nose to the window again.

She sighed. "Ethan said you were unofficially investigating an unusual case that sort of appeared on your doorstep. How's that going?"

"Slow. Yesterday I fired up my computer and downloaded an investigative program that allows me to run a state-by-state check by date of birth. I started with Arizona, since it's where the suitcase was found. I discovered there were a lot of babies born that day. So far, I haven't found any named Katie, Kathryn or Kathleen who died the same day they came into the world."

Regan raised an eyebrow. "Ethan thinks you're wasting your time. I'm inclined to think it's worth the effort. I hope you succeed. It's an intriguing puzzle."

"It's more, Regan. Don't freak out when I say this, but I feel like…like the baby's…well, not her guardian, exactly. Maybe…emissary."

"After all the years I've worked in social services—plus all the case studies I've read—I've come across far stranger stories."

"Hey, Gilly's here." Mitch started to turn from the window, then cupped his hand against the glass again to screen out the kitchen light. "What's she doing? She's not getting out. I'd better go see. Maybe she's not sure she's at the right house."

Regan joined him at the window. "You said she was bringing dessert. She's probably getting it out of the back seat. Nope. Looks to me like she's drumming her fingers on the steering wheel. Hmm. I'd say she's having second thoughts about coming in. Why? She's parked right behind your pickup. She obviously knows you're here."

"If she's seen me driving anything, it's probably the Vette." Mitch thrust his half-drunk glass of wine into

Regan's free hand. "Anyway, she's kind of shy. Don't overwhelm her, all right? And whatever you do, don't psychoanalyze her." Once he'd delivered that lecture, Mitch hobbled down the hall, leaving a speechless Regan behind.

Afraid Gillian would take off before he could reach her and persuade her to stay, Mitch walked so fast a pain struck deep in his side. It stole his breath; when he pulled open Gilly's car door, he couldn't speak, wasn't able to allay the fear that caused her to jerk away and cry out.

For a long moment, Mitch stood, breathing hard, blinking at Gillian, who cowered against the passenger side of her car.

"What's wrong?" Razor instincts—honed to a fine edge through his years as a cop—kicked in, restoring Mitch's ability to breathe. "Were you involved in a fender bender or something?"

"No." Gillian's fingers flexed around her seat belt, already stretched to its limits. "You scared the daylights out of me, yanking my door open without saying a word. Why did you pounce on me like that?"

"Why are you sitting in your car instead of coming to the door?"

Guilt flooded her face.

"Aha! You considered standing me up, didn't you?"

After a shake of her head, she said, "I gave my word."

Mitch didn't look convinced. "I watched for you out the window. I know how long you sat here after driving up."

"I, ah, was bolstering my courage to meet your friends. I'm not good in crowds."

"There's only going to be four of us. Hardly a crowd."

"Oh, so one of the Knights parks in the street?"

"I told Regan you wouldn't know my pickup. I use it mostly to haul hay and stuff. Tonight, I brought kibble for Trooper and I didn't want him getting into it."

"Oh. Well, I still need to work up nerve to get cozy with your friends."

Mitch's eyes darkened sympathetically as he leaned inside and took her hand. "This is supposed to be a fun evening, Gilly. Not a supreme ordeal."

"I know." She slid out, clutching her small handbag. "Flo said the same thing. By the way, Bert helped me make dessert. Strawberry flan. It's a work of art. Don't ask me where he got fresh strawberries this late in the year. We ought to take it out of the trunk and put it into a refrigerator."

"Give me your keys. I'll carry the container."

She extracted a single key from her jeans pocket and handed it over. That was when Mitch noticed how the soft blue denim of her jeans outlined her long legs. He'd never seen her in anything but one of Flo's uniforms. Mitch had known she was slim, of course. He hadn't known she was so much leg. Damn, he'd always been attracted to leggy women.

"Do I have strawberry juice on my clothes?" Gillian tugged at the front of her bright-red T-shirt, trying to identify where she might have a spot.

"You're fine. Great, in fact. I'm glad you didn't dress up. I meant to tell you gatherings in Desert City are generally casual."

"Good. Most of the clothing I have with me is knock-around stuff."

Mitch's head was in the trunk, muffling his reply. "Wow. This is enough to feed half the neighborhood. I hope Regan has room in her fridge. Follow me," he added, awkwardly closing the trunk with an elbow. "Regan's waiting on the porch."

Gillian fell in behind him. She craned her neck to try to see something of the woman married to Mitch's best buddy. Gillian had meant to ask Flo for more information, but the café was extra busy and she didn't get a chance. All she knew was that Regan Knight had met and married Ethan in a whirlwind courtship. Oh, and her career was in social work.

Around Mitch's bobbing broad shoulders, Gillian glimpsed sleek blond hair, gold earrings and black linen slacks topped by a white silk blouse.

Her steps slowed. Worrying about how her oldest jeans would stack up against linen and silk, Gillian ran right into Mitch, who she didn't realize had stopped.

Reaching behind him, he clasped her hand and tugged her against his side, where she could see and be seen by Regan Knight.

Gillian opened her mouth to respond to her hostess's greeting. The words stuck in her throat. She grabbed Mitch's arm to keep from fainting. Her ears buzzed and stars danced before her eyes. Her attention froze on a child clasped in Regan Knight's arms. A girl in ruffled pink rompers—very near the age her own baby would have been. Gillian had systematically avoided all children in the ten months since she'd lost her own. Why, oh why, hadn't she asked if the Knights had a family?

"Gilly! Gilly?" Mitch's voice bombarded her from afar. Her name swam at her through waves of nausea.

Regan descended the steps. "She looks ill. Mitch, take the dessert into the house before you drop it all over the sidewalk. Look after the kids, please."

As if he hadn't heard, he plunked the flan container

down on the steps and hooked a supporting arm around Gillian. "You worked two shifts again, didn't you?"

She nodded, endeavoring to quell the initial shock.

"Skipped breakfast and lunch, too, I'll bet." Glancing up at the worried Regan, he continued in a proprietary manner. "Getting her to eat is like spinning your wheels. It's like—"

"You've known her *how* long?" Regan broke in, her left eyebrow disappearing into her bangs.

Gillian let their argument swirl around her until the worst of the unexpected jolt had passed. Her dizziness had lessened and her churning stomach began to settle. She needed an extra minute to collect her scattered thoughts. Think! What could she tell them so Mitch's friend wouldn't consider her a complete screwball?

"If you don't believe me, Regan, ask Flo," Mitch argued. "Gilly doesn't eat enough to fill a peanut shell. You've got eyes. You're skinny, but she's thinner."

"Stop, Mitch. You're embarrassing her," Regan scolded. "Here, take Cara. Give us a minute alone. We'll bring the dessert when we come in."

Mitch seemed reluctant to let go of Gillian. "Don't badger her, Regan. I already asked, and she told me she doesn't have one of those eating disorders."

This time both of Regan's eyebrows shot up. She employed the look she'd perfected to get subordinates to do her bidding. Mitch took Cara from her, slanting Gillian a last troubled glance before he limped up the steps and into the house.

Ever direct, as she had to be in her job as a social worker, Regan struck while Gillian's defenses were lowest. "Are you pregnant?"

"Wh-a-at?" That was the last question Gillian expected.

Regan ticked the symptoms off on her fingers. "Dizzy. Nauseated. Off your food. My husband said Bert told him you decided to dig in here in Desert City because you ran out of money. Mitch mentioned you're divorced. I'm in private social work now, Gillian, but I still have connections if you need help."

Floored by the amount of information Regan Knight had at her fingertips, and by the sincerity of her offer, Gillian crossed her arms and rubbed away a chill. What had made her think she'd be safe hiding in a nest of cops? Clearly they'd already begun to add up various details they'd learned about her. Every instinct went on red alert. She ought to...*wanted* to give Flo her notice and take off again. But a very cold place inside reminded Gillian why she couldn't. She wasn't going anywhere without doing every single thing in her power to locate Katie's urn. Her terrible loss was tied to the men in the blue car, whom she'd last seen leaving Mitch Valetti's lane. If that meant she had to perfect covering her tracks and lying—that was what she'd do.

"I'm...not pregnant," she told the woman drilling her with all-seeing blue eyes. "I was ill for a while before and after my divorce. Not an eating disorder," she hastened to add. "Emotions did affect my physical state," she said, reverting to honesty. "If you don't mind, I'd rather not get into it. I'm trying hard to put the past behind me." She mustered a smile, however feeble.

"Boy, do I understand where you're coming from on that score. I've recently overcome a long-standing phobia toward dogs." Regan curved a bracing hand around Gillian's upper arm. "I won't lecture, Gilly. I will say I thought I could handle my fears alone, but after meeting Ethan I learned how much easier it is to share the burden with someone who loves you."

Gillian laughed nervously. "I'm happy to hear what worked for you. My case is different, though. No one can solve my problems but me."

She sounded so adamant, Regan let her hand fall away. "No man is an island," she reminded. "That also applies to women. Mitch wants to be leaned on, you know."

"I, ah, you have our relationship all wrong. He's not interested in me romantically. Even if he were, I can't— no, it's impossible." Gillian tightened her arms around her middle as though folding herself into a cocoon.

"Then it's your loss. Don't hurt him, though, he's—" Regan almost added that Mitch had recently been hurt. But he opened the screen door. In his arms, he held Cara and one of her brothers.

"Is everything all right?" he asked anxiously. "Ethan phoned. He'll be home in fifteen minutes. He asked if I'd help feed the kids and get them to bed in order to keep the evening on schedule. I volunteered Gilly's services, too."

"You have twins?" Gillian murmured, her gaze zeroing in on the children in Mitch's arms. The shock wasn't as great this time, even though one of the babies wore some type of brace. Anyway, how could a person not respond to such precious little beings?

Regan wriggled four fingers in front of Gillian's face. "Quadruplets. I'm surprised Flo and Bert didn't tell you. Or Mitch. He was shot in an attempt to help Ethan protect the babies from their abuser. We could have all been killed by that maniac. He wasn't the father—they were his girlfriend's children. Anyway, DeSalvo killed a cop, so he'll never get out of prison. Their birth mom's been institutionalized for a mental disorder. Ethan and I are fostering the kids. We've petitioned to adopt. It's looking more promising, considering everyone knows they were neglected.''

Gillian mounted the steps. ''It's beyond me how any woman who carries a child for nine months could—could—''

''Mistreat them?'' Regan bluntly finished Gillian's sentence. ''I have stories that would curl your hair. As do Mitch and Ethan. That's how Ethan and I met. He established an underground safety net for abused kids in the city,'' she said with unmistakable pride. As she spoke, she bent to pick up the flan.

''Regan's former boss tried to force her to stop Ethan's unofficial foster placement program,'' Mitch said, abruptly transferring the baby boy into Gillian's arms.

She could do little but gather in the soft, sweet-smelling bundle. *This is what it would've been like to hold Katie.* Tears formed and demanded release.

''Oops. Have you got him?'' Mitch, seeing the baby had slipped a little in Gillian's grasp, cupped a large, warm palm over her hand to secure her grip on Rick's heavily diapered bottom.

Determined to master her panic, Gillian fought against letting any tears escape. ''I wasn't prepared,'' she said. ''You didn't warn me. I…haven't got any experience with kids. Oh,'' she said, consciously changing that subject. ''I hope we didn't let the flan sit out here too long. It needs to go in the fridge.''

''I'll do that now and check my tamales. Odella—she's my partner, Gilly—helped me before she left our office. We work from this house. Now, Gilly, if you and Mitch would please put the babies in night diapers and pajamas, I'll fix their bottles. With luck, we'll have them ready for bed around the time Ethan gets home.''

Gillian nodded.

"Will do." Mitch hefted a third baby who sat in the middle of the hallway banging a large spoon against a metal lid. He growled against the little boy's neck, making the boy shriek wildly.

Overwhelmed by the presence of so many children, Gillian wasn't sure she'd be able to deal with even routine diapering.

Because neither Mitch nor Regan had a clue as to the very real anxiety assailing Gillian, no one paid attention to her fumbling efforts to follow Mitch's lead. Therefore, she was able to watch what he did and quickly learned to secure the diaper tabs.

Ethan and Taz showed up as Regan sat in the rocker, prepared to feed both boys. Mitch and Gillian each held a girl apiece. Gillian had conquered the worst of her jitters. She loved the feel of the warm little body snuggled close to her heart, and smiled at Angela's efforts to keep her eyes open. Could anything in the world be sweeter than having these tiny dimpled fingers clinging to her own?

Ethan tiptoed in and then out of the room, after stooping to hug each baby and exchange murmurs and a quick kiss with his wife.

Gillian happened to glance away from the Knights, and discovered Mitch observing her just as intently. The look he wore sent an undisguised shiver of need straight to her heart. He sparked a longing she'd really thought she'd never feel again. Not just a desire for sex. Gillian knew Mitch Valetti had triggered that hunger in her already. This feeling was different. A deeper yearning. An ache to make a baby with someone who loved kids as much as she did.

Dumb! The word rattled around inside Gillian's head. So what if Mitch was staring at her with a soft, sensual look in his eyes? Looking at her the way she'd hoped Daryl would when she'd excitedly informed him they were pregnant.

Regan Knight rose gracefully, interrupting Gillian's trip down memory lane. "We did it, guys," Regan whispered. "All four are fast asleep. I'll put Mark and Rick in their room and come back for the girls. Unless you two want to do the honors," she added as if noticing that Gillian had curled Angela more tightly to her breast.

Stirring, Mitch wiped a sappy expression off his face. "I'll show Gilly which crib. Can you believe she's the same woman who claimed not to have any baby experience? Gilly's a natural when it comes to handling kids, isn't she, Regan? Somehow I don't think Flo needs to worry about how Gilly spends her free time from now on. It's plain you'll be seeing more of her. At this rate, I'll probably never convince her to come out to the ranch to go riding. Horses can't compare to babies."

Gillian went still. "When did you invite me to your ranch?"

Mitch grinned. "I'd planned to wait until you were totally relaxed—after Regan's delicious meal and several glasses of wine. Actually, I was hoping to lure you out of the city tomorrow. Bert said you have Sundays off."

Gillian didn't know what to say, how to react.

"Do you ride?" Regan asked her, motioning them down the hall toward the babies' rooms.

"It's been years. I rode every summer as a girl. My mother's parents owned a farm. They kept a really gentle mare for me."

"A farm as opposed to a ranch? So you didn't grow up in the Southwest? Where did you live, Gilly?"

"In the Midwest. My grandparents lived in Ohio." She cleared her throat, realizing she'd revealed more than she'd intended. Was Ethan Knight's wife pumping her for information, or had she asked a simple, natural question?

"Years ago I had a boarding-school roommate from Chicago. Your accent is nothing like hers. You have a bit of a drawl," Regan said, pausing outside the door to the boys' room. "I'd guess you spent some time in the Deep South. Is that where you lived before you came here?"

"I have one of those eclectic accents. I only have to be around a person a little while to begin talking like them. And I never totally lost my childhood accent." Gillian tried for a casual shrug. She was determined not to give them any information they might use to trace her and find out she was a fraud.

"Hmm. I'm pretty good at picking out where a person's from. Now you've gone and spoiled my record."

"Why are you three standing in a dark hallway?" Ethan Knight stuck his head around the kitchen archway. He hadn't yet put on his shoes, and his hair was damp and tousled from his shower.

His wife smiled. "We're just chatting. Gilly spent her summers on a farm in the Midwest. I was saying that her accent doesn't sound to me as if she's lived there recently."

"We could probably discuss stuff like that while we eat. I hate to rush anyone, but I missed lunch. My stomach's caved in to my backbone. Hey, Mitch, I noticed Trooper in the yard. Did you bring puppy food, or shall I put out some of the kibble I feed Taz?"

"His food and bowls are in the bed of my pickup. Will you grab them?"

Ethan glanced in the opposite direction. "Oops—you spoke too late. I'm afraid Trooper's at the back door licking his chops. Looks like he already scarfed up Taz's food.''

"At least Taz didn't gobble *him* up. Give me a minute to get Cara down and I'll give both dogs a little more."

"Never a dull moment if you raise kids and dogs," Regan put in. "When you moved home, Mitch, I distinctly recollect someone making noises about missing all the action we have around here. I even told Ethan I thought you sounded serious about settling down, maybe getting married. Was I wrong?"

"Now, how should I answer that?" Mitch glared at Regan as he shoved open the door to the girls' nursery. "I bring a new lady to meet you, having already admitted I want to coax her out to my ranch. If I let her think I have marriage in mind, it'll scare her off for sure. Be good, Regan. Your smile may be angelic, but you have a devilish streak a mile wide. And Gilly doesn't know you like I do."

"Since I took Ethan off the dating market, you're the most eligible bachelor in town. You delude yourself if you think any woman would try and escape from you. Isn't that right, Gilly?"

Mitch turned red. He didn't bother answering Regan. Executing an abrupt about-face, he grabbed Gillian's elbow and whisked her into the girls' bedroom.

She knew Regan had been teasing him, but she felt bad for Mitch all the same. Goodness, she hoped he *didn't* have marriage in mind. Once had been enough for her. And yet she was glad he'd offered her a good excuse to return to his ranch—a chance to examine the lane in daylight. She'd hate to go on false pretenses. Before tonight ended, she'd definitely accept his offer; tomorrow she'd make clear that she had no interest in a relationship.

Gillian's arms felt empty after she'd placed Angela in

her crib. She hadn't expected it to be such a wrench and bent to place a kiss on the downy head. As she pulled back, it occurred to her that she ought to feel guilty for bestowing kisses on another child—kisses that belonged to Katie.

Daryl had insisted she'd kissed her baby goodbye. He said she'd been too ill to remember. Gillian had simply never believed it was true because she couldn't recall the act. But just now, as her lips brushed Angela's soft hair, it stirred a memory. Daryl hadn't lied. She'd held her baby briefly. Katie had been so cold and still, but so very beautiful.

Gillian tried desperately to hang on to that fleeting glimmer from the past. It proved impossible, especially after the two couples sat down at the table and mundane talk rose around her.

"Are you feeling unwell again?" Mitch asked during a lull in the conversation he, Regan and Ethan had been carrying on without her.

"What? Oh, no." Gillian realized the others had almost finished their tamales, while she'd done little more than poke at hers.

"Maybe she doesn't like tamales." Regan looked truly sorry.

Ethan stopped with his fork poised over his second helping of steaming corn husks. "I guess we should've asked if you liked Mexican food."

"I do," Gillian assured. She piled some of the corn mixture on her fork and popped it into her mouth, hoping to divert attention from herself.

"Something's wrong," Mitch insisted, not to be deterred. "You haven't said one word since we sat down."

It was true. Gillian had her reasons, but she didn't plan to share them.

Regan must have read her distress. "The three of us know each other so well. I suspect we can be mind-boggling to a newcomer."

"Is that all it is, Gilly?"

"I don't mind," she was quick to say.

Mitch reached for her left hand. "Well, I do."

Then it happened—what she'd feared most in coming here. Ethan lifted his wineglass and studied her over the rim. "We aren't deliberately excluding you, Gillian. Tell us about yourself. Where did you come from and what did you do before landing in Desert City?"

Her hand trembled inside Mitch's. Not realizing it, she implored him with huge eyes.

"Our lives may be open books," Mitch snapped at Ethan even though he wasn't fully certain what Gillian was imploring him to do. "Other people prefer privacy. Shall we find an impersonal topic?"

She telegraphed him a grateful smile.

"Work is an impersonal topic," Ethan argued stubbornly.

Gillian reacted to an undercurrent radiating toward her from Mitch's best friend. "Uh, waitressing is pretty boring compared to what you and Regan do. And ranching must be more exciting than waiting tables." Pulling her hand out of Mitch's long enough to pick up her glass of wine, Gilly smiled at him, ignoring Ethan. "What can you tell me about your ranch, Mitch? I mean, if I'm going riding with you, I'd like to know if I should be prepared for sand or rock or worse."

"You're really coming out? No kidding?" Delight danced in Mitch's eyes. "Is eleven o'clock good? I'll fix sandwiches to take on our trail ride. There's a spot up the mountain where you can view the whole valley. Remind me to draw you a map before we leave tonight."

"Oh, I kn—" Gillian clamped her lips shut. She'd been about to say she knew the way. "I need to buy an area map," she finished lamely.

"Sounded to me as if you were about to admit you knew where Mitch lives," Ethan accused.

"It's no secret," Mitch said sharply. "Ethan, I'm sorry if the chief pulled you in to work on your day off. Don't take your bad mood out on Gilly. Maybe we should forget playing cards, and call it a night after dessert."

"I'm not the one going off the deep end. I'm beginning to wonder if DeSalvo's bullets severed a connection to your brain. What do you know about her?" Ethan demanded resoundingly, even though everyone at the table sat gaping at him. "I haven't figured out what game you're playing," he said, leaning into Gillian's face. "But if you're not on the up and up, my advice is to pack it in, darlin', and move your operation to another town."

Mitch jumped up, knocking over his chair. Grasping Gillian's wrist, he yanked her up, too. "Ethan's not himself tonight. Thanks for dinner, Regan, but Gilly and I are leaving."

"Mitch, I'm sorry." Regan threw a frustrated glance at her husband, who calmly cut a third tamale. "Ethan, Gillian brought flan for dessert," Regan hissed.

"You keep it." Gillian smoothed back a flyaway curl. "Mitch, why don't you stay?" She eased out of his hold. "Your dog's still in the backyard. I can find my own way. For the record," she muttered, "Bert gave me your address." That was true enough—even if it wasn't the *whole* truth. "But I'll understand if you'd rather withdraw your invitation to go riding."

"Not on your life!" he said explosively. "Give me a minute to collect Trooper. While I'm gone, I'll expect

Ethan to apologize.'' Aiming a last glare at his former partner, Mitch limped out the back door and slammed it hard.

Gillian had disappeared by the time he returned with the dog and his food and bowls. Nor was Ethan anywhere in sight. Only Regan, who sniffled as she scraped nearly full plates of food down the garbage disposal.

''Did Ethan tell Gillian he was sorry?''

Regan raked a wet hand through her hair. ''Don't... Mitch. Ethan thinks you're making a mistake. He says you've always paid attention to his hunches. I wish you'd both take stock of what you're doing. Please, don't let this woman—a virtual stranger—ruin a solid friendship.''

''Ethan's hunch is wrong this time, Regan. He's too pigheaded to admit he's not infallible. I'll see you around, but I doubt if it'll be any time soon.''

''Mitch...'' Regan trailed him to the door. Once he'd marched stiffly through it, she made no effort to say more. Instead, she stood and watched him drive away.

CHAPTER SIX

GILLIAN WENT to the café at 5:00 a.m. to work the breakfast shift. She could have had the day off, but the extra money would come in handy.

During a lull she cornered Flo. "Earlier you asked how my evening went. Then we had a rush of customers so I couldn't really answer. It started out okay, but ended badly. Mitch's friend doesn't like me."

"Regan?"

"No, she was nice. And the…babies…are adorable. Ethan—he'd rather I hadn't come to dinner. Has Detective Knight said anything to you about me? I mean, does he normally interrogate newcomers so rudely?"

Flo hesitated a fraction too long.

Gillian's heart began to pound. "He's said something? Tell me. I can't answer charges if I don't know what they are."

"Honey, it's nothing. Ethan will be the first to tell you he operates a lot on intuition. Some say he's right a majority of the time. Not *all* the time, mind you."

"Are you saying he met me and intuitively dislikes me?"

"See, it even sounds silly. He said red flags went up the first day he met you. Your first day at work, when Mitch made such a big play for you. Ethan's hung up on the fact that he ran your name through their office computer and nothing came up. It's a super-duper machine the city paid thousands of dollars for. Ethan claims the database has the poop on everybody who lives in this country. Obviously his shiny new toy isn't so omnipotent if your name didn't even show up.''

She wished to heaven she'd never brought up the subject. ''I'm not sure what that means,'' Gillian ventured hesitantly. ''And…why is he looking up my name, anyway?''

''That's what I told him. If a person's done nothing wrong, why would they be in that dumb old database? I love these cops, but you can't tell 'em a thing. And they're a tight bunch. Almost like a brotherhood. So few of their marriages last, which is why they're concerned about the women their friends date, if you see what I mean. Ethan's a fair man. Eventually he'll figure out you're good for Mitch, and he'll come around.''

''I have no intention of marrying again.'' Gillian frowned pensively. ''Don't any of them date casually?''

''Sure…but…'' Flo tugged at one earlobe. ''I probably shouldn't open my mouth. Mitch was sweet on someone who eloped with another man. His friends wouldn't want him hurt again. Ethan's happy. Maybe he feels guilty about that.''

Gillian's mouth dropped open. ''Because *he* feels guilty and he doesn't like me, he's honor-bound to make sure Mitch dislikes me?''

''Like I said, cops are a unique bunch.''

''*Unique* isn't the word. *Juvenile* is more like it. If I knew how to reach Mitch, I'd cancel out on our horseback ride this afternoon.''

''Now, now, Gilly girl. Why punish Mitch? Or yourself, for that matter. You two go have fun. You both deserve it.''

"If he's interested in marriage, I'd never want to give him the wrong impression."

"I've known that boy for five or six years. Haven't seen him stampede to the altar yet, though enough women have tried."

Gillian's shoulders relaxed. "In that case," she said, shedding her apron, "I'd better go. He's expecting me at eleven."

"Have fun. Don't be falling off a horse, though. It's hard to waitress if you're wearing a cast."

At last, Gillian found something to laugh at. Waving, she dashed out.

SHE'D LEFT her boots in the car. Changing into them provided a legitimate reason for stopping halfway down Mitch's lane in case he had the spot under surveillance. Although, why would he?

Learning that Ethan Knight had run her phony name through his computer had made her extra jumpy. And it had crossed her mind that he and his former partner might have been pulling some sort of good cop, bad cop routine on her last night. After all, they didn't know she'd seen the men who'd followed her from New Orleans leaving Mitch's ranch.

If he and Ethan wanted to keep tabs on her, though, why would Ethan say anything to Flo, who might fire her? Then what would they have gained?

Gillian's head ached from trying to second-guess them. Pushing aside the muddle of her thoughts, she slowed and stopped near the grove of trees. It took her a surprisingly short time to search the brush on either side of the lane. There was no sign of her suitcase. *Someone* had already found it. The disappointment crashed over her, wave after wave of it.

Until this moment, Gillian didn't know how fiercely she'd been hoping the case had merely been knocked into the tall grasses bordering the lane. One reason was simple—she wanted her belongings, wanted Katie's urn. The other shocked her. She wanted to absolve Mitch Valetti of any connection to those men in the blue car.

Gilly trudged back to her vehicle and was climbing in when a beat-up silver pickup came toward her from the direction of Mitch's ranch. She experienced a moment's fright, but stood her ground.

The truck slowed to an idle. An elderly man with a shock of white hair stuck his head out the driver's window. "You lost, miss? This is a private road."

"I'm, uh, looking for Mitch Valetti. Have I made a wrong turn?"

"Nope, you're headed right. Is your car acting up?"

"No." The man studied her so intently, Gillian thought she'd better appease him. "Well, I felt a thunk and thought maybe I'd hit a chuckhole and damaged the front end. I checked, but found nothing wrong."

"Hmm. I didn't see any holes going in. But I was in a hurry. Ask Mitch to take a gander at your front-end alignment. If the frame is sprung, you'll want it fixed. Ruins tires fast otherwise."

"Thanks. I'll be sure to mention it to him. Well…he's expecting me at eleven."

The old codger waved, revved his motor and drove up on the right bank near the fence to squeeze past her. It hadn't occurred to Gillian earlier that Mitch might have a lot of visitors. Any one of whom could have picked up her case thinking they'd found a prize.

She felt more dejected than ever. But since the man was probably still watching her in the truck's rearview mirror, Gillian started her engine and proceeded down the lane.

As she pulled into Mitch's circular drive, she winced. Directly ahead were the broken split rails where she'd plowed through his fence. She'd been sure he would've fixed it by now.

Sitting there a moment, tense and awash in guilt, she noticed Mitch exiting the barn and walking toward her with the rolling, cowboy gait that had first intrigued her. When he drew near, she saw he looked positively unkempt. There was blood on his shirt and jeans, and the sight took her aback.

"Gilly," he called, sounding out of breath when he opened her car door. "I phoned, asking Flo to give you a message. She said you'd already left. I have to cancel our ride. I had a mare go into labor around two o'clock this morning. She's had a rough go of it. You must have passed Doc Bishop, my vet, headed out. He's been here since three."

"Oh, Mitch. Is your mare all right?"

He nodded—a slow smile creased his stubbled cheeks. "Her colt's a beauty. Want to see him?"

"I'd love to, if it's not imposing." She slid out the open door, then drew back. "Wait. You were going to the house to fall into bed, weren't you?" As he moved closer, she'd been afforded a clearer look at his bleary eyes.

"Yeah," he admitted scrubbing a hand across his unshaven chin. "I probably look like crap, and smell worse. If you can stand being around me, I'm dying to show off Pretty Baby's handiwork."

"Okay. I'll only stay a minute. I've never seen a baby horse," she said, completing her exit from the car this time.

They walked in silence. Due to Mitch's more pronounced limp, their upper arms brushed with each step. Beyond the barn, Gillian noticed that the ground leveled out into a huge green pasture where a dozen or so horses grazed contentedly.

"Is all of that yours?" she asked, shading her eyes against the sun.

"Don't I wish? My neighbor, Dave D'Angelo, and I split a lease on eight hundred acres that we seed for grazing. He runs steers on his portion, the horses are on mine. I hope to breed and sell good saddle horses. Someday," he added.

"Building a business is grueling, time-consuming work," she remarked absently.

"Spoken like someone who's been there and done that." Curiosity tinged his face as he opened the barn door and stepped aside, holding it open for her.

Gillian moved into the dark barn, pausing to let her eyes adjust. She heard her heart pounding in her ears. *Another wrong step.* Darn, she continued to stick her foot in her mouth around Mitch. "I thought I told you my husband started his own CPA firm," she said haltingly, weighing her words carefully.

"Your ex-husband, you mean?" Mitch let the door bang shut at his heels. He bumped into her as he cut in front to take the lead again.

"Yes, of course I meant my ex." She squinted as he flipped a switch turning on a bank of overhead lights. Gillian might have elaborated, but she opened her eyes and caught sight of the mare and her spindly-legged foal. "Will you look at that? He's positively the cutest thing I've ever seen!" She leaned against the gate that blocked the stall. All ears, eyes and long legs, the sorrel colt with the white blaze on his face wobbled toward them on splayed feet.

"He's smaller than I imagined a baby horse would be," Gillian said in hushed tones.

Mitch placed a booted foot on the lowest rail and rubbed the mare's velvet nose. "He's a runt, all right. But he's a fighter, and he'll grow." Turning, Mitch lifted the lid on an oak barrel. He reached in and pulled out an apple, which he fed to the mare.

"I didn't mean to sound negative. He's lovely, and I appreciate your bringing me out to see him. I'd better go now and let you get some sleep."

"You'll give me a rain check on the trail ride, I hope?"

"Uh…sure."

"So, what'll you do with this unexpected day off?"

She shrugged. "Either go back and work the afternoon shift for Flo or catch up on my laundry."

"Laundry? Now you've really made me feel bad. I wouldn't send my worst enemy off to do that dreary chore. Tell you what. Let me catch a few Zs, and I'll drive over and we'll take in dinner and a movie."

"There's no need," she protested.

"I want to, Gilly. Do you like Italian food? I know this great place. Nothing fancy to look at, but the pasta…" He kissed the tips of his fingers. *"Bella."*

She laughed. "I'm sold. What's the address? Name a time, and I'll meet you there."

"I could pick you up at your place," he said, sobering.

"I know. But I'd rather, uh, meet you."

"When I take a lady out, I like to see her safely home."

"Mitch." Gillian gripped the top rail of the stall.

"Your friend Ethan is right. You don't know anything about me."

"Okay, so tell me. What don't I know?"

She peered through her lashes and met his stubborn gaze. "For one thing, I'm not sure how long I'll stay in Desert City. For another, I'm not looking to get serious."

Mitch hauled in a deep breath, and rammed his hands in his back pockets. "If you'd said that last night, Ethan wouldn't be so worried thinking you've got your eye on my property and my pension. Me, I like a plainspoken woman. I still want to take you to dinner. Next week, if you're still around, we'll do the trail ride we missed today."

Gillian sighed. "You're tenacious, I'll say that."

A smile found its way to Mitch's lips. "*Mulish* is how my former partner put it. So, are we set for dinner then at Pagglio's? Say eight, or would you rather go earlier?"

"Eight is fine. Pagglio's is in the phone book?"

"You sorta remind me of a mule yourself," he muttered.

Smiling, she patted the mare and murmured goodbye to the foal. An easy silence fell between them as they left the cool barn, walking into a splash of fall sunshine.

"Gilly, the least I can do is offer you a cold drink before you head back to town. I've got iced tea or lemonade."

"I'm fine, Mitch. I don't need anything. You, on the other hand, look ready to drop. I'll leave now. Go grab some sleep." They'd reached her car. Mitch was quick to open her door.

"I guess you couldn't help noticing the chunk missing from my fence. I'd planned to spend this morning splitting new rails to patch it. Pretty Baby had other ideas."

An invisible hand squeezed Gillian's lungs. "Is repairing a fence hard? If it takes two people, I could help on my next day off.''

''I wasn't hinting,'' he said dryly. ''I was merely pointing out that some idiot flattened it and took off through the desert instead of using my road.''

Gillian's nerves were suddenly too jumpy to let her comment. She hoped he didn't reflect back and think it odd that she slipped behind the wheel and gunned her motor without further comment, leaving him eating her dust with little more than a feeble wave.

He might be wondering. She noticed he didn't move— at least not while he remained in her rearview mirror.

All the way back to town, she told herself how many kinds of fool she was to get involved with Mitch Valetti. She had to end this, she vowed.

Considering her resolve, she couldn't really explain why, at seven-fifteen, she hauled out the phone book and looked up the address of the Italian restaurant.

At seven-thirty, she changed into one of the only two dresses she'd brought from the town house she'd left so hurriedly in New Orleans. Dresses Daryl had packed...

At 8:10 she pulled into Pagglio's parking lot. Unaccountably, joy tumbled through her veins when she saw Mitch seated in his Corvette.

Getting out, he flagged her into a vacant, adjacent parking spot.

Darn, what was there about him that sent her common sense into a tailspin?

He was good-looking, yes. Like a lean wolf. Hair, slightly longer than dictated by current fashion, all but dared her to muss the dark curls with her fingers. Rich, coffee-colored eyes erupted in a smoky fire each time they cruised over her. Eyes that didn't roam when another woman came on the scene. It was something that made

Gillian feel special, and it had seemed so long since she'd felt special. Nor did it hurt that Mitch Valetti wore his clothes well. Rack items took on new life on his rangy build.

Tonight, Gillian was glad she'd worn a dress. Mitch had shaved and changed into black slacks and a brick-red shirt with the sleeves rolled midway up his muscular forearms. He had on his trademark cowboy boots, but this pair was more formal—highly polished snakeskin.

"You made it worth the wait," he said. He took her hands and held her steady at arm's length. His low, very masculine growl of approval brought heat to her cheeks.

"Like cotton candy. That's what your dress reminds me of. The pink stuff I used to buy as a kid at the county fair. Hey, I thought redheads weren't supposed to wear pink."

Caught. When she'd left home she'd been her normal blond self. Fortunately, she was spared an explanation by the arrival of a van-load of noisy, chattering women. All seven in the party knew Mitch.

"Are you coming or going?" one of them asked Mitch. The women showed definite curiosity about his companion.

"We're on our way in." Mitch took a minute to introduce Gillian. "Erica, Jenny, Melissa, Katherine and Elizabeth…uh, Lizzie," he corrected when the pretty brunette doubled her fist and socked him on the shoulder. "Ouch. These are some of Ethan's sisters," he informed Gillian. "Jessica is his cousin, and Lexie, here, is married to his brother, Matt. What's the occasion?" he asked.

"Girls' night out," the most elegantly dressed of the seven said. "Don't worry," she added in an undertone, "Amy couldn't make it tonight."

Gillian noticed that the announcement had all of them gazing on Mitch a bit sadly.

But if *he* noticed, he didn't mention it to Gillian. He simply cupped her elbow in a warm, steady hand and led the way into the restaurant. All the same, harkening back to what Flo had said, Gillian was curious about the missing Amy.

"Mitch!" A swarthy, heavyset man standing behind the cash register glanced up in dismay. Mitch released her to shake hands with him.

"They're not all with me, Vincente," Mitch said quickly. "I'm here with Gillian," he added, doing that thing with his eyes again, caressing her without a touch.

She squirmed inside, knowing they'd drawn the attention of this man, Vincente, as well as Ethan Knight's relatives.

She groaned silently. In the Desert City phone book, there were five pages of restaurants. Murphy's Law, Gillian thought, that the family of a man who detested her and seemed possessive of Mitch, would all show up at this one tonight. However, it stood to reason that if they were all good friends, they'd frequent the same establishments.

Her jackhammering heart settled some after Vincente showed the boisterous sisters into a separate room. When he returned, he led her and Mitch to a table secluded by potted palms.

Mitch ordered wine before Vincente lit the candle in the middle of their table, handed them gilt-edged menus, bowed and left. Setting the menu aside, Mitch toyed with the container holding the candle, which had already mushroomed out in many layers of bright color.

"I guess you're wondering who Amy is. She's Ethan's

youngest sister. Works at the station as a police dispatcher.''

"Six girls. Wow! So what's significant about Amy?'' she asked casually.

"We dated off and on. Nothing serious,'' he said, surprising himself because he suddenly believed it. "Last month she eloped with the county D.A. Rocked the police community.'' He shrugged. "We shouldn't have been so shocked. She was nuts about the guy.''

Gillian heard what Mitch had left out, and what Flo had hinted at. Amy Knight's elopement had hit him hard. She reached for his hand and squeezed it. "The heart takes a long time to heal, Mitch. But given time, it *does* heal. At least according to what I've read.''

He patted his left shirt pocket. "Mine's all in one piece now,'' he said.

A waiter brought their wine. Mitch tasted it. "Go ahead and pour, Leo. How are Mariella and the kids?'' The two chatted as Leo filled both glasses.

"Shall I give the lady a minute with the menu, Mitch? You, I know, will order lasagne.''

"I hope you don't have anything against predictable,'' Mitch muttered to Gillian as Leo withdrew.

She thought for a moment, letting go of his hand to taste the wine. "Mmm. If the food you recommend is as good as the wine, I'll suffer through predictable.''

Grinning lopsidedly, Mitch threw an arm over the back of his chair and visibly relaxed. "Glad you like the vino. I aim to please. As for the food, you can't make a bad choice.''

"In that case I'd like the cannelloni. House dressing on my salad, please.''

Mitch motioned to Leo and gave their order, never averting his eyes from Gillian.

She didn't know how long it had been since she'd held one hundred percent of anyone's attention. Not even in the early, happier days of her marriage had she captured Daryl's entire focus. From the moment they met in college, his mind had been on his career. In the end, it had stolen what affection they'd had for each other. Sad, but even in death, Daryl's business continued to manipulate her.

Mitch snapped his fingers in front of her face. "I lost you. I hope you aren't still thinking about Amy. At the time, her elopement bothered me. I swear I'm fine now."

"You know what they say about people who protest too much, Mitch. Who could blame you? They're all gorgeous women. If Amy resembles them…well…"

He gathered Gillian's hands. "Have you looked in the mirror lately?"

She flushed and pulled away. Actually, she hated looking in the mirror since she'd deliberately changed her appearance. "Looks are such a small part of a person's total package."

"Believe it or not, I heard you laughing with Flo, and that's what first caught my attention. You laugh, yet your eyes are always so serious." He frowned. "I'm not explaining this very well."

"It's all right, Mitch. Who can explain what attracts two people? Let's just accept that we're here together because we want to be."

"You bet. I'm not interested in psychological mumbo jumbo. While I was recovering at Ethan's, I listened to Regan and her office partner, Odella Price, analyzing people. They had to know why a person acted the way he did. In Ethan's and my work it was a simple matter of separating good from bad. I tend to think the bad should be put away, regardless of why they veered off track.''

A pit yawned in Gillian's stomach again. ''Sometimes there are extenuating circumstances that alter people's choices, Mitch.''

He grimaced. ''You're starting to sound like the defense attorneys who try to get slimeballs off with a slap on the wrist. Daddy drank and mama did drugs. Society ought to understand that's why they bought a gun and blew away their wife and kids.'' Mitch glanced up and saw that Gillian had gone pale and had an iron grip on the stem of her wineglass. ''Hey, forget it. Badasses aren't my concern anymore.''

His descriptions had transported Gillian back to her experience in Flagstaff when she'd seen the blue car ruthlessly run down Pat Malone. The same men had left Daryl McGrath lying on his doorstep in a pool of blood. If Mitch Valetti really believed all the stuff he'd just spouted, then he wouldn't have anything to do with that sort. *Would he?* If it was coincidence that they'd happened to be in his lane, then maybe she could trust him.

Maybe.

Leo delivered their food on piping hot plates. He grated Parmesan cheese over both orders, and refilled their wineglasses before he moved to another table. With eating uppermost on their minds, talk turned from police work to Gillian's job at Flo's.

''You ever done anything besides wait tables?'' Mitch asked.

Gillian weighed the wisdom of being truthful. She was so very tired of making up stories. ''I've worked with flowers.''

When Mitch paused with his fork halfway to his mouth and his eyebrow arched, she expanded. ''I've crafted and sold floral arrangements, dried centerpieces, funeral sprays and all the flowers for bridal parties.'' She didn't tell him *where* she'd worked or that at one time she'd had her own shop.

''Which job did you like best?''

She pretended to give it some thought, even though it was no contest. She had loved everything about flowers—until she'd been the recipient of too many bouquets when she'd lost her baby. She'd probably never smell roses again without wanting to throw up. ''Food service is basically happy. People send flowers for a lot of sad occasions.''

''Hmm. I never thought of that. Cops learn to turn off their emotions.''

''So your motto is Don't Get Involved?''

''Not exactly,'' he said. ''Some cops get involved. Take Ethan. I know you didn't walk away with the best impression, but he does a lot for abused kids. He bucked the system and built an underground network of safe houses. Until I got hurt, I coached underprivileged kids in basketball and football at St. Margaret's Church. I started the program because I hated seeing poor kids hanging out on the streets. I always tried to scrounge up hot soup or chili at practice. Some kids wouldn't have had anything hot in their bellies, otherwise.''

''Contrary to how it might seem, Mitch, I don't dislike your friend. And you just explained why he's protective of you. It's his nature.'' She set her fork down and picked up her wine again with unsteady fingers. ''Maybe you should heed his advice. Ethan's right. What do any of you know about me, really?'' She felt somehow obliged to give him an opportunity—a second opportunity—to back off.

''Have you murdered anyone?'' he asked abruptly.

"No," she gasped.

"There you go." A smile kicked up one side of his mouth. "I happen to think Ethan should give me more credit for being able to judge a person's character. Let's not hear anymore remarks of that type. Okay?"

Gillian flinched when Mitch clinked his wineglass against hers. Nevertheless she felt a sense of relief even though she'd tried warning him off. Again she was gripped by a strong sense that Mitch Valetti was a man to be trusted. It was the first time in over a month that she'd felt any measure of safety. *That's it,* she decided. This man made her feel safe, and it was a good feeling.

They talked about inconsequential things throughout their meal. Thank goodness he hadn't asked too many personal questions about her past. Most were generalities comparing their childhoods.

"My two sisters are older," he admitted. "No one suggested I was an accident, but I figured that out. My parents were busy stockbrokers, rarely home. Gran Valetti took care of me. She died when I was nine. I had nannies and housekeepers after that. And my folks wonder why I didn't have a burning desire to join their brokerage." He shook his head. "I hope you have better family support. Have your parents been understanding about your divorce?"

She hesitated, not wanting to lie, but not wanting any roads to lead back to her past life. "My parents are…gone," she said, crossing her fingers behind her back in a childish attempt to cancel out her lie. "My father sold insurance. Mom did mending for a dry-cleaners. She brought the work home. They wanted more children but apparently couldn't have any. The summer I graduated from high school, they went on vacation without me. A Carribean cruise. Their small sightseeing plane shouldn't have been flying in the aftermath of a hurricane. Wind sheers, I was told, dashed the plane against a rocky island coast.'' She knew she was leaving the impression that both her parents had died. Her father had. Her mom was never the same afterward. She lived life at a breakneck pace. Gillian didn't blame her, but she'd never really understood, either. Oddly, maybe now she better understood her mother's need to have... someone to count on.

Mitch's eyes darkened. ''That must have been rough.''

''It was. Dad's affairs were a mess.'' That much was true. ''He'd borrowed against his life insurance to pay for the trip. He'd second-mortgaged the house to prepay my college tuition at his alma mater. Did I mention I met my husband there? In some ways, we were kindred spirits.'' That, too, had been true. ''His parents died when he was young, in a commuter train accident.''

''We've hit on morbid dinner conversation. It seems to have stolen your appetite. I don't suppose you want dessert?''

''No. I'm not big on sweets. But you go right ahead. I'll take coffee. That wine sneaked up on me. It's making my head fuzzy.'' In reality, Gillian was sick over weaving so many tangled webs. When would one catch up with her?

''Maybe I'll have coffee, too. Sweets are my weakness, but it's a weakness I can't afford, since I've skipped my normal exercise routine since the surgery.'' Mitch signaled Leo and ordered their coffee.

''What about playing ball with the kids at the church? Will you eventually be able to go back and coach them?''

''I hope so. A guy doesn't have to run to coach.''

''You have much to be thankful for. You're lucky to

be alive,'' she said, leaning back while the waiter poured the rich black coffee.

''Who's been talking out of turn?''

Gillian suddenly caught herself. She'd been obsessing over Daryl's death again. ''No one. I gleaned a few bits and pieces at the café.''

''I feel a whole lot luckier since I met you.''

She smiled and sipped her coffee, oddly content. And yet, deep down, she felt as if she were using him. Right now, though, he provided the only lead she had. Her suitcase had disappeared from the private road leading to Mitch Valetti's ranch. Plus, her only sighting of the thugs since she'd left Flagstaff had occurred on the same lane. Whether she liked it or not, she was inexplicably tied to her handsome escort. And sticking close to him certainly wouldn't be a hardship.

As if he'd read her mind, Mitch brought up their next meeting. ''I need to hang out at home and take care of some overdue chores next week. I've neglected a case I sort of…accepted on the side.'' He peeled bills for the check out of a money clip and dropped them on a silver tray. ''The offer to join me for a horseback ride on your next day off is still on the table.''

''I'd like that. Next Sunday? Same time? Is eleven good?''

''Great. I can't wait.''

They stood, and he placed a hand on her back to guide her through the tables to the front door.

They'd stepped outside, laughing at something Vincente had said to Mitch. Gillian glanced up, saw a big blue sedan pull into the lot. Her laughter died on a squeal of alarm. She gulped in a strangled breath and dodged behind Mitch.

He paused, buttoning his wallet into his back pocket.

Frowning, he followed her wide-eyed gaze to the car. A well-dressed elderly couple climbed out and started toward them. Feeling Gilly glued to his back, hanging on with trembling hands, Mitch twisted and stared at her over his shoulder. Her eyes remained dark with fright. "Gillian? Do you know those folks?"

By now the tottering man, easily in his late seventies, had moved to where he could grasp the handrail on one side and his companion's arm on the other. The old guy made an inane joke about aging. Only then did Gillian slacken her death grip on his shirt.

"Darned high heels," she said, trying for a breezy air. "I'm not used to wearing them. Sorry to grab you, Mitch." Moving around him, she skirted the elderly couple and walked swiftly down the steps.

Mitch would stake his reputation as a good detective on his belief that her cowering behind him had little to do with tall shoes. Since all he had to base his conclusion on was a gut instinct that had lain dormant for a while, he let it go. Just as he ignored the sock to his senses that suggested maybe Ethan's instincts about Gillian Stevens were more correct than his own.

Her nerves still jittery, Gillian unlocked her car before turning to tell Mitch good-night.

She bumped up against his chest, shocked anew when he suddenly bent and kissed her. His lips were warm and soft and electric. The keys trickled from Gillian's hand and clattered on the pavement. She curled her fingers in the fabric of Mitch's shirt, rising on tiptoe rather than lose the physical connection between them.

He had thought to keep the kiss simple. But he'd been dying to kiss her from the moment she arrived wearing that candy-pink dress. When she moved against him, he tested her lips with his tongue, and felt lightheaded at being allowed entrance to her mouth. It was way too late for songbirds to be out, yet Mitch could swear he heard them. Spanning Gillian's narrow waist with both hands, he lifted her, bringing her closer. Eventually his lungs screamed for air, forcing him to raise his head. Not before both he and Gillian were thoroughly rattled by the kiss, however.

"I...you...caught me by surprise," she mumbled when he released her. She knelt to retrieve her keys from the ground.

"Do you want to slap me?" Mitch thrust out his jaw and tapped a point on his chin. His eyes were serious.

She dragged her top lip between her teeth. Averting her eyes, Gillian broke into a shy smile and shook her head. "I wouldn't change anything about the evening," she admitted, sliding into the driver's seat.

Mitch fumbled his keys out of his pocket. "You acted...I don't know...frightened a minute ago. I'm following you home to make sure you get there safely."

"That's absurd! My place is a mile out of your way. I'll be *fine*."

She sounded so firm, Mitch backed off. He barely managed a wave as she roared out of the parking lot. Damn, but she confused him. She had mood changes the way a chameleon shifted colors.

He took his time leaving the lot, waiting until she turned the corner. He even made a circuit around the dark-blue sedan—a newer-model Lincoln, pricy but otherwise unremarkable. He hadn't imagined Gilly's reaction. Something about that car made her jumpy as a frog. *What?* he wondered.

CHAPTER SEVEN

GILLIAN'S MIND remained on Mitch's troublesome kiss all the way home. *A mutual kiss,* nagged an inner voice.

"I only kissed him back because it's been too long since anyone kissed me," she grumbled to herself after parking and tramping up the back stairs. "Idiot! You can't afford to get romantically involved." She slammed her apartment door behind her far harder than necessary.

Not even a long hot shower succeeded in washing away the feel of his lips. Nor could it remove the scent of his aftershave from her nose. Mitch wore something subtle, not citrusy as Daryl had. Though with Mitch, Gillian detected a tangy spice toned down with a dab of— sage, perhaps? On Mitch it smelled yummy, Gilly mused, slipping into her nightgown and flopping down on top of her bed.

"Yummy?" Her tone was disgusted. It was a word she'd never before used in connection with a man. But in the next moment she wryly admitted that Mitch Valetti's lips tasted good enough to eat.

Then, girl, you'd better pretend you're on a strict diet!

Snapping off the light, she heaved a sigh and beat her pillow into a lump before burying her head underneath.

THE FOLLOWING Thursday dawned with dark clouds rolling in across the nearest mountain range. By midafternoon it was pouring buckets of rain. And the next day, too.

Gillian knew that when it rained this hard in New Orleans, things could easily be left dripping for three or more days. She latched on to the storm as a sign—a legitimate excuse not to go horseback riding with Mitch on Sunday.

In true desert fashion, the sun rose clear and bright the very next morning. Gillian glanced outside when the lunch crowd arrived, and saw that the ground had completely dried. She had no justification for not going unless she flat-out wanted to slight Mitch.

"Do you need me to work tomorrow?" Gilly asked Flo hopefully before her last shift ended on Saturday night.

Flo winked. "Not if you've got something better to do. I know you're our one and only waitress, but you need some time off."

"I like working here, Flo. And I made enough in tips this week to get ahead a little bit."

"You deserve good tips, honey, the way you hustle. Take tomorrow off. Enjoy yourself. Could you work two shifts next Wednesday, though? I have a doctor's appointment."

"Nothing serious, I hope."

"Nah. The yearly overhaul."

Gillian laughed. "I'll work all three shifts if you'd like. Wouldn't want you to miss getting lubed and oiled."

"Speaking of cars," Bert popped out of the kitchen in the middle of their conversation. He obviously didn't understand why that sent the women into peals of laughter.

"Listen up, ladies. This isn't funny. I've seen the same two men cruising this neighborhood. They look kinda shifty-eyed, ya know what I mean? You two be careful."

Gillian gave a start, almost dropping the plate she'd taken off the warming shelf.

"Didn't mean to scare you, Gilly. They could be bumbling tourists, but it's never a bad idea to stay alert. There's a lot of funny business goes on in this old world."

"Yes." Gillian made sure she had a solid grip on the plate this time. "Did he happen to say what color car?" she asked Flo. Bert had gone back to the stove.

Flo ducked her head into the pass-through and asked him. "He's not sure. Dark." She rolled her eyes at Gillian. "Bert says streetlights distort colors. He's colorblind, you know, and hates to admit it. Faked his way through the military. He said if he sees them again, he'll try and get the license number. It's easy enough to have one of the guys from the station run it through their system."

Nodding, Gillian hurried off to deliver the plate before it needed reheating. *A dark car. Could it have been blue?* She felt cornered. Were the men hanging around the city hoping to get lucky and find her? Or had they found her and were merely biding their time?

Leaving work, she scanned the street carefully before dashing to her car.

Later, locked inside her apartment, Gillian spent the evening trimming and coloring her hair again in order to maintain her disguise. She'd been so careful to cover her tracks. How could they have run her to ground so fast?

Easy, if they'd had the help of Mitch Valetti.

Which might explain why the goons were cruising around the café. Thank goodness she hadn't given Mitch her home address. And it was a good thing she had put off applying for an Arizona driver's license.

Darn, she didn't want Mitch to be part of this mess. If

he was, though, then it was time she quit playing mouse to his cat. She didn't have that damned key. So the killers' secrets would never be exposed. Unless Daryl had hidden the notebook in a bank that audited inactive safety-deposit boxes years down the road. By then, everyone involved would be old and gray. Oh, it all seemed so hopeless.

The next day, Gillian wasn't exactly looking forward to meeting Mitch. She felt ambivalent about him. The part of her that enjoyed his company and his kiss woke up eager to see him. The saner part waved all sorts of warning flags. Underneath it all lay a desperate need to find her suitcase and go into hibernation.

Once again, after her drive to the outskirts of town, she parked short of the curve in Mitch's lane. This time she searched thoroughly along both sides of the fence. If by some miracle she'd overlooked her case before and found it now, she'd retreat and quietly leave town. She'd go pack her bags and light out for someplace new. Someplace far from Desert City. Far from the handsome, sexy, troublesome Mitch Valetti.

No luck. The missing bag remained missing. Her spirits plummeted. Depression washed over her as she drove the remaining distance to the ranch.

Mitch had apparently anticipated her arrival time. She'd barely shut off her engine when he led two saddled horses out of the barn. A barn gleaming with new paint, Gillian noted. The broken fence had also been repaired. He'd obviously been busy this past week, she thought as she climbed from her car and studied his renovations. The horses in the back pasture looked fat and sleek.

Seeing her, Trooper streaked past Mitch toward her. Barking incessantly, the pup pounced on Gillian and began licking her face.

"Trooper, get down!" Mitch dropped the reins and rushed over to Gillian, who was trying to escape the rambunctious dog. He grabbed Trooper's collar. "Sit," he ordered. "You're late," he said to Gillian, using almost the same tone. "I'd about decided maybe I'd jumped the gun saddling our mounts in advance."

"You really asked me out here to ride horses?"

Mitch stripped off his cowboy hat, slapped it twice on his leg to dislodge dust, then resettled it on his head. "Well...yes. I thought that was the plan."

"The whole plan?"

"I suggested a picnic on the mountain. Food's already in the saddlebags. I left them in the house where it's cooler. I thought you might, uh, need to use the facilities before we take off."

She glanced nervously toward the house, but saw nothing out of the ordinary. No eyes peered furtively out from behind his curtains. No blue car half-hidden behind his barn.

"Gilly, is your sudden hesitation about our, uh, kiss?" he asked uncomfortably.

What would you say if I told you it was about two men who drove a big blue car? She wanted so badly to toss that back at him. Which would quash any hope she had of getting him to deliver a message to his pals. After all, Mitch Valetti, ex-cop, had no doubt learned to turn any situation to his advantage.

"Sorry, I wasn't really listening, Mitch. The fact that you kissed me last weekend had all but slipped my mind," she said breezily. "To answer your question, though...no, I don't need to use the facilities. I'm ready to ride. Are we going alone?"

Well, she'd certainly put him in his place. If he'd had second thoughts about how far they might progress beyond that first kiss…well, he was obviously the only one giving it a high priority.

"You mean are we taking Trooper? I'm not making a lot of headway teaching him to heel when I whistle. He's sort of a pain in the butt at times. All the same, I'd hate to risk losing him on the mountain."

Gillian smiled faintly at his admission. "The little guy has you wrapped around his paw, I see."

"Yeah." Mitch sounded guilty. "Don't let him hear you say so. The truth is, I wonder how I managed to live here alone for so long."

"He knows we're leaving. He looks sad. Let's take him. Unless the trail is too overgrown. If it's not, how hard could it be to keep him on a leash?"

"I hope I won't regret this. Okay, we'll give it a whirl. There's a long, sturdy leash hanging on a hook just inside the barn. Will you nab it while I collect our lunch?"

"Don't forget to bring water for him."

"There's a stream where I plan to eat. It should be running well after Wednesday's storm."

Shading her eyes, Gillian stared up the sloping hills. "A stream. In the desert? So…can a person camp out in these hills?"

"If the person likes sharing a bed with scorpions and rattlesnakes."

Gillian acted so squeamish, Mitch rethought his decision regarding the pup. "You know, that's another reason not to take Trooper. He's liable to stick his nose into a den of rattlesnakes." Mitch bent and lifted the wriggling pup. "I'll shut him inside. Mount up on the pinto. I'll be right back with our supplies."

Gillian hated snakes. She didn't know anything about scorpions. But she couldn't very well renege on the outing now. Doing as Mitch said, she climbed awkwardly into the saddle. It'd been years since she sat on a horse. Had they always been this far off the ground?

"How's the length of those stirrups?" he asked on his return as he limped past her to toss leather saddlebags across the rump of his sorrel gelding.

Gilly noticed Mitch eying the way she handled the mare. "The fit's remarkable." To prove it, she stood in the stirrups.

"I thought you and Amy were similar in height. That's the saddle she used. Outside of oiling, it hasn't been off the rack since the last time she stopped by to ride."

"When was that?" Gillian regretted her curiosity. Mitch Valetti's relationship with Amy Knight wasn't any of her business.

"More than six months ago. After she met ol' Creighton Henner and began hanging out at the country club, Amy developed an aversion to the smell of horses. And me." He laughed, but his joke didn't seem humorous to Gillian.

"Then I'd say Amy needs a nose adjustment. When we met for dinner, I remember thinking your aftershave or cologne smelled fantastic."

"Is that a fact?" Stepping into a stirrup, Mitch's smile revealed pleasure—and sensuality. He casually swung his leg over the saddle.

Blushing, Gillian kneed her horse into a turn. She cursed her instinctive remark. And his reaction, which had made her heart beat faster.

The two rode side by side across the pasture stretching out behind Mitch's barn. Every so often his leg brushed hers, sending Gillian's pulse into high gear. If her life depended on it, she couldn't have repeated a single thing they talked about during the entire trek across the field to the foothills. And if they hadn't soon joined a narrow trail that led upward, forcing them to ride single file, Gillian thought she might have dissolved into a mess of steamy hormones. Never in her entire life had she been this aroused by a man's look or mere touch.

She'd always thought she and Daryl had a fairly normal sex life. Looking back, though, it dawned on her that he'd never been very demonstrative. Busy expanding her flower shop, she'd often arrived home exhausted. Skipping sex hadn't seemed any big deal. She couldn't imagine skipping sex if Mitch was waiting at home.

Had she changed so much? Every free minute at work she had dreamily relived Mitch's kiss. At home, in her bed, she'd gone way beyond that in her imagination. Embarrassingly beyond, if she was being honest.

"You okay back there?" he called, ejecting her out of her illicit meanderings.

"Go-ood. I'm enjoying the view." His broad back and slim hips provided excellent scenery, as a matter of fact.

"You get turned on by sand and limestone?" A low, sexy laugh floated over his shoulder.

"Are you angling for a compliment, cowboy?"

"Were you flirting?"

To her shock, Gillian realized she'd been doing just that. "I guess I was," she admitted, deciding to play it straight. So much of her life seemed to be swaddled in lies. "But I'm sure you know what an attractive picture you make." She wanted to be testy, dammit.

"You're awfully direct when I can't get my hands on you." Mitch craned his neck to keep her in view. All of a sudden, he swore and grabbed his thigh. Doubling over, he loosed a series of dark mutterings.

"Mitch? Is it a stitch in your side? Can you get down? Maybe walking would help."

"I haven't ridden this long since my surgery. Hang on.

We're almost at the overlook where I planned to stop. I'd rather wait and get down there.''

"But if you're in pain—"

"I'm always in pain. Some days are worse than others. My theory is the faster I get back to a normal routine, the quicker I'll heal."

"Spoken like a man. What does your doctor say?"

A drawn-out silence answered Gillian. But she wasn't in any position to scold or even offer advice. If she'd adopted his attitude toward pain—and she had suffered severe emotional pain after losing Katie—she probably would have healed much faster. Instead, she'd let anguish drag her down. Now she feared that she bore full responsibility for everything that had followed. If she'd healed emotionally, Daryl might not have taken a mobster's account. If he hadn't taken the account—

No, that wasn't true. Daryl was driven by money. He always had been. Chances were, he'd have accepted the account with dollar signs in his eyes, anyway.

They rounded a corner and a panoramic vista opened up. Gillian reined in her horse. "Oh, my. It's so beautiful! Look at the red, yellow and purple streaks in that sky. Oh, oh, it reflects off the cliffs. I've never seen purple mountains before." She slid from the saddle, eyes raised to follow a red-tailed hawk making loop the loops against the splintered rays of the sun.

No matter how badly he hurt, Mitch derived immense satisfaction from watching Gillian's reaction to his favorite haunt. He took his time dismounting. As his pain eased, he loosened the girth on his saddle and limped back to do the same with hers.

"Mitch, Mitch! Come quick. Are those your horses running through that rocky canyon? Oh, they'll be killed." Gillian clapped a hand over her mouth. Mitch recognized the low keening sound she made as fear for the animals.

Slowly, he limped up behind her and pulled her back against his chest. "That's a sight few are privileged to see, Gilly. Our local band of wild horses. The white stallion leading them has been king for a decade. As far as you can see is reservation land. The O'Otam people call him Winter Smoke."

"So they're Indian horses?"

"Nope. They're free. Thousands of wild horses still run free on public and reservation land in Arizona. Some ranchers want them destroyed. Here, we take turns hauling out feed for them in the winter."

"Don't they steal from your herd?" She leaned against him, tipping back her head to meet his eyes.

Mitch gripped her upper arms hard, fighting the temptation to turn her around and kiss lips whose taste he vividly recalled. "My hope is that Winter Smoke knows I care about him. I like to think we have an understanding. If I'm wrong and one day he steals a mare or two from me, I hope my herd will have grown to the point that I can say *so be it.*"

Gillian turned his words over in her mind. His credo was diametrically opposed to Daryl's, to whom money in the bank meant everything. Mitch's outlook more closely matched her own belief—that it was better to share wealth. She'd frequently given an impoverished child flowers to present to mom or a favorite teacher. She'd discreetly discount bouquets for elderly women who carried worn purses and counted out each penny. More often than not, Daryl yelled at her when he did her books. "You're awfully softhearted for a cop," she murmured, carried away by memories.

"Cops are no more alike than…say, waitresses."

"Touché." Gillian sighed, afraid she was enjoying the feel of his chin pressing down on her head a little too much. "The horses are gone. So is the hawk. What are we looking at now?"

"Whatever's out there." He swayed her gently from side to side. "I just like holding you." He blew softly on a curl that framed her ear. "You cut your hair. It's sexy this way."

She stirred. "Mitch…" Gillian felt him nibble at her ear. His warm breath tickled her, and she ducked her head to her shoulder. He simply moved his lips to the other side of her neck.

Alarm coiled in her stomach when he began to press openmouthed kisses from the hollow under her ear to her collarbone. It wound tighter as he nuzzled her T-shirt out of the way. Shortly, though, alarm changed to languid pleasure. Gillian felt her body go limp—warmed by the afternoon sun and made weightless by Mitch's onslaught. Her nerves hummed along with the soft sounds—the whicker of the horses, the melodic call of birds flitting among the trees. The buzz of honey bees and the laughing rush of water from a nearby stream.

The stream. She'd forgotten Mitch said they'd picnic beside a stream. "Listen," she begged, sounding breathless. "Do you hear the water?"

He raised his head fractionally. "Yeah." He sighed. "I guess we'd better take the horses to the creek and let them drink. I usually do that first thing. Shows how you scramble my brains."

"Not on purpose."

"No? I suppose not. Am I moving too fast?"

She slipped out of his arms. "Any movement along those lines is too fast for me, I'm afraid. And yet…"

"Finish," he urged, halting his progress toward the horses to stare at her earnestly.

Gillian linked her hands behind her back while she studied the trees, the horses and finally, the seamless blue sky. "You...uh...scramble my brains, too."

Mitch wished she hadn't sounded quite so reluctant. Not knowing what he needed to do to convince her he wasn't an ax murderer, he gathered both sets of reins and let Gilly think he was satisfied with her response.

After seeing to the comfort of their horses, he spread out a blanket that had been rolled up behind his saddle. Sinking down on it, he chewed a piece of grass, giving Gilly time to exclaim over the beauty of the mountain stream. He waited until they'd unpacked the sandwiches and apples from his saddlebags, and she'd joined him on the blanket before he switched into investigative mode. "Tell me about your ex-husband," he asked, springing the question on her out of the blue.

Gillian had just bitten into a chicken-salad sandwich. The bread and filling went neither up nor down, but stuck in her throat, making her cough. "There's nothing to tell," she finally squeaked. "We were divorced this past May, but the marriage disintegrated long before we took legal steps. He's since...died," she managed to add without sounding too shaky.

"Rough, huh? Is that why you pulled up stakes and lit out for parts unknown?"

Gillian had known, of course, that this type of questioning could come from allowing him to get too close. She ought to have been better prepared. But she wasn't prepared at all.

"Daryl's death played a role in my...change of locale. Look, I'd rather not talk about any of this if you don't mind."

"Hoo…kay. Tell me about when you were a little girl, then." Mitch ran the tuft end of his grass down her nose. "Did you have freckles and long red curls?"

Again Gillian's throat tightened. Mitch appeared to have a one-track mind. She thought it was obvious that red wasn't her natural hair color. "I was homely. I had skinny arms and legs and knobby knees, okay? Little boys like you avoided me as though I were contagious."

"Hmm. You know what I was like as a boy?"

She decided it was time to throw back some of the baloney he was dishing out. "I'd guess you were a smaller version of the audacious, handsome devil you are today."

Mitch tipped back his head and laughed. "A devil, anyway. It's a cinch you don't know about the horrible tricks I played on my piano teacher."

"You play the piano?" Gillian's tone accused him of fibbing.

"No." He shook his head, apparently trying to appear remorseful; if so, he failed. "I wanted to play drums in the worst way. My parents wouldn't hear of it. In their circle of Wall Street friends, kids played piano. I hated to practice scales, so I pulled evil pranks on the teacher until he quit. He passed the word in the music community. My mother couldn't find another teacher who'd take me on as a pupil."

"I wish I'd known you when I took ballet. My mom was convinced lessons would help me get over being awkward and shy. Having to perform onstage only made my insecurity worse. I swore I'd never force kids of mine to do anything they weren't comfortable doing. And I won't."

"Same here. Then you do want kids? When we were at Ethan's, I couldn't decide how you felt about babies."

"You certainly handled diapers like a pro." Gillian thought if she could turn the conversation away from her and back to him, there'd be less danger of cracking her fragile network of lies and half truths.

Mitch polished off half a sandwich, then unscrewed the tops of two bottles of water he'd brought. He handed her one, then took a swig himself before settling a shoulder against the same tree trunk Gillian leaned on. He began a pared-down version of his sojourn at Ethan's home. "I might have drifted into feeling sorry for myself after my accident if not for the quadruplets. Compared to the trauma of abuse they suffered, my aches and pains seemed insignificant."

"Flo said you had three bullets in you. That's hardly insignificant. You have a right to the occasional bout of self-pity. Especially since you had to give up a job you loved."

"I could have stayed on the force at a desk job. I decided to quit, instead. Anyway, we weren't discussing me, Gilly. The point I'm making is that spending a couple of months around Regan and the babies changed my thinking a lot."

"How so?"

He hiked a shoulder negligently and recapped his water. "I've learned what's important." Sliding down to rest his head on Gillian's lap, he laced his hands over his chest and closed his eyes. "Now, this is my idea of the good life."

Gillian tensed the minute his head touched her thighs. Relaxing minimally, she fought an urge to rearrange the dark curls that dipped over his eyebrow.

Opening one eye, Mitch squinted at her. "You make a perfect pillow. But there's room on the blanket if you'd care to join me for a nap. We've both worked like fiends all week. I think we deserve to squander some time resting, don't you?''

The rock-solidness of the man, combined with the music of water skipping over rocks and the dance of warm sunlight filtering through tree branches—they all served to tempt Gillian. Maybe if she pretended everything was fine, it would be…

Uttering a soft sigh, she eased out from under his head, scooted down alongside him and rested her cheek in the crook of her arm. ''There's a safe feeling to this place, Mitch. I wish I could stay here forever.''

Raising himself on one elbow, he let his gaze roam leisurely over her flushed face, the enticing curve of her breast, the gentle swell of her hip. Something wound tight in his belly at the forlorn tone of her voice, and he felt a resounding need to keep her safe. From what, he didn't know; in fact, Mitch couldn't even venture a guess. While he judged her far from helpless, he sensed that her nerves were strung tight with fear.

His original plan hadn't included a nap under the shade of the old mesquite. Inexplicably snared by the picture Gilly presented, Mitch lay down and ran a finger over her nose and cheek, trying to capture her interest. The minute her eyes popped open and he was sure she understood his intent, he kissed her. Kissing was his only goal until her fingers brushed the hair at his temples and then whispered along his neck.

His breathing thickened, as did Gillian's. Soon he felt the sweep of her tongue demanding entrance. The noisy acceptance exploding from his throat drowned out the rustle of their clothing as they both fumbled with buttons in a desperate need to touch skin.

She murmured. Not a protest, he hoped. He was pretty

sure it wasn't when she unbuckled his belt, all the while struggling to discard her shirt.

"Uh, wait a sec." He reached for his billfold and finally extracted a small dog-eared packet. "Dang, this is pretty old."

Gillian examined it. "The wrapper's mooshed, but still intact. It's probably all right."

"Yeah." He tore away the foil, and handed it to her. She began to slide it on. He distracted her, though, with kisses. Then, when he felt his tension build to unbelievable heights, he helped her finish the job.

Gillian let the passion of the moment carry her beyond the niggling voice that asked what in heaven's name she was doing. Too many lies and half truths lay between her and Mitch. She shouldn't proceed. But it'd been years since she'd felt a tenth this alive. Years since she'd been swept away by sensations. Of sun on her face, the rush of wind against her bare flesh. Of strong arms holding her gently—promising to keep her safe from harm. Desire welled into insurmountable yearnings as he eased on top of her and urged her to hold him close. She wanted him, and opened for him without hesitation.

He filled her, easily, deliciously, completely.

Trembling, Gilly wrapped her legs around his narrow hips and chanted his name like a mantra.

Any doubts lingering in the back of Mitch's brain evaporated in that instant.

He gathered her against his chest. His heart. As close as one human being could be to another. The throbbing pain in his side vanished as all thoughts dissolved except one. To make this the best ride of Gillian's life. Of *his* life. He gave all he had, until he was lost in her. Until he couldn't distinguish a difference where he ended and she began. Until they were completely lost in each other.

She shattered around him. Felt pieces of her heart and soul break loose. And imagined a warm healing light raining down on them as Mitch exploded within her a pulsing second later.

They lay joined without stirring for quite some time. When at last Mitch started to lift himself off her, Gillian tightened her arms around his waist. "Please. Not yet. Don't let reality intrude." She felt a sense of contentment she was reluctant to give up so soon.

He remained arched above her, staring at her tightly closed eyes. Her lips were swollen from his kisses. Happy and relaxed, Mitch waited, holding his breath, wishing she'd smile. Wishing she'd admit *this* was reality.

Her eyelids fluttered open at last, but there was no lightness in her gaze.

"Tell me that what's going on behind your eyes isn't regret."

Gilly ran her fingers up the smooth surface of his back and down again, touching each of his bony vertebrae. "Not regret. But..."

"Good. No buts. It was meant to happen," he said softly, rolling off her at great expense to his injured hip. "Damn. I knew that condom was old. Gilly, I'm sorry— it split."

"When?"

"Maybe now as I tried to protect my sore hip." He pulled her into his arms, whispering her name as his lips tugged softly on her ear.

Plenty of objections, reasons they shouldn't have gotten so carried away, beat against Gillian's mind. She figured that by the time she got back to town, she'd carry guilt enough for both of them. Right now, she preferred to pretend that neither one of them had any cause for regret. Here, in Mitch Valetti's arms, the world as she knew it to be, filled with danger and risk and death, had ceased to exist. "It's probably okay, Mitch. My, uh, periods have been hit-and-miss for a while. Let's forget it, okay?" She cuddled into his warmth.

Yet no matter how hard Gillian tried to banish reality, clouds eventually drifted over the sun and kicked up a chill wind, which forced her and Mitch to part and seek out their scattered clothing.

She turned her back on him, huddling into herself while she slipped into her underwear. She knew her shyness was absurd—hadn't they already explored every inch of one another? But she couldn't help it.

At ease with his own body in the aftermath of sex, Mitch stretched and took his time finding his briefs.

He ambled over to her, stark naked, to rebutton her blouse. Gillian had done it up crookedly. "It's a little late for modesty," he said around a grin as she shied away.

"We just—how can you…" Her protest ended in a yelp as his lips closed over hers and she was dragged against his chest.

Giggling, she managed to dislodge him. "Mitch, stop. Do you hear that helicopter? If we don't hurry and dress, some poor pilot from the air base is going to hover over us and drop his teeth."

Mitch stepped into his briefs. "He'll think I'm a damn lucky guy. And I am," he reiterated stoutly.

"Chopper isn't from the air base," he said a moment later after he'd pulled on his jeans and moved out from under their tree to wave at the craft. "Border patrol. They're always on the lookout for clandestine meetings." Noting Gillian's shocked expression, Mitch winked. "Relax. The type of meetings I meant don't involve lovers but illegals and drug runners. Anyway, they know my horses.''

Her cheeks burned, even though she had to admit she and Mitch could be termed *lovers*. Distracted, Gillian folded the blanket and went busily about tying it behind Mitch's saddle.

''Do you want one of these apples?'' he asked casually. ''If not, I'm going to treat the horses before we head back.''

''No…really, I couldn't eat anything. I wish we hadn't finished off all the water, though. I'm horribly thirsty.''

''We'll take a shortcut home. I've got beer. Also iced tea, or maybe lemonade, in the fridge. A neighbor lady who cleans my house generally leaves me a full pitcher of each.''

''There's a lot to be said for having nice neighbors.'' Gillian was remembering the phone call she'd received from an old neighbor, telling her of Daryl's death, warning her to flee.

''Yeah,'' he agreed, tightening the cinch. ''Dave and Barb D'Angelo are nice folks. Dave's been a huge help, feeding and watering my stock while I was laid up. Barb plies me with bread and cookies she's baked. She thinks I need a wife. Don't be surprised if she gets nosy when you two meet.''

''Why would we meet?'' Gillian asked as she levered herself into the saddle.

Mitch climbed onto his horse, unsettled by Gilly's cool remark. But maybe he'd read too much into what they'd just shared. He thought it had been pretty special. If she didn't…well, damn.

He nudged his gelding around her mare and led the way to a trail that cut several miles off the route they'd taken up the mountain. This path was wider and smoother, but not as appealing. Suddenly, however, Mitch was interested in getting home as quickly as possible. If Gillian couldn't wait to be shut of him, he certainly wouldn't stand in her way.

The grueling pace Mitch set almost jarred Gillian's teeth out of her head. To say nothing of how sore other parts of her anatomy would be by morning. He seemed to be in a desperate rush and she hadn't any idea what possessed him. The gallop must be killing his hip. Hers were uninjured, and already her joints protested.

She was totally winded by the time they cantered to a halt outside his barn.

"I'll unsaddle and rub down the horses," he said. "I won't keep you from getting back to town."

Slow to slide off, she frowned at him over the saddle. "I...thought...you offered me a cold drink."

"I did. But you sounded as if you were in too much of a hurry."

"Sorry. I didn't mean to. I'm dying of thirst."

"Go on up to the house and help yourself. I'll look after the horses."

"I won't go poking around in your kitchen. Either I'll help you here and we'll both go, or we can forget it and I'll head on out."

Relenting, Mitch motioned for her to loosen the mare's cinch. Between the two of them, they made short work of tidying up. Mitch strode out ahead of her, but he stopped on the porch and held the door open to let her pass. He tried to keep Trooper from knocking Gilly over in his excitement. "Down, boy," Mitch gasped, nevertheless accepting the lap of the dog's sloppy tongue. "Okay, go outside and sniff around."

They both watched the pup race in circles around the vehicles, then charge a shrub where he scattered a covey of quail. Trooper ran back to Mitch and shot between his legs, into the house.

"Looks like he's had enough. Don't pay any attention to the condition of my living room, Gilly. I'm working on a case, and I've set the computer up on my coffee table. There's papers all over. Feel free to dump them on the floor. I'll get our drinks and be right back."

Gillian nodded, her eyes adjusting to the lack of light in the dark-paneled room.

Mitch had disappeared through an arch, leaving her alone in the room. The first thing she saw tore the breath from her throat. *Her missing suitcase.* It sat open on the coffee table next to Mitch's laptop. Gillian's heart thundered like a cannon blast in her ears.

On his fireplace mantel, there in plain sight, stood Katie's urn.

Gillian tried to muffle an aching cry. Instinct told her to snatch her belongings and make a clean getaway before Mitch returned. In her haste, she tripped on the edge of a braid rug and banged her knee into the coffee table, sending papers flying.

Oh, God, what if the noise brought him to investigate? Fear bore down, crushing her chest. She fought to breathe as she reached over to slam the lid on the case with hands that shook. The lid stuck. It wouldn't close. Her lungs refused to expand. The room began fading in and out. Gillian's legs turned rubbery as darkness engulfed her. Despite valiant efforts to scoop the small case into her arms, her knees gave way and she crumpled to the floor.

CHAPTER EIGHT

GILLIAN CAME TO ON Mitch's couch. His pup stared at her with anxious, liquid eyes, ropy tail thumping rhythmically on the thick rug. Someone—Mitch, she assumed—had placed a cool compress on her forehead. He hovered over her now, patting an icy washcloth on the insides of her wrists.

When he saw Gillian's eyes flutter open, the fear hammering inside Mitch's chest subsided. "You fainted. I heard you cry out, but you hit the floor before I got here to catch you. No, don't sit up yet." He gently pressed her down again. "Your heart is racing a hundred miles an hour."

"I've never fainted in my life," she insisted weakly.

"You've never lived in the desert. Our low humidity dehydrates some people more rapidly than others. I should have insisted you drink more water. Here, take a swallow of this sweetened iced tea."

Gillian had to tear her attention away from the mantel. Why was he trying to sell her a story about fainting because of low humidity? If he hadn't wanted to shock her, why had he allowed her inside? God, he'd had her suitcase all along. He and his pals from the blue car. How could she have let herself be blinded by Valetti's easy charm? How could she have made love with him?

"You're still white as chalk and you're shivering. Would hot tea be better?"

She sat up, furtively noting the layout of his doors and windows. She'd lost the chance to grab her suitcase and get away. But it appeared that Mitch was prepared to carry on the charade. Should she play along a while longer? "I tripped on your rug. I'm afraid I knocked over your suitcase and scattered a lot of your papers." Bending forward, she collected a few of the fallen sheets.

"Don't lean down like that. You'll get dizzy again. Those papers are expendable—evidence from a case I'm attempting to solve. Nothing official, even. I thought I'd mentioned it to you."

"No. What kind of case?"

He stared at her for a minute. "Intriguing to me. No one else agrees. It's nothing, really. I won't bore you with it."

"Fine. I'll finish the drink and leave. I feel silly, fainting like that." Gillian picked up the glass. The sweet tea did seem to calm her galloping nerves.

Although…she would've expected Mitch to hide the evidence while she was out cold. Why hadn't he? Was he telling the truth? Could it be possible that he wasn't aware of her connection with the suitcase?

She felt better knowing it was intact and here for the taking. *Stealing,* warned that nagging voice.

Gillian shivered. Was it stealing to take something that was yours?

"You're far from being steady enough to drive, Gilly. I'll run you home. Your car will be okay left here. Give me your keys. In the morning, I'll drive your car to the café and have Ethan or one of the other guys in the department give me a lift home."

Gillian opened her mouth to object. Then she realized that picking up her car provided a perfect excuse to come back here for the suitcase. "You said you've let chores go around the ranch too long as it is. If you're kind enough to take me home, the least I can do is come get my car without imposing on you further.''

Mitch curled her hand over his and kissed her knuckles. "What kind of talk is that? I'll do anything I can for you. You scared the life out of me just now.''

She offered a wan smile, all the while sneaking a peek at her baby's urn. *Anything.* He said he'd do anything. Wouldn't it be great if she could dump the whole lousy mess her life had become into Mitch Valetti's lap? But of course she couldn't.

Aware of her slight, restless move, Mitch caught the shift of her eyes to his mantel. "Oh, hey, I didn't stop to think you might wonder…'' His breath stalled a minute. "Is that what happened? You walked to the fireplace and read the information on…'' He waved a hand toward the mantel. "Baby Katie isn't mine,'' he said, squeezing Gillian's fingers too tightly. "She belongs to *somebody,*'' he said, his voice cracking. "I'm trying to find out who. I'm not making much headway, though.''

Mitch's attention seemed to drift.

"I don't understand. Wh-why is the urn on your mantel?'' It took a huge effort, but Gillian managed to get the words out.

Mitch stood and dug a ring of keys out of his jeans pocket. Trooper, who'd dropped down beside the couch, sat up and barked loudly.

"Come on, Gilly. I'll explain on the way to your place. Believe me,'' he muttered, "it's probably going to sound screwy to an outsider.''

"Outsider?'' Gillian passed so close to her baby's ashes, she could have touched the vessel. Instead, she wrapped her arms around her midriff and let Mitch lead her out, followed by the dog.

Her heart sank as he locked his front door. Why wasn't he one of those rancher types who didn't see any need for locks?

"I don't mean outsider the way you obviously took it, Gilly. I probably should've said lay person. Cops get jaded. Nothing surprises us, uh, them. Like, only a cop or ex-cop would make a federal case out of finding a suitcase of baby things."

"F-fed…eral c-case?" Gillian stumbled and almost fell, even though Mitch had a firm grip on her waist as he was set to help her into the cab.

"Another figure of speech. Look…you're way too shook up for me to go into detail. I shouldn't anyhow. Wouldn't, if I was still with the force. Can you manage that step into the truck? My Vette's in the shop being tuned."

Trooper bounded inside, nosing Gilly aside. The pup sat in the center of the seat, which suited Gillian, who clung to the door.

Mitch rounded the hood and climbed in on his side. "Where to? I know you live near the café. What street number and which block?"

Gillian rattled off her address, all the while trying to decide if Mitch was playing her for a sucker. She wondered if he was laughing silently at reeling her in and out like some dumb trout on a line. It hurt to think he would, after everything they'd shared on the mountain. But to some men, sex meant nothing more than personal gratification. It shamed her to think that the only man she'd given herself to, outside of the one she'd married, might be so callow.

Daryl's brother, Conrad, said she was gullible. Actually, he'd called her an airhead. He'd never liked her, and she'd hate for him to be right about anything. He'd done his level best to talk Daryl out of marrying her. She realized now that she hadn't called Conrad before fleeing Louisiana. He was probably stewing—no doubt even blaming her for his brother's death. And considering the way she'd disappeared, he probably had every right. Maybe she should call and ask his advice.

"I'm glad to see you're getting some color back." Mitch cast a quick glance in her direction before returning his attention to the Sunday-evening traffic. "I shouldn't have raced downhill so fast. Why didn't you yell at me to slow up?"

"I thought of it. I had visions of a black-and-blue bottom in the morning. The pinto mare does not have a rocking-chair gait."

"She's the least feisty of my saddle horses."

"It's okay, Mitch. I'll live. Wait, you missed the turn. My building's on that one-way street."

"I know. But the next street over allows access into your parking garage. I'm walking you to the door, Gilly. So don't try talking me out of it."

Strangely enough, Gillian wouldn't have. She'd been nervous ever since Bert's warning about two strange men hanging out near the café. Not only had she kept a sharp lookout, she'd been fighting a strong feeling that they knew exactly where she lived but were biding their time. They'd probably lost her trail during the week or so she'd laid low. They must have figured out she'd dug in somewhere around here. It wasn't as if towns in Southern Arizona were plentiful.

Mitch suddenly jammed on his brakes as a car shot out of a driveway that led to a tavern. He reached out a hand to keep Gillian from flying forward. "Jerk," he snarled. "They wouldn't get away with that if I still had my badge."

Gillian, anticipating a collision, grabbed Trooper. As the car and truck barely missed scraping sides, her panicked gaze flew to the offending vehicle. At once her stomach did cartwheels. *It was them. The two from Louisiana.* She slid down in her seat, feeling awfully close to throwing up.

Trooper whined and stuck his cold nose in her ear, shooting her upright again.

Mitch slowed to a crawl, straining to see in his side-view mirror. "Damn, I can't read their plate. That car could benefit from a good washing. The passenger had on a business suit, otherwise I'd guess they were cowboys gathering for next week's rodeo," he muttered. "That car looks like they've been out in the desert. Hey, are you okay?" He gave a guilty laugh. "Once a cop always a cop, unfortunately. Okay, I admit, once in a while I miss having a badge."

"My parking space is number fifteen," Gillian said. He seemed to be taking his time turning into her below-ground parking garage. Seeing the blue car so close to her residence rattled Gillian more than she cared to admit. Darn, she *liked* working for Flo and Bert. Had even grown complacent, always a dangerous thing. She sensed her world crumbling again.

As Mitch found the right spot, stopped, hopped out and rushed to help her from the truck's cab, she sneaked a look at her watch. "I didn't realize it was so late."

"Is that a hint for me to take off?"

"Actually, I thought about inviting you up for a bite to eat." Even sharing a table with a known enemy was preferable to sitting alone waiting for the unknown to strike.

Mitch eyed Trooper, who'd responded eagerly to the rattle of his leash. "Okay, but if you feel up to eating, we could walk down to Flo's. Bert will give me a big soup bone for Trooper to gnaw on.''

Her heart sank. ''Uh, I'd prefer to go upstairs. You don't have to stay if you'd rather eat at Flo's. Pets are allowed in my building, though. Trooper can have the leftover hash Bert sent home with me yesterday. But don't let me twist your arm.''

''Twist away.'' Mitch kissed the tip of her nose. ''Trooper will love the hash. I'll order pizza for us. While we're waiting for delivery, you can soak in a hot tub. That ought to stave off the sore muscles you were worried about.''

''Sounds great. Except I don't have a TV. How else can you occupy yourself while I soak?''

''Um.'' Mitch wagged his eyebrows. ''Scrub your back?''

She'd started up the stairs. At his announcement, she stopped. ''Mitch, I—maybe this isn't such a hot idea, after all.''

''You do have regrets about our time on the mountain,'' he accused.

''No.'' She shook her head. ''Not regrets, exactly. It's more that…well, there hasn't been anyone but my husband—until us.''

Mitch gently scraped the back of one knuckle along the hollow of her cheek. ''I had that figured out, Gilly.''

She felt his hand leave her face and settle on her hip as he reached over her head and opened the heavy door. His touch set new wildfires racing across her skin. Wildfires she had to keep in check. ''I'm not placing blame, Mitch. I was a willing partner.''

''Glad to hear it,'' he said, yanking open the same kind of door on the third landing. He waited for Trooper, who'd stopped to sniff the wooden floor. ''I care about you, Gilly. We'll take whatever's going on as fast or as slow as you'd like.''

"How can you care when you know nothing about me?''

He tugged the dog into the hall by his leash and let the fire door slam shut. "Ethan asked the same thing. I didn't have an answer for him, either. Look, let's just work through this hour by hour if need be. I'll make coffee while you shower, okay?''

She led the way down the hall to the last apartment. Mitch helped himself to the key she dug out of her jeans pocket. He jabbed twice before hitting the keyhole.

"Gilly, did you know there's a light out at the head of your stairs? Have you called maintenance?'' Mitch glanced up and down the hall. "Muggers love shadowy corners like the one over there.'' He pointed to the blackness at the end of her hall.

"Thanks,'' she drawled, her years in the South more noticeable than usual. "I chose this building for its proximity to the police station. Wouldn't a mugger be too smart to strike this close to a bunch of cops?''

"Gilly, Gilly. People who break the law usually aren't rational.''

She stepped inside and turned on a lamp, barely able to suppress a convulsive shudder. Mitch could well be describing the men who believed she had information she didn't have. Those two possessed the tenacity of killer sharks. And she felt their razor-sharp teeth inches from her throat. Quite possibly, he was in cahoots with them.

Mitch came in after her, shut and locked the door. He rammed his hands in his front pockets and stood blinking in the brighter light. The room had stark white walls and a nondescript beige carpet. A single pole lamp stood between a horrid orange plaid couch and a lime-green chair.

The coffee and single end table, both bare, looked like early Salvation Army rejects.

"It's not much." Gillian shrugged.

The understatement of the world. Mitch bent to unsnap Trooper's leash, keeping his thoughts to himself.

Gilly crossed to a window overlooking the street that ran past her parking garage. Her bedroom window looked out on the opposite street—the one at the building's entrance. Standing to one side, she depressed a slat on the miniblinds and scanned the street below before closing the blind tight.

Mitch considered her behavior rather odd, but he wasn't a woman living alone. She'd probably developed a nightly routine. He wandered into her kitchen, which had even less character. Enameled white walls looked bleak against dark wood cabinets. The only color in the room came from straw mats on a table tucked into an alcove.

"The place was already furnished," she offered after handing him a small canister of coffee and two clean cottage cheese cartons.

"That's a relief. I'd hate to think our tastes were that different. What am I doing with these?" He waggled the empty cartons.

"They're for Trooper's food and water. Are you sure it's okay for him to eat hash?"

"I won't give him much." Filling one bowl with water and setting it on the floor, Mitch made an offhand remark. "So Desert City really is a stopgap for you?"

Gillian heard the question mark at the end of his statement. She wasn't sure, after their near-collision with the men who were tailing her, if she wanted to embark on this conversation. But she had to say something. "I told Flo—and you—that this is where I ran out of money."

"I know. You've lived here—what? Almost a month already?"

"Yes. So?" She raised her head, her blue eyes wary.

He took the coffeepot out of her rigid fingers and filled it with tap water. "So, it's none of my business, but most of the women I know can't be in an empty room ten seconds without plotting where to hang pictures and set knickknacks."

Even when I had a place, I didn't keep my baby's ashes on my mantel. Lacing her fingers, Gillian clamped her teeth together to keep from lashing out.

For a minute Mitch thought he'd pushed her too far. She looked fragile enough to splinter into a million pieces. That hadn't been his aim. He only wanted some idea of where he stood. Where *they* stood. "Go shower," he said, his voice only slightly gruff. "Point me toward the phone and I'll order our pizza. Unless you'd rather eat something else. There's a Thai place not far from here. We used to call them and order in at the station if we had to work after Bert and Flo closed."

Opening a drawer, Gillian took out a phone book and a cell phone. "Suit yourself, since you're paying. Oh, don't give them my name, please. Only the apartment number."

"Sure, but why?" Her eyes reminded Mitch of baby owl's he'd seen at the ranch. And suddenly her lips looked so kissable, he forgot his question.

"Are you vouching for the character of all pizza delivery drivers?"

"What are you afraid of, Gillian?"

She was oh, so tempted to tell him. Tempted to tell him everything that had happened to send her running away from all she knew and loved.

Her laugh sounded brittle. "That's a question cops

shouldn't have to ask a woman living alone. But you aren't a cop anymore, are you, Mitch? All the same, if more women worried about the strange men they let into their lives, wouldn't there be fewer Jane Does in the morgue?''

In the silence that ensued, all that could be heard was the gurgle of brewing coffee and Trooper lapping vigorously at his water.

Mitch riffled through the phone book. ''Ethan would tell you I'm better behind the scenes than with interrogation. Sorry if I sounded skeptical. Before you head for the bath, tell me what pizza toppings you like.''

''I'm not wild about anchovies. Anything else is fine. Chicago-style, if that's an option. And extra cheese.'' She looked guilty. ''And don't nag at me about clogging my arteries. I eat pizza once in a blue moon. When I do, I want the full gastronomical effect.''

The strain that had developed between them dissolved at last. Mitch threw back his head and laughed. ''You're talking cop-style pizza. Gut-busters we call 'em. Best washed down with beer.''

She left the kitchen, but stopped after reaching the hall on the other side of the living room. ''If you need something to pass the time while you wait, there are magazines in the drawer of the end table. You can probably figure out which ones I bought. *Biker* and *Tattoo* were here when I moved in. They're kind of interesting—if you like bulging muscles and tattoos. And,'' she said drolly, ''...those are the women.''

The pup padded after her as she disappeared. ''Lucky dog,'' Mitch mumbled to himself. Those rare glimpses of Gillian's humor were one thing that kept him intrigued. That and the air of mystery about her, he supposed. A definite air of mystery.

After he phoned for the pizza, he ambled down the hall looking for Trooper, and paused outside a door where he heard water running. Tapping lightly, Mitch glanced into a room across the hall that must be Gillian's bedroom. "Hot pizza will be here in fifteen minutes," he called when the water stopped. "I think I'll go to the bar at the corner and pick up a six-pack of beer."

"All right. I'll be quick, but feel free to start without me."

Mitch hadn't intended to snoop in her room. Except, he told himself, he should make sure Trooper wasn't chewing her shoes. Again he was struck by the austerity. Four off-white walls. A double bed, covered with a cotton spread. Sort of a rosy-pink shade. Again, the only color. Peering into the open closet, he whistled softly for Trooper. What stunned Mitch was the scarcity of clothing. He'd been in a few women's bedrooms. Their closets overflowed with dresses, blouses and shoes.

A pair of sneakers and a pair of sandals sat beside Gillian's work shoes and the boots she'd worn riding. Above, on the closet shelf, stood an open suitcase and an unzipped duffel bag. She certainly wasn't attempting to hide anything—like a million bucks in stolen cash.

His wry smile turned into a frown as Trooper crawled out from under the bed, his nose stuck in a white sock. He looked so funny, Mitch had to chuckle. He dragged the errant pup out of the room and pulled the door closed, at once forgetting the frugality of Gillian's closet.

Gilly heard her bedroom door whisper shut. Was Mitch checking to see if she had knickknacks in there—or had he been searching for Daryl's key? Maybe he'd hoped to find it for his buddies. Well, she wished him luck. She'd even ripped the lining out of her suitcase trying to find any sign of that key.

Knowing he'd probably urged her into the bath in order to go through her things dampened Gillian's enthusiasm for the evening ahead. She lingered until the water got cold. Sometime after that, she heard Mitch return with the beer, then heard the pizza arrive. Finally, she got out and dried off. Wrapped in a towel, she eased open the door, glancing right and left before she dashed across the hall. Sure enough, the bedroom door she'd left ajar was now closed.

Mitch called down the hall, reminding her that the pizza was there. "I'm getting a head start on the beer," he added.

"I need another minute or so."

"Okay," he yelled back.

Inside her room, she made a cursory check. Nothing seemed out of place—except for a sock, which lay in the center of the floor. Where had it come from? She took her time dressing, all the while trying to decide whether or not she'd say anything about his intrusion. He must not have been much of a cop. He'd left a trail an idiot could follow.

"Find what you were looking for in my bedroom?" she blurted out the minute she entered the living room.

Mitch sat on the couch with one of the motorcycle magazines spread on his lap. Glancing up, he crushed an empty beer can and automatically opened another. "Yes," he said mildly after indulging in a long drink. "Trooper sneaked in there and went under your bed. He came out with a stray sock. I didn't check to see if the mate's still under there."

"Oh." She fought an uncomfortable wave of heat that climbed up her neck.

"Is it me you don't trust, Gilly? Or men in general?" Mitch put down his beer.

The timer on the oven buzzed, saving Gillian from answering.

"I put the pizza in the oven to keep it warm."

"I'll get it." Turning, Gillian tripped over Trooper. He barked sharply, and Mitch gave a command in Dutch to quiet him. The dog sank to his haunches at once, his ears pointed and twitching.

"I'm impressed. Maybe I ought to get a dog." She didn't say for protection as well as companionship.

"You have your food," Mitch scolded Trooper when he put a paw on the box Gillian was sliding the sizzling pizza back into.

"What's in the sack?" she asked, pointing to a bag on the kitchen counter.

"I conned the tavern out of plates and napkins. No sense dirtying your dishes for a meal like this."

"You think of everything. Um, maybe I should keep you around." She felt bad for accusing him of snooping. This was her attempt to lighten the mood.

Mitch carried the hot pizza box to the couch, and left Gilly to bring the plates and napkins. Making room for her on the middle cushion, he pulled the tab on a beer for her. He served her a slice first, ordering Trooper in English to sit. A sad-looking dog flopped on his belly at Gillian's feet. Dropping his nose on his paws, he gazed at her from soulful eyes.

"Can he have a bite?"

"No. He's been trained not to beg, according to Ethan. I'd hate to mess up his training."

"Ethan trains dogs?"

"No, Ethan bought him from the kennel that trained his dog, Taz."

"I met Taz, remember?"

"Right. Not for long, though. Ethan acted like a total jackass that night."

"He looks after your welfare. I think that's commendable."

Mitch shut the box lid and took a pull from his beer as he slid closer to Gillian. "That's what Regan said. We could all four be friends, if Ethan would shape up."

Gillian ate her piece of pizza except for a bite of crust, which she left on her plate even though she was tempted to sneak it to Trooper. Satisfied, she settled back to nurse her beer.

"One skinny slice and you're done?" Ethan stared in amazement at the woman seated beside him. He couldn't explain why he felt nervous around her tonight. Generally he knew what to say to women. Gilly was different, he acknowledged.

"Don't stop eating just because I'm full." As if to prove it, she broke off a piece of pizza and fed Mitch little bits.

"This has distinct appeal," he mumbled. Especially since she paused to pick off the mushrooms as he'd done with his first wedge.

Swallowing the last bite, Mitch grabbed her wrist, then leaned over and took his time kissing her thoroughly and wholeheartedly.

Gillian told herself she was playing with fire. Kissing Mitch Valetti led to more, and that was a bad idea. As she tried to hold on to that thought, her hand went limp. Her toes curled into the carpet. On his lips, she savored the taste of cheese, marinara sauce and malt from the beer. A feast, she decided.

Trooper filched the pizza crust on her plate. Scrambling to his feet, he loped off to his bowl in the kitchen.

Mitch sensed what the pup had done, and after flailing with one hand, made sure the box was firmly shut.

Mitch found he was no longer hungry. At least not for pizza. Lifting Gillian, he brought her onto his lap. At once he felt the visceral hardening behind his jeans zipper.

Gillian felt it, too. This was the time to call a halt, to make excuses.

Then Mitch slid both hands under the fleece top that matched the sweatpants she'd hurriedly donned after her bath, and the moment to make excuses passed.

He'd guessed correctly that she didn't have anything on under the zippered sweat top. His pleasurable growl said plainly how he felt about being right.

Thought of any kind failed her once he'd snaked the zipper down and skimmed his palms over the aching tips of her breasts. Loud warnings sounded inside her head. *Don't do this!* And yet…

Their arms and legs tangled pleasurably. But as Mitch shifted her again, Gillian attempted to pull away. The narrow, lumpy couch was exceedingly uncomfortable. Twice Mitch inhaled on a sharp moan and finally released Gilly to massage his badly aching side. When he yelped, swore, ending with an "Ouch!" Gillian sat up.

"This isn't working, Mitch." She pulled down her fleece top.

"You're right. Why are we going through these contortions when you have a perfectly good bed down the hall?" Grinning, he stood up and held out a hand.

"I mean…it's not working. You're in pain and I'm…out of the mood."

"Oh. That kind of not working." He studied her. "I should go then."

But he swayed and grabbed for the arm of the couch

to keep from pitching headlong into the pizza box. "Whoa!" he exclaimed, straightening a little at a time. "Must be more tired than I realized. And after a couple of beers... I guess I'm done for."

"You have a ways to drive, too. Uh...I have an extra blanket," she said, watching him stifle a yawn and move unsteadily toward the door.

Sleepy-eyed, he turned to watch her test the couch cushions with one hand. They both heard a spring pop. "Thanks, Gilly, but my side's already giving me fits. I'll be okay. It's not that far from home." He fumbled his pickup keys out of his pocket as he called to Trooper, hoping Gilly would invite him to stay. If not, maybe he'd phone and ask Ethan to come get him.

Gillian plucked the keys out of Mitch's hand and dropped them on the coffee table. "I guess my bed's big enough for two. If you really are as sleepy as you seem," she said, eying him cautiously.

"I really am. Not something a guy likes to admit to a gorgeous woman."

"I'm not gorgeous. And all flattery will get you tonight is half a soft bed and a pillow to yourself."

"You're on," he said, struggling to maintain some dignity. "Don't take this wrong, Gilly, but I won't be sleeping in these jeans. They're killing my bad side and my hip."

She wondered, when she agreed to his terms, if she ought to have her head examined.

Mitch managed to shut off the lamp before trailing her down the hall. True to her word, the bed was feather-soft. He let her douse the bedroom light before he tugged off his jeans and rolled into one side of the bed. He'd thought it would be hard to share a bed and not touch her. He was wrong. The strenuous horseback ride, the lovemaking on the mountain and the subsequent worry over her fainting—added to the beers he'd downed too fast—had taken a toll. Soothed by her scent on the sheets and her warm body by his side, Mitch fell into a deep, untroubled sleep.

Gillian lay awake much longer. She didn't drift off until Trooper had crawled onto the foot of the bed and settled at her feet. And she still wore her sweats.

Some time later, slamming car doors on the street below, accompanied by Trooper's low growl, awakened her from a twilight sleep.

She sat up and strained to see the clock sitting on the table near Mitch. Almost four o'clock. Muffled voices rose up from the street below through her open window. Gillian would have lain down again, but the pup's constant whining under the window prompted her to get up and see what was going on outside.

What she saw started her trembling. Two men, one chubby and one thin, stood next to a blue car arguing. Arguing and gesturing at her building. *It was them!*

Gillian's first instinct was to wake Mitch. *And say what?* Her story was so wild that even if he *was* trustworthy, those men would show up before she could make Mitch understand. *If* she could make him understand. They might well shoot him first and ask questions later. *No, they wouldn't.* They were thick as thieves, all three of them. She didn't want to believe it but she had to.

She stood looking down on his sleeping form, loving the boyish way he curled around his pillow. A yearning for everything that might have been billowed around her. Deliberately, she turned away, steeling herself against what she felt for the man she doubted she could trust. Who was she kidding? Of course she couldn't trust him!

He had her suitcase. And she'd seen the blue car exit his ranch.

Her blood running cold with fear, Gillian took a jacket from the closet and collected her boots. Quietly she made her way to the living room, where she stopped and stepped into them. If she left now, she'd have a decent head start.

Oh, no! Her car. Mitch had driven her home. She threw up her hands and paced. Those goons wouldn't argue forever. And since Trooper had begun to whine louder, Gillian reacted without taking time to think matters through. She snatched Mitch's keys off the coffee table, hissed at Trooper to stay and let herself out of the apartment.

The men would probably come in the main entrance and take the clunky old elevator to her floor. She tugged silently at the fire door and ran headlong down three flights of stairs. Not until she reached Mitch's pickup and sorted through his keys to find the one that fit the ignition did she realize she also had the key to his house. Nothing stood between her and retrieving Katie's urn except the time it'd take to detour past Mitch's ranch.

Whispering a shaky prayer that her plan would work, she started his vehicle and drove out into the black of night, leaving Mitch to explain her absence to his pals.

CHAPTER NINE

MITCH JERKED AWAKE to a noise that sounded like someone kicking a wall. He threw his legs over the edge of the bed, reaching simultaneously for his pants and the lock box that held his service revolver. Coming up empty on both counts, he grasped his head in both hands, attempting to rid himself of disorientation.

The sounds grew louder. Brusque male voices now accompanied the pounding. Beyond, in the blackness, Trooper growled menacingly. A warning, low and insistent, in the back of his throat.

Fighting free of the last covering, a tangled sheet wrapped around his waist, he inhaled the faint scent of an appealing perfume. *Gillian. He was in her apartment. In her bed.* Smiling, he patted the spot where he'd last seen her. Pillow and sheet were stone-cold.

More confused than ever, he finally located a lamp. In the subsequent flood of light, he saw a heap of denim, which luckily turned out to be his jeans. He pulled them on, yelling, "Pipe down!"

"Boy, apartments suck," he grumbled, hoping Gillian wasn't getting mixed up in some drunken neighbor's brawl. Whoever was making the racket was outside in the hall. Zipping his pants one-handed, Mitch jammed sockless feet into cold, stiff boots.

"Gilly?" Hobbling down the hall, listening to doors slamming and people grumbling, he called for her. The bathroom was empty. Likewise the living room and kitchen. By now, he'd determined the pounding was someone trying to cave in her front door. Snapping on the one pathetic pole lamp, Mitch cursed the fact that her door didn't have a peephole.

He'd left his watch on the bedroom night stand so he hadn't a clue as to the time. Where the hell was Gillian? But before he solved the mystery of her disappearance, he needed to stop the fools outside from doing serious damage to her door. He didn't know how early or late it was; perhaps she'd already gone to work. He knew Flo's breakfast shift started at an indecent hour.

Bringing Trooper to heel with a word, Mitch released the first lock. He left the chain on when he opened the door. "Whaddya want?" he growled. To his shock, a well-placed foot splintered the casing that held the chain. Two men in wrinkled suits, both holding automatic weapons, burst through the opening, forcing Mitch to leap back. Only his quick thinking let him stop Trooper from doing what he'd been trained for—saving his master.

"Who are you?" demanded one of the men. "We're looking for Noelle McGrath."

Although Mitch clutched the dog's collar, Trooper barked ferociously and strained toward the strangers.

"Shut the pooch up," the tallest of the two ordered.

Mitch again told Trooper to cease and desist. "You've obviously got the wrong apartment." He tried to keep his voice calm and his tone even. Not easy, since he kept seeing the fiery bullets that had belched from Tony DeSalvo's gun—a weapon similar to those aimed at him now.

"Search the place," the tall man commanded his stockier pal.

"Hey!" Mitch barely let his eyes move as he watched

the heavier man waddle down the hall. A few minutes later, he came back, carrying the suitcase Mitch had seen in Gilly's closet. The skinny dude opened the case, then swore and tossed it to the floor. The silky lining of the bag appeared to have been hacked to pieces with a carving knife. Mitch grimaced, wondering if that was fatso's work.

"She's been here all right. Little Noelle has found the key and flown the coop. If you know what's good for you, pretty boy, you'll tell us where she went."

"I don't know any Noelle," Mitch said carefully. By now they could all hear the wail of sirens moving closer to the building.

The fat guy gave an ugly laugh. "Trying to tell us those are your panty hose hanging over the shower stall?"

"No, they belong to Gillian. This is her apartment."

"Gillian?" The tall man glanced nervously toward the window. He clearly wanted to flee the approaching sirens. "Maybe that's why she's been so tough to find. After she doubled back at the border, I told the boss she was smarter than he gave her credit for."

"This Gillian, is she a blue-eyed blonde looker?" asked fatso, jamming his gun barrel in Mitch's midriff.

"Redhead," Mitch grunted, still unable to piece together what the hell was going on. "She's a waitress I met recently. So, what's this Noelle woman done, anyway? And who are you guys? Feds?" he asked, knowing full well they weren't part of any law enforcement. Mitch hoped they'd fall for his dumb boyfriend routine and provide some information as well as breathing space.

"None of your beeswax who we are," snarled the obvious leader. At the same time his partner sneered in Mitch's face, "Whatever she calls herself now, bud, or however she's changed her looks, I wouldn't get too chummy with the little lady. Cops in New Orleans have a warrant out for her—for murdering her husband.''

"Shut up!" The man who'd been giving the orders motioned to the door. "Let's get the hell out of here, Lenny. And you—" he stabbed the gun at Mitch "—had better conveniently forget you saw us. We've got long memories, and we'll come looking for you."

They melted into the hall shadows. Mitch heard them clattering down the back fire stairs as two cop cars squealed to a stop in front of the building. He knew there were two because one of them was slower in turning off the high-pitched scream of his siren.

He also knew it'd be a while before the teams made their way upstairs. He used the interlude to grab his watch, slip into his shirt and decide whether or not, like the toads with the guns, he was going to take a powder. About the time he'd decided to leave, he discovered his car keys were missing.

"Dammit!" he shouted, doubling a fist to strike the coffee table where he distinctly remembered Gillian putting them. "Gilly stole my pickup."

He stalked into the kitchen and yanked open the drawer to see if she had, in her haste, remembered to take the cell phone.

It was still there. He quickly punched in Ethan's home number. "Damn, damn, damn," he muttered, pacing the small kitchen along with his pup. "I'm really gonna hate swallowing all of Ethan's I-told-you-sos."

Regan's sleepy voice whispered a groggy hello. "Regan, Mitch here. Sorry to disturb you at this hour, but I need to talk to Ethan fast." He listened a moment, thanked her, then hung up and punched in another string of numbers. Maybe luck was in his corner after all. Ethan had gone out on a call. He'd checked in with Regan ten minutes ago, promising he'd be home as soon as he'd tied up a couple of loose ends.

Mitch connected with his former partner fully five minutes before the uniforms finished taking statements from residents on the floors below and finally made it up to his level.

"Well, well, Valetti. If you're involved in this nuisance call, you'd better have damned good cause." The not-so-rookie cop of the two glared at Mitch from eyes that had seen a long night.

Mitch invited them inside and fed them the trumped-up story he and Ethan had quickly concocted. "Look, Mike. This is what happened. Trooper and I dropped by here last night to have pizza with a friend. We talked late into the night. I had a couple of beers. She offered her couch so I wouldn't have to drive home." He pointed to a blanket he'd had time to rip off the bed. It and a pillow lay crumpled on the couch. "My friend works an early shift. She must've tiptoed out and left me sleeping. Hey, you know how it is..." Mitch offered a lopsided, sheepish grin.

Mike asked for the woman's name.

"Would you kiss and tell, old buddy? The jerks who caused the disturbance had nothing to do with her. They banged on the door and woke me up. I smelled booze the minute I cracked the door. They thought I was some dude horning in on their babe. One of 'em ripped the chain out of the wall. I convinced them they had the wrong building, then I phoned the station to report the incident." Mitch raked a hand through already mussed hair. "Out of habit, I rang my old line. Ethan was there. He took my report."

"Ethan did do that," came a deep voice from the door.

Mitch glanced up and met his friend's cool smile. The other two cops had arrived—Ron Glendenning and Brian Fitzgerald from his old precinct. Taz barked, which meant Ethan was here, too. Trooper bounded over to greet the older dog.

"Hey, Ethan. If you're picking up this call, much obliged," Brian said. "It's been a crazy night. The complaint came in as we were heading off duty."

Ethan clapped one of the officers on the back. He walked them to the door and accepted the notes from Ron's clipboard. He didn't turn and look at Mitch until the others had gone.

"Don't say it." Mitch held up his hands.

Ethan's eyes were dark and sympathetic. "You ought to know me better. Doesn't mean I understand why you're protecting her when I offered to put out an APB on your truck. You know it's the best, maybe the only chance we have of nabbing her."

"Listen, those bastards who barged in here had mob written all over them. What if she's accidentally mixed up with them? You know as well as I do that with their police contacts, she's less safe in jail."

"The woman steals your wheels and you want her kept safe? Aw, man, I thought when you phoned and asked for my help you'd learned your lesson."

"First, I think she only stole my pickup as a way of getting out to the ranch to collect her car. I figure she must've gotten up to use the bathroom and maybe heard those fools. She probably got scared and took off."

"I won't even ask why you were sleeping here."

"Don't. Ethan, if we leave now and take the shortcut to my place, we may catch up with her."

Ethan opened his mouth, then as quickly heaved a sigh and closed it again. Pulling out his keys, he jingled them to gain Taz and Trooper's attention. "I'll phone Regan from the Suzuki. I'm due home right now. It's coming up on four-thirty."

Mitch followed him out, pausing only long enough to snap off the lamp and latch what was left of the door. "Wait up. Listen, Ethan, those jokers may have been blowing smoke to throw me off track. But after you touch base with Regan, I wonder if you'd log on to the station computer and run an NCIC search in Louisiana using the name Noelle McGrath."

"That name sounds familiar." Ethan's brows knit. "Hot damn! Gillian Stevens is an alias. I should've figured. That explains why she came up totally blank when I ran her through the National Crime Information Center. Come on, Mitch. Are you thinking with something other than your brain here? I'll phone Villareal over at the county and have him pick her up. He can ask the questions and keep us out of it altogether."

"If I could handle this alone, Ethan, I'd never have called you. I can't explain it, but I'll stake my reputation—and my life—on Gilly being clean."

Unlocking his dusty Suzuki SUV, Ethan shooed the dogs into the back seat. If he had anything else to say on the subject of his former partner's stubbornness, he kept it to himself.

GILLIAN WAS SHAKING so hard, she could barely open the door of Mitch's pickup. She just prayed she'd be able to sneak out of the garage while the thugs from the blue car were entering her building via the front. The truck's engine sounded so loud in the quiet of the early-morning hours, she was afraid she'd faint again. The air inside the cab grew close from her rising fear.

Gillian expected men with guns to jump into her path

from behind each shadowy car she passed. She made it to the garage entry without mishap, fully recognizing the dangers of driving onto the street without headlights. This was, after all, only two streets away from the police station. Cops were always out and about in this area, starting and ending their shifts. But if she could reach the intersection without using lights, there'd be less chance of the thugs seeing her drive away.

Maybe they wouldn't connect her with this truck. Then again, maybe they would.

A half block more and she'd be at the intersection. Once she drove through it, she'd be home free. Up ahead she saw the traffic light turn yellow and then red. Damn, she hadn't wanted to stop. As she drew closer to the stoplight, twin beams crested a rise in the next block. Sweat popped out on her forehead. In the unfamiliar pickup cab, she fumbled around until she found the switch for the lights. She turned them on just as the other vehicle, a taxi, pulled to a stop across from her, and the driver blinked his lights as a reminder.

Gillian bent over the steering wheel. She wished her hair was longer so she could hide her face behind it. During the interminable wait for the light to turn green, she noticed a low fuel light blinking at her from Mitch's instrument panel.

Wasn't it just her luck to steal a truck that needed gas?

What to do about it? She'd run off without money. Not only didn't she have her phony driver's license, she didn't have a dime to her name.

Almost fortuitously, a streetlight illuminated the inside of the cab. From the corner of her eye, she caught the reflection of light off something silver in Mitch's console. With a trembling hand, she scooped up a stack of change.

Quarters, nickels and dimes. Almost four dollars, if in her haste she'd counted correctly.

At today's prices, how much gas did that buy? Two gallons, she decided dismally, passing a service station. It was closed. So, she could buy two gallons of gas, provided she found a station open at—she glanced at her watch—four-ten in the morning. That much gas would carry her to Mitch's ranch. From there she'd switch to her own car. At least it had a full tank.

God, she needed to factor in the time it'd take to pump two lousy gallons. The fuel needle was sinking more into the *E* by the second. Really, she had no choice.

For once, luck rode on her shoulder. Halfway down the next block, at which point Gillian had already determined she'd have to abandon the pickup, she caught sight of a combination convenience store-service station. And it was open!

Nerve-racking though the flashing low-fuel sign was, the worry had served to take her mind off her larger problem. Like what to do once she reached the ranch and switched cars?

Careful as she'd been to keep ready cash on hand at her apartment—preparing for this very eventuality—Gillian found it hard to believe she'd left without any of the essentials she needed to disappear again. That showed how thoroughly Mitch Valetti had addled her brain.

While she pumped her two gallons of gas, she kept a wary eye on the street. *Done at last!* She hurried inside and dumped her sweaty handful of change on the counter, gave the pump number and started to dash out again.

"Sheesh, lady," grumbled the zit-faced teen at the register. "What did you do, rob your kid's piggy bank?"

Gillian hunched her shoulders to ward off his sarcasm. Yet she didn't turn back. If someone came looking, the less she stood out, the better. It was a cinch the boy wouldn't soon forget her, though. With luck, however, he might not have gotten a clear look at the vehicle she drove.

To keep from making a U-turn in front of his window, she backtracked two blocks down a one-way street, circled the station and emerged several streets beyond where she'd bought the gas. Time ticked. Jeez, almost four-thirty.

MITCH DRUMMED his fingers on Ethan's dashboard, nervously awaiting the report he expected to pop up on Ethan's laptop CAD screen.

"Anything yet?" Ethan, who knew the best routes to navigate Desert City, sped down an alley guaranteed to take ten minutes off their drive.

"Nothing. Wait, something's coming up now." Mitch tilted the screen to see it in the light of the car's dash.

"Well?" Ethan demanded when the silence expanded and Mitch continued to stare.

"Hold your horses. There's no criminal record on Noelle McGrath, although there's a warrant for her in Louisiana. She's wanted for questioning in the drive-by shooting of her husband, Daryl. The way I read this, she disappeared suddenly, leaving furniture, clothing and a car behind at her town house. Dispatch put me on hold while they scan in a newspaper article and a driver's license photo ID."

Ethan tossed Mitch his cell phone. "When you get the birth date off the license, ask them to run searches on a mix of the two names. See if we can pick up a definite connection between the McGrath woman and your Gillian."

"There's no need," Mitch said, closing his eyes and

rubbing at the frown lines forming between his eyebrows. "The picture's grainy. She's got really light hair in the photo and it's longer. But it's Gilly, all right. There's no disguising the shape of her face, or her smile."

Reaching across the seat, Ethan gave Mitch's shoulder a bracing squeeze. "I'm sorry. I really am." He let his foot off the gas. "Shall I phone Villareal, and we'll turn back? Regan told me to bring you to the house for breakfast," he said placatingly.

"I know it looks bad on the surface, Ethan. But I refuse to believe that Gilly or Noelle—or whatever the hell her name is—did anything criminal. I won't be satisfied until I hear the story from her own lips. If you don't mind, I'd prefer we try to catch up."

"I don't mind as long as you're prepared to accept the consequences."

"You mean, watch while you cuff and book her?"

"You wouldn't be so foolish as to try to interfere, would you, Mitch?"

Mitch's expression was pained. "Who I am hasn't changed because I turned in my badge. I'm still one of the good guys."

"Okay. I've got to admit," Ethan growled, "that lately you've had me worried. But then, I've hardly made a secret of the fact that from the first day I met her, I've been uneasy about your Gillian Stevens."

Mitch didn't bring up the few times he'd felt she was holding back, or hiding something. The last thing he wanted to do was change Ethan's mind about helping him locate Gilly.

"So what's the game plan?" Ethan asked once they'd reached the outskirts of town and were headed down the perimeter road toward Mitch's ranch.

"Let me think a minute. If she *is* there and we roar

down my lane, she could climb in her car or my truck and light out across the desert—like that driver who left the suitcase.''

''I thought you said you'd fixed the fence.''

''Yeah. Except Gilly was out here yesterday. She'll know it's a matter of circling around the toolshed and the black walnut tree to skirt the fence.''

''Damn.''

''Yeah.''

''Okay. We need an alternative plan.''

Mitch closed the laptop computer and set it aside. ''I wish I knew how much of a head start she had.''

''What are you thinking? Spit it out.''

''It'd take longer, but we can stop at Dave's, saddle a couple of his horses and ride to my place across the back pasture.''

''Sounds workable to me. I'd suggest we leave Trooper with Dave. We can take Taz. He might distract her if she's armed.''

''She's not going to be armed!''

''You don't know that, Mitch. Louisiana wants to question her about a drive-by, for God's sake.''

Mitch stared at his friend in the dusky morning light beginning to filter into Ethan's Suzuki.

''Have it your way. Slow down, or you'll miss Dave's drive. There, turn. I guess we'll know soon enough which one of us is right.''

''I'm sorry, Mitch. Honest to God, I wish it hadn't ended this way.''

''Nothing's ended, Ethan. First, I want to hear what Gilly has to say.''

Ethan's snort voiced his opinion as effectively as any words.

IN GILLIAN'S HASTE to reach the ranch, collect her belongings and be on her way, she missed Mitch's lane. Because it was still pitch-black out, she also missed the narrow crossover between the two lanes of the divided road. She knew the crossovers weren't meant to be used by motorists. There were signs everywhere saying they were for emergency vehicles only. However, this perimeter road was so sparsely traveled, she didn't think there was much chance of anyone seeing and reporting her indiscretion.

She did grow extremely nervous when it proved to be five miles down the road to the next crossing to a path that was barely defined. But cross it she did. Afterward, she heaved a huge sigh, wanting badly to step on the gas and speed all the way to Mitch's ranch. However, from the moment she'd pumped gas into his pickup, she'd cautioned herself to obey traffic laws, no matter how great her urgency.

Halfway down Mitch's lane, she turned off her lights and crept forward. She'd come this far; it wouldn't pay now to get careless. Until yesterday, she hadn't realized how close his house sat to his neighbor's. Now that she knew, and also knew the men watched out for each other's property, she didn't want to risk his friend seeing her lights and maybe coming to investigate.

She slowed even more when she drove out from the covering of trees. Faint light, beginning to break in the east, made it easier to assess what lay ahead. Her car stood exactly where she'd left it. Her key would be inside on Mitch's kitchen counter. There was no light on in the house. Gillian shut off the ignition and sorted through his keys for the one most likely to open his door.

It shouldn't feel like breaking and entering. But it did. Her stomach thrashed and bile rose when she slid out of the pickup. For maybe the first time since the start of this debacle, she considered giving up.

What would Mitch do if she turned around now, went back to town and threw herself on his mercy? It was tempting. So very tempting. Of course she couldn't. It'd be too unfair to involve anyone she cared about in this unholy mess.

Startled, she realized she *did* care for Mitch Valetti. A lot. More than someone in her position ought to. The best thing she could do for both of them, she decided with an increasingly heavier heart, was to disappear permanently from his life.

As she stumbled up his porch steps, she was unable to see Mitch's front door for the blinding flood of tears.

"HI, DAVE." Mitch hopped out of Ethan's SUV and hailed his neighbor, who'd just come from his barn leading a saddled horse.

"What brings you two out here before daybreak?" Dave met them with an outstretched hand and a grin.

"You seen any activity around my house this morning?"

Dave gave a shake of his head. "You got trouble over there again?"

"Maybe, maybe not. Ethan and I need the element of surprise. Would you mind keeping Trooper and also lending us two horses? We thought we'd ride in the back way and sneak past my barn."

"This have anything to do with the guys who tore out your fence and scared the daylights out of your pregnant mare?"

Mitch tugged at his lower lip. "Doubtful." But now he wondered if it tied in with Gillian. He'd thought at the time it was joyriding teens.

"I'll need a few minutes to saddle an additional horse. Want me to go with you?" Dave asked hopefully.

"Like the cavalry?" Ethan said with a grin. "We aren't anticipating trouble, Dave. If we run into any, I'll signal the county for back-up. Technically, this is their territory. I don't even have jurisdiction, although I can hold someone if need be. Mitch is involved strictly in the capacity of property owner. Aren't you, Mitch?" he reiterated when Mitch failed to agree verbally or even nod.

"What? Sure, Ethan. I said up front that you're calling the shots. So let's get at it. Dave, don't bother with a saddle. I'll ride bareback."

"I haven't ridden a horse in so long, I hope I haven't forgotten how." Ethan mounted the saddled horse, watching Mitch swing up on the second one Dave led out.

"My hip's feeling the effect of being in the saddle so long yesterday," Mitch said, grimacing. "My whole side is sore."

Ethan didn't reply until after they'd left Dave's land. "You know, Mitch, if you'd stuck to just riding horses yesterday, your hip might not be so stove up."

Mitch scowled. "Needle me all you want. I'm not telling you if I slept with Gilly or not."

"I wouldn't be much of a detective if I didn't pick up enough clues at her apartment to know the answer to *that,* now would I?"

"Then kindly keep your remarks to yourself."

"Did I say anything in front of Dave?"

"No. And we'd better shut up. Sounds carry out here. The reason we're bouncing across the field like this is to take Gilly by surprise."

"Just one more question. Do you think she'll switch

cars and take off like a shot, or are you guessing she'll go inside first?''

"Her car key's in my house. Plus, she left her place with nothing, as far as I could tell.'' *Not that she had much to begin with.* Mitch wanted to tell Ethan about her meager material possessions. On the other hand, he didn't want to say anything that might damage Gillian further in Ethan's eyes. Detective Knight had a soft heart when it came to kids. Adults who broke the law didn't fare so well.

Mitch had held the same views. Funny how turning in his badge made him see things differently. Or was his thinking skewed just where one woman was concerned?

They topped a rise looking down on Mitch's property. He saw Ethan jab a finger. "My truck's there,'' he muttered. "So is Gilly's car. Looks like we hit pay dirt, partner.'' Both his tone and his heart were wooden.

"Can we tie up behind the barn and split up? One go in the front door and one in the back?'' Ethan asked quietly, bringing Taz to heel with a hand motion.

The big dog's ears pricked forward. His shoulders rippled with tension the way they did when he went on full alert.

"Okay,'' Mitch said without inflection. He dug a coin out of his pocket. "Heads I stop her at the front door, tails I go in the back.''

Without looking at it, Ethan snagged the coin in midair as they dismounted. "I'm the only one here with a badge.''

"I know that.'' Mitch failed to turn away fast enough to conceal the pain in his eyes.

Ethan clapped him firmly on the shoulder. "I promise, unless she pulls a piece, I'll be gentle.''

"Yeah.'' Mitch ducked his head.

"You won't have to hike so far over rough ground if you take the front door. Taz and I'll go in via the kitchen."

Nodding this time, the men exchanged a thumbs-up. Still, Mitch felt a hole open up in his chest as Ethan bent double, skirted the barn and hugged the ground in his effort not to be seen from the house. He'd taken his weapon from his shoulder holster, which made him appear too damned official.

"I'm counting on you, Gilly babe," Mitch whispered stonily. He didn't think he'd be able to live with the consequences if he'd read her wrong and Ethan got hurt doing him this favor.

Though it was near impossible for him to crouch, Mitch knew he had to, since he'd be passing two windows. Gilly could look out either one and see him sneaking up to the porch. If she spotted him first, she had the shorter distance to dash to her car. Then they'd never get answers.

Most of all, Mitch wanted answers. Whatever mess Gillian was in, he wanted the names of those bastards who'd broken into her apartment.

Halfway up the porch steps, his leg cramped. He fell to one knee. Gritting his teeth against the pain, he hobbled the remaining distance. Breathing hard, he reached for the doorknob and muttered a final prayer. Sucking in a last massive gulp of air, he planted his shoulder against the door and burst inside.

He'd got there before Ethan, whom he now heard jiggling the back door.

It was hard to tell who was more shocked, Mitch or Gillian, as she screamed and spun away from his fireplace. In her hands she held baby Katie's urn. As Mitch advanced, she maintained her grasp on the silver vase and edged steadily toward the kitchen, which led to a back door. She hugged the urn protectively against her breasts.

Mitch heard Ethan splinter the lock to his back door—a noise that seemed to occur in a remote section of his brain. His sweeping gaze had landed on the suitcase still sitting on his coffee table. Neatly repacked, the blanket and frilly pink dress lay folded as they'd been when the bomb squad had first let him open the valise.

Finally, his breathing leveled and his knees felt strong again. Mitch lunged for Gillian, grabbing her none too gently. "What in hell are you doing with baby Katie?" he demanded, his grip so tight Gillian cried out in pain.

Ethan's words came at him through a thick bank of fog. "You're hurting her, Mitch. Let go. It's pretty obvious if you ask me. At least one mystery here is solved."

CHAPTER TEN

GILLIAN APPEARED ready to bolt. From wide, stricken eyes, she darted panicky glances between Mitch, who blocked the entry to a bedroom door to the kitchen where even now Taz stood guard. The instant Ethan filled the archway, Gilly wrenched out of Mitch's hold and sank wordlessly to the floor.

"Explain!" Mitch, still hurting from the stress he'd placed on his healing wounds, stared coldly down on her bowed head.

"Would it do any good?" she asked in a shaky voice. "If you're working with them, I doubt my telling you I don't have the key will make an impression."

Mitch and Ethan exchanged bewildered glances.

Taz sank to his haunches, teeth no longer bared. His tail made swishing sounds on the hardwood as he awaited some kind of signal from his master.

"Them who? *What* key? Gillian—if that's even your name—" Mitch shouted in exasperation, "for God's sake, get up and sit on the couch instead of cowering on the damn floor. Ethan and I aren't going to hurt you. We just want to know what the hell is going on."

"I'm not cowering." She tried to get up, but her knees refused to support her.

Noticing that she quailed all over, Mitch reached down and gently helped her to her feet. He escorted her to the leather couch where just yesterday she'd lain in a faint.

Ethan sauntered up to the heavy wood coffee table. He swept aside an untidy stack of computer paper, then sat in the spot he'd cleared. "It usually helps to begin at the beginning," he said, not making eye contact with Mitch. "If you'd prefer to have a lawyer present before you say anything, that's your privilege and your right."

She blanched at that. "I don't have a…a…lawyer. Well, Daryl had one for the business." She raised a badly shaking hand to scrape back a curl now drooping over one eye. Her hold on the urn remained tight.

"I haven't done anything wrong," she said, almost to herself. "Or maybe I have. I ran. First, because Daryl was convinced I'd be killed. Later when Patrick…when Patrick…" Gilly's voice trailed away as her eyes filled with tears. "Someone else who tried to help me was viciously run down."

Mitch and Ethan shared a second look. "Maybe you could start over and tell us who's chasing you," Mitch suggested, tossing aside a pillow to make a place beside her on the sofa. She flinched when he sat down, and that hurt.

"You don't know?"

"Why would I?"

She stared blankly up at him. "I don't know who they are, Mitch." Backed into a corner of the couch, she hugged the urn for dear life, and haltingly told her sorry tale. She began with the wrenching loss of Katie, briefly touched on her misery and her divorce, then described the full events on the night Daryl had arrived at her rented town house. She quickly told them about her flight, ending with her coming to Desert City.

"Where was his CPA firm?" Ethan asked, pulling a battered notebook from his jacket pocket. "Louisiana, right? And your name wasn't…uh…isn't Gillian Stevens.''

Lifting her head in surprise, Gillian shrugged her shoulders. ''Legally my name is Gillian Noelle Talbert McGrath. Daryl never liked Gillian. So from the time we started dating, he called me Noelle. After we got married, he insisted I use Noelle McGrath on everything.''

Ethan scribbled faster in his book. ''Flo said you showed her a driver's license and social security card in the name Gillian Stevens. Are they stolen? Or phony?''

''Phony, I imagine. Daryl provided them. They were in an envelope in the glove compartment of a car he must've bought out of state. At least, it had Mississippi plates that matched the driver's license. Stevens is the name of my third stepdad. He d-died of cancer, but he gave me away at my wedding. That's how Daryl knew him. Mom's remarried again. We've grown apart.''

Mitch choked and sputtered. ''Then the story you fed me about your folks dying in a plane crash was a lie?''

''Partially,'' Gillian admitted, rallying in her own defense. ''My dad died in the crash. Mother survived. She married the doctor who saved her life. He was my first stepdad. She's not…strong, and she missed my dad so much. Oh, this is pointless. What does any of it matter? Lock me up, or extradite me to New Orleans. I'm tired of having to pile lies on lies.'' She fingered the lettering on the urn. ''I have Katie back. That's all I really care about. I hoped I could help put away the men who killed Daryl. Only I don't know anything. Not even their names. Beating them is impossible.''

Ethan closed his notebook. He dug in his jacket pocket, and came out with handcuffs.

''Now hold on a damned minute.'' Mitch reached across the coffee table and jerked the gleaming steel out of Ethan's hands. "So far nothing she's told us adds up to cold-blooded contract murder, interstate chase scenes or stolen suitcases."

"It's *my* suitcase. I had to change a flat tire, and I took my suitcases out of my trunk. Then I saw headlights on the road behind me. I was afraid it was them—the men who'd followed me from New Orleans. I didn't manage to get everything back in place. I've been searching the underbrush along your lane—until yesterday, when I saw you had all this." Her hand swept the case and the urn.

"What were you doing on my property in the first place?"

Gillian gazed at Mitch. She seemed near shattering. "On the freeway, I saw a car in my rearview mirror—a big blue car like they drove. I panicked and took roads at random, hoping…trying to lose them. I think I always knew they wouldn't give up."

"Okay," Mitch said. "I'll buy that. But later, when you saw I had this…" He stabbed a finger at the case. "Why not explain to me then?" What he didn't say in front of Ethan, but the accusation he left hanging between them, hinged heavily on the personal intimacy they'd shared earlier that same day.

She licked her lips, hesitating a long time. "The day I started working for Flo, I drove out here hoping the suitcase had simply been knocked into the underbrush along the lane. I…saw…the men who were after me go toward your house. After a while, they drove out again. You weren't far behind. I hid, but you got out and started searching the area with a spotlight. I ran away. Tell me, what would *you* have deduced? I assumed you worked with them, and your befriending me was a setup."

Anger appeared in Mitch's dark eyes. "I stuck my neck out making sure baby Katie didn't get forgotten in the precinct's evidence room. You think I lied when I said I'd find out where she belonged?''

Gillian dropped her gaze guiltily. She knew what he was really wondering: how she could have slept with him if she thought he was mixed up with crooks and killers. His beautiful dark eyes were windows opening straight to his heart.

She squirmed. With Ethan looking on, she wasn't going to explain how Mitch affected her—how, with a mere touch, he stripped away every vestige of her good sense.

Ethan snatched his handcuffs out of Mitch's limp hands. ''Gillian, you must've been mistaken about the identity of the men you saw leaving Mitch's.''

''Wait! Maybe not.'' Mitch remembered back to the night in question. ''One evening I thought some kids were messing around my corral. It was the same night you brought Trooper, Ethan. I chased after the car. I thought I saw a person—a silhouette in the trees—so I stopped to have a look.''

''You weren't looking for me because those men said they'd seen me?'' Gillian asked.

''No.'' Mitch seemed thoroughly stunned.

Ethan leaned toward him. ''If they were the same guys who barged in on you at Gillian's apartment this morning, and they dig deeper and start adding things up, we could have company here before we know it.''

Gillian jumped to her feet. ''Whoever they are, they think my ex-husband gave me a key to a safe-deposit box or a locker or something, where he put evidence that'll send their outfit to jail.''

When Ethan and Mitch stared at her, Gillian continued. ''Daryl implied in an e-mail to a friend that he'd uncovered a big money-laundering operation, and that he'd hidden evidence. Daryl hinted I'd bring this man some kind of key. If I have one in my possession, I can't find it. But I can't…*won't* let them destroy all I have left of my baby. Please, Mitch, could you put Katie someplace she'll be safe, no matter what happens to me?''

"Lord, Gilly. You've finally given us information we can understand." Mitch got to his feet and paced. "Ethan, I won't let you throw her to the wolves. Are you with me here, or do I have to try to hang these bastards on my own?''

Ethan stroked the beginnings of a shadowy beard on his chin, obviously contemplating Mitch's request.

Gillian set the urn carefully and lovingly between the quilt and the dress in the little suitcase before closing the lid. "I can't let you involve yourself, Mitch." In a rush, she explained how Patrick Malone, a kindly cop in Flagstaff, had tried to help. "Because of me," she concluded, "he was probably killed."

Ethan's head shot up. "Stop. You're saying these guys found you in Flagstaff? And in broad daylight they mowed down a cop in the precinct parking lot?''

Gillian nodded unhappily. "Except the sun was going down, so it was hard to see."

"I saw a fax come into our office on that incident. The cop didn't die. I think he's recovering. The fax didn't say he was in a safe house, but reading between the lines, I think the chief has him under wraps."

Tears filled Gillian's eyes. "Thank heaven. Sergeant Malone was like a father to Daryl. The man was just weeks away from retirement. All this time I've thought he…thought those men…" She sank back on the couch, buried her face in her hands and wept huge, gulping sobs.

Mitch and Ethan both seemed at a loss. Finally, Mitch pulled her up and into his arms. As he rocked her silently,

Ethan shifted from foot to foot, gazing uncomfortably on the tender scene.

After a few minutes, he leaned down and picked up the suitcase. "Look," he said, sounding a bit raw himself. "There's enough to this situation to warrant investigating. Can't do that if our primary witness turns up dead. Mitch, since your ranch and Gillian's apartment are known to these bastards, I think we ought to pull up stakes and reconvene at my house while we talk this through."

"Good idea," Mitch agreed. "First on the agenda is to find a more secure place to hide Gilly. With all the traffic Regan and Odella have in and out of their home office, it'll be hard to keep Gilly safe there. Besides, we don't want you guys to be their next target."

Stepping away from Mitch, Gillian blotted her eyes. "I wouldn't stay. Your family was in jeopardy once, Ethan. I'd never knowingly let something like that happen again on my account."

For the first time since meeting her, Ethan gave her a genuine smile. "I appreciate your thoughtfulness. However, today is Regan's day without appointments. That gives us several hours to knock together some kind of plan."

"I'll work on that," Mitch volunteered. "You're the one who has the official capacity to dig up goods on the guy in New Orleans who's calling the shots."

"What do you mean?" Gillian's eyebrows rose. "Aren't the men who're chasing me clients of Daryl?"

"Doubtful, sweetheart." Mitch stroked the back of Gilly's neck. "Sounds to me as if your ex stepped into the middle of a great big dirty operation. Before I transferred to Desert City P.D., I was involved in a sting in Philly aimed at bringing down a mob boss. They're adept at keeping layers of underlings between themselves and the action on the street. It's rare to compile enough documentation to nail any of the head creeps.''

"It's been done," Ethan said. "By men like your ex, Gillian. It takes a witness who can track the money trail."

"You're talking about the Mafia! I can't believe Daryl would… Well, you'd have to know him." She continued to look horrified.

"We can't say for sure this involves organized crime," Mitch told her soothingly. "All this talk of gangsters is upsetting Gilly, Ethan. Can we save it for later? Right now, let's clear out of here."

"Sure. Why don't I drive Gillian to my place in her car? I have a couple of other questions. You return the horses to Dave. I left keys to the SUV in the ignition. Bring it to my house, okay?"

When Mitch seemed about to object, Ethan added, "I expect you'll want to ask Dave to keep Trooper, and cover your ranch. Probably better to be vague about your plans. Tell him you're moonlighting on a case that's liable to take you out of town."

"Goodness, look at the time," Gillian exclaimed. "I'm due at the café in twenty minutes."

"No, Gillian!" Mitch and Ethan exclaimed explosively.

Mitch completed their joint thought. "As much as Flo's going to want to pound on me and Ethan for spiriting you away, the only smart thing is for you to call in and quit."

"I can't do that! Flo hired me without references. Her niece left her high and dry. I won't do that to her and Bert. They deserve better.''

"Sweetheart, you aren't thinking straight," Mitch argued. "Those guys—and by the way, Ethan, one of them's named Lenny—aren't new at their job. They've tracked you halfway across the United States. I'm betting they've figured out where you work.''

''True,'' admitted an ashen-faced Gillian. ''Bert's seen two suspicious men around the café. I was afraid it was them. All right,'' she agreed reluctantly. ''But do you think Regan might know someone who might help Flo out, at least till she can hire someone new?'' At his nod, she said, ''That's good. But someday, I hope I can tell Flo the truth.''

''You will if I have my druthers,'' Mitch said. ''Ethan, I'm leaving Gilly in your hands until we meet at your house.'' A strong, unspoken message underlay Mitch's statement. Gillian was important to him, and he charged his best friend with keeping her safe.

SOME FORTY MINUTES later they all reconvened in Ethan's kitchen. Regan had fed the quadruplets breakfast before they arrived, and was putting the last child down for a morning nap. ''There's coffee, and cinnamon coffee cake Odella brought this morning,'' Regan announced. She and Odella had worked together at Desert City's Child Help Center. They'd left, believing they could help more children privately, without all the government red tape.

An elegant black woman rose gracefully from the table, having accurately read the tension in the faces of Ethan and his friends. ''If this is private, I can make myself scarce,'' she offered.

''If Mitch doesn't mind, I'd like you to stay.'' Ethan deferred to Mitch, adding for his ears alone, ''Gillian and I talked some more on the drive home about what happened to Pat Malone up in Flagstaff. If the guys tailing her are up to their ears in organized crime, they might have moles in several police departments. Odella's son works vice in Flag. He could get us Malone's status easier than I can go sticking my nose in up there."

Mitch nodded. "If possible, I'd like to talk to Malone." Spinning on his heel, he stalked to the kitchen table where Regan had just handed Gillian a steaming mug of coffee. "Gilly, is Pat Malone clean?"

"Clean? Oh, you mean above reproach?"

"Exactly. Sometimes guys close to retirement get anxious about their future and make a last killing on the take."

"Daryl trusted him implicitly. Patrick was on an important undercover operation at the time of our wedding. Even though he and Daryl were like family, I'd never met Patrick until I looked him up, per Daryl's instructions. I felt he was as frustrated by the few clues Daryl had provided as I was. And he advised me to hide out and trust no one. That was after he'd been struck by the car and in a great deal of pain."

"He's our best lead," Ethan mused aloud.

"I don't know what this is about, and I don't want to," Odella said, glancing around at the long faces in the room. "I can vouch for my son's integrity. Write down what you want me to ask and I'll phone him."

Regan cut Odella's coffee cake and passed slices to people who weren't interested in eating. The men were focused on Odella's side of the telephone conversation.

"Sergeant Malone had chest injuries, plus a broken arm and leg," the older woman announced after hanging up. "You could probably tell my son was curious. He said none of the cops in the parking lot that day got a good look at the car. Except Malone—who claims everything happened too fast for him to see anything. He's staunchly maintained that the woman he was talking to on the sidewalk was an innocent bystander asking for directions. Officially, the case is closed. Malone has gone to his sister's home in Phoenix to recover. That's privileged information,'' she said, handing Ethan an address she'd written on a memo pad.

"Then it's true he is alive.'' Tears stood in Gillian's eyes again, tears of relief.

Mitch relaxed in his chair. Some of his tension had lifted, and he used the moment to sample the cake. After complimenting Odella and downing a swig of coffee, he got back to the case at hand. "I saw Lenny and his sidekick up close and personal. Give me an hour with mug shots of known mobsters operating in the South and Southwest. I might be able to pick those two out.''

"While you do that, I'll take Gillian to pay Malone a visit.''

Mitch acquiesced, albeit not happily. "Before you take off, I have a question for Gilly. I'd like to have another look inside your suitcase. Are you okay with that?''

She nodded.

He turned to her again once Regan and Odella had left the room. "When those guys came to your apartment, Lenny, the short, fat dude, dragged your larger bag into the living room. If you hadn't already ripped the lining out, he did. Hunting for the key, no doubt. We'll want to give your car another once-over, too.''

"I pretty much ruined the other suitcase myself, Mitch. And the car I'm driving isn't the one Daryl bought.'' She described how she'd spent the two weeks following her mad flight from his lane. "I searched every nook and cranny inside the car and also tore apart the trunk. Before I sold it and bought a new car in Douglas, I removed the seats, vacuumed and felt under every rug.''

"Maybe they hit your ex before he had time to stash the key."

Gillian twirled her cup on its coaster. "You'd have to know Daryl to see the fallacy in that. Before he embarked on anything, he'd plan it down to the tiniest detail. He was like that. You know the papers you had spread out on your coffee table?" she said to Mitch. "Those piles would've driven Daryl nuts. The first time I saw the inside of your house, I was struck by the contrast between the lived-in look of your place and the way Daryl made us live."

"Mitch is a slob." Ethan grinned, and Mitch turned red.

Gillian countered quickly. "Nothing of the sort. Daryl was a neat freak."

"You must've known what he was like when you married him." Mitch tossed out the remark with careless abandon.

"We met in college and both lived in dorms. Maybe I should have had an inkling based on the fact that he had his sights set on becoming a CPA. But I wasn't complaining about him, Mitch. I was trying to point out why I naturally assumed I had the key. I think it's also why Patrick Malone believed I had it. Probably why the men chasing me think so, too. If Daryl worked for them, they'd know he was like that."

"Shall we quit arguing and get cracking?" Ethan asked. "I have other cases needing attention. My partner's going to send out the Saint Bernard with the brandy if I don't check in with him soon."

"Speaking of checking in—" Mitch wagged his coffee cup at Gillian "—don't forget you need to phone Flo."

"I did. First thing when Ethan and I got here. She was so kind, I feel just terrible."

"What excuse did you give her?"

"I said someone out of my past had caught up with me and I was going home. The lie stuck in my throat, but Ethan wants her and Bert not to know anything in case someone comes by asking questions about me. And Regan's promised to ask around to see if she can locate someone who'll take my place."

"You sound defensive." Mitch hiked an eyebrow. "Did I say you acted improperly?"

"Not in so many words. It's more the way you've...been looking at me since you found me in your house."

"How am I supposed to look at someone who's a walking lie?"

Ethan whistled between his teeth. A sharp, annoying sound, Gillian thought. But it served to distract her and Mitch.

"Mitch is right," Gillian said, lacing her unsteady hands together on top of the table. "I'm sorry about everything. But I won't offer excuses. Given that—" she sighed heavily "—Ethan, I don't like taking you away from your family and work. Honestly, I'd feel more comfortable if Mitch took me to visit Pat Malone. Although I'm sure it's the last thing he wants to do."

"I *do* want to go. I didn't pitch a fit because Ethan's way saves time. These guys may have connections in Desert City. Possibly even on the force. Money talks at all levels of government, and the mob infiltrates from top to bottom. They're not long on patience, either. Lenny and company are hot on your trail, Gilly. Thanks to my sleepy-headed goof, they know your alias now." He slammed a fist on the table. "I'm mad at myself. I wouldn't have given them squat if you'd confided in me."

"I explained why I didn't. In hindsight it's easy to say I'm sorry, Mitch. But it's frightening to find yourself in the middle of something, not knowing who to trust or where to turn. Patrick said I should trust no one. He also pointed out that some cops are crooked."

Regan had stepped back into the room to refill her cup. "If you ask me, and no one did, you've got to stop blaming each other, or this case is going nowhere but down the tubes."

Ethan beamed at his wife. "Wise words from a wise lady. I vote we listen to her. Beating up on each other won't solve this case. I owe Gillian an apology, too."

"About damn time," Mitch sputtered. "But I'm no better. I didn't stop to look at this mess from Gilly's point of view. From where you sit, sweetheart, it must look like a damned Chinese puzzle."

Gillian's irritation with him for using meaningless endearments began to melt away. "If our roles were reversed, I'd be mad at me, too. It must seem as if I schemed and took advantage of your feelings for me. I swear I didn't. This whole thing unfolded one step at a time. It was one shock coming after another."

Odella entered the kitchen carrying a sleepy-eyed Cara who, when she saw Ethan, grinned sweetly and held out her arms, saying "Da." One little arm was still in a Velcro brace. Seeing her reach out to him, after a man she'd trusted had abused her so cruelly, touched everyone in the room, including Gillian.

Mitch watched solemnly. "These thugs chasing Gilly remind me of Tony DeSalvo." He glanced at her. "DeSalvo's the nut who abused the quadruplets and shot me."

Mitch saw that her hands had begun to shake again. He took them between his warm fingers and began to gently chafe her skin. "I'm willing to put everything behind us, Gilly. Ethan and I have a good record of cracking the cases we worked on together. Will you let us have a go at solving yours?"

Gillian gazed on his face with such longing and affection, he couldn't possibly miss how she felt about him. If he did, he was the only one in the room. Which was entirely possible, she supposed. Because the moment she pulled away and nodded, he switched into police mode and began snapping out orders.

"Make a list of the things you want from your apartment," he said, leaving the table to rummage in Regan's sideboard. He plunked paper and pen in front of Gillian, tapping a finger impatiently on the tablet, indicating she should begin.

"Odella, would you go to her place for us and collect her stuff?"

"Sure. Oh, boy. Wait until I tell my husband I get to be a decoy," she said, rubbing her well-manicured hands together. "After the shootout with DeSalvo, I complained to Roger that you guys have all the fun."

Gillian dropped the pen. "You think those men might be watching my apartment? Mitch, I'll have to go myself. I refuse to put anyone else in danger."

He ignored Gillian's plea. "Take a folded shopping bag, Odella. Or something that won't draw suspicion. So, Gilly," he added, "list only the bare essentials."

She turned a pasty white. "Why won't you listen to me? I mean what I say, Mitch. I'm not writing another word." As if to underline her point, she ripped off the page and crumpled it.

"Take it easy, Gilly," Ethan warned mildly. "Mitch is thinking straight. There's no reason for anyone to be suspicious of Odella. Even if those thugs monitor who comes and goes from your building, it's a big complex. They can't recognize every resident. Odella, I'd suggest you park in a visitor slot in the underground garage. From there, walk around to the front, go upstairs, load up the stuff on Gillian's list, then leave by the back stairs. They give access to the garage.''

''Brilliant,'' Regan exclaimed. ''That's my husband's fine mind at work.'' Reaching up to take Cara, she lingered to kiss Ethan.

''Ummm.'' He followed her mouth as she broke contact. ''You three won't mind carrying on without me for a while, will you?'' He ran a hand over the curve of his wife's hip.

Laughing, Regan said, ''Down, boy.'' That drew a sharp bark from Taz, who flopped next to Ethan's chair.

Everyone laughed, and it helped Gillian relax. ''I know you're trying to ease my stress—thank you. I still think you're all crazy to get involved, but since nothing I've said has deterred you, count on me one hundred percent. After I make my short list—'' she emphasized *short,* her eyes landing on Mitch ''—what's next?''

Across the room, Ethan delivered a last kiss aimed toward Regan's lips. Instead, he grazed her cheek and Cara's forehead. The baby giggled.

Turning serious as quickly as Mitch had, Ethan dug a cellular phone out of his shirt pocket. ''Amy's on dispatch today. I'll have her run through the directory with the address Odella got for Malone's sister and get us a phone number. Gilly, you call him and see if he's okay with Mitch hauling you to Phoenix for a visit. Don't identify Mitch as an ex-cop. Just say you've found somebody you can trust to help you, and he has questions to run past Malone. Make the call short and sweet. We won't give him time to put a trace on it. If he's not on the up and up, we should find out soon enough.''

"Then you think we should visit Malone before I go through the mug shots?'' Mitch asked.

"If he's clean, and he got any kind of look at the car's occupants before it hit him, his department may have already ID'd the bastards.''

"Ethan,'' Regan cautioned, hugging Cara against her chest while she covered the baby's ears.

"Sorry,'' he muttered, sounding contrite. "I'm trying to clean up my language before the kids start to talk.''

"That means I've gotta clean up my act, too,'' Mitch said, shooting a glance between his friends.

"Neither of you are so terrible,'' Regan ventured. "But I think being aware of it will help you cut down on the swearing in front of the children, anyway.''

"I'll feel the same when I have kids,'' Mitch alleged. "Cussing comes with working the street.''

Odella looked stern. "Social workers are hip-deep in the problems of the street, Mitch Valetti. Environment's no excuse. We're each responsible for our words and actions.''

"Bravo!'' Regan grinned. "I don't recommend tangling with Odella Price, guys. She's been there, done that and lived to lecture you about it.''

"Wow! Here I was worried about sending you to my apartment,'' Gillian said, gazing at the woman with admiration.

Odella smirked and flexed her muscles. "I took karate lessons with my sons. 'Course, they left me behind at the orange-belt stage. The lot of them are quick to remind me to stay away from situations I can't get out of by using only my brain. Collecting a few items from an empty apartment, I can handle.''

They all laughed. Gillian made her list while Ethan phoned Amy. Odella had barely left with the list when Amy called back, giving him a number for Patrick's sister.

As Ethan instructed, Gillian didn't spend a long time on the call.

"You did good," Mitch said. He'd listened in on a second line.

Ethan, the first to hear the other kids waking up, disappeared into the boys' room and came out carrying Rick and Mark. Behind him, Regan now held Angela, as well as Cara. Ethan collided with Mitch as he left the dining room. "What's your read on Malone? Is he okay, or not?"

"He sounded really happy to hear from Gilly—er, Noelle." Squinting at her, he murmured, "It was odd hearing you call yourself, Noelle. Is that the name you'd prefer we use?"

"I like Gillian, or better yet, Gilly." She spoke guardedly. "Gillian *is* my real name," she assured them, as if she might not have convinced them earlier.

"Then Gilly it is," Mitch rushed to say.

"Oh, I wish I had time to stop and play with the babies." She sounded wistful. "Mitch had me tell Pat Malone we'd be there by one o'clock."

Ethan checked his watch. "Not unless you're planning to fly."

"Yeah. I figured we should take precautions in case Malone's a good actor. This way, he won't believe he has time to notify his bird dogs and get them there."

"Are you always so distrustful?" Gilly asked him.

"Don't judge all cops by me. I'm more cynical than most. I learned early not to count on people's promises. When I was a kid my folks were always promising to show up for school activities or whatever and then forgetting all about it.''

Again Gillian glimpsed the disappointments a young Mitch had suffered. Deep in her heart, she regretted failing him, too. She saw now that he wasn't as thickskinned as he tried to let on. She'd make it up to him if she could. But until her position changed or improved drastically, she didn't have any right to either take hope or to offer it. They might never have more than the few precious hours they'd already shared.

Realistically, even if Mitch and Ethan managed to find Daryl's key and ensured that the bad guys would be put out of commission, she'd left obligations behind in New Orleans. Daryl's affairs, including their joint holdings in his CPA firm, had to be dealt with. There might be a court case, too, if those thugs were tried for murder.

By his own admission, Mitch Valetti was ready to settle down, find a wife and raise a family. In the time it would take her to discharge her obligations, he'd have found someone else. And she couldn't blame him. Not considering the way she'd lied to him.

Looking into his eyes, Gillian could tell that the same thoughts had struck him. What hurt so much was knowing she desperately wanted what *he* wanted. A home and family.

Spending time in the company of Mitch and his friends, Gillian saw that they were living her dream. All she'd ever wanted was a husband and children. But as she'd discovered in the most brutal way, people didn't always get what they wanted.

She realized that Mitch had decided, just as she had, that the chances of a future together were unlikely at best. There was an invisible stepping back by each.

Gillian felt like crying. But she couldn't afford to break

down now. "I'm ready to leave anytime you are," she said, collecting Katie's suitcase before she brushed past Mitch, heading out the front door.

Ethan clapped Mitch on the back. "I've gotta spend an hour or so in the office. I'm behind on paperwork. Take my Suzuki. If you need me for any reason, you'll have the radio. I know you won't like going through Amy, but she is on duty today."

"I'm over Amy," Mitch declared. His tormented gaze followed Gillian's retreating form. "It's the God's honest truth," he said bitterly. "For all the good it does me. If the visit with Malone goes off without a hitch, I'll bring Gilly by the precinct later so I can check the mug shots. The faster we get to the bottom of her problems, the sooner she's out of my hair and I can get back to building my herd."

Ethan opened his mouth, but his wife thrust a sharp elbow in his rib.

Mitch stomped away, locked in his own black world.

CHAPTER ELEVEN

A TALL, slender woman with snowy-white hair answered Mitch and Gillian's knock. They identified themselves before she unlocked the screen door and invited them in.

"Thank goodness you've arrived in one piece," she said, blue eyes sparkling. "Patrick's been fussing like a mother hen since you phoned. Follow me, he's in the den watching TV. Lord love him, he wants to be well, and isn't. His chief ordered me to hog-tie him if need be."

"I heard that," complained a gruff masculine voice from the room they were about to enter. "This is what I get for having teased my sister when we were kids. Noreen's been waiting fifty years to get back at me for the tricks I played on her. Come closer, Noelle. Let me look at you—and the man you've decided to inflict Daryl's mess on. I've been worried about you."

Gillian squeezed past Mitch. "Sergeant Malone, I'm just glad to see you alive. I left Flagstaff thinking the worst."

"I thought I was a goner, too."

"I've told him he's too tough to die before his time," Noreen said, wiping her hands on a white apron she wore over a lavender print dress.

The man winced when his sister snapped off the TV and opened the curtains. His eyebrows dived together in a frown. "What have you done to yourself, Noelle? Have I lost my mind? Weren't you blond?"

Gillian patted her hair. "I cut and colored it. If you don't recognize me, I must've done an okay job of disguising myself."

"Humph. I guess your voice is the same."

Mitch leaned a shoulder against the door and surveyed the steel-haired man hooked up to a variety of ropes and pulleys. Bruises, though fading, marred one side of a grizzled face. Mitch felt an immediate kinship. Not too long ago he'd undergone a similar recovery. He hadn't needed traction after leaving the hospital, but he'd been trussed up like a Thanksgiving turkey for longer than he cared to remember. Judging the old guy harmless, Mitch pushed off from the door.

Malone's sharp gaze tracked the younger man's halting progress into the room. "Glory be, son, did they get you, too?"

"Nah. I stopped a few slugs from another lowlife. I was a cop, too. I've joined you in retirement, however."

"That's a shame. The force needs strong, honest men like yourself."

Mitch crossed his arms over his chest. "Not so strong anymore, Sergeant Malone. This wasn't my first tangle, either. Started me thinking I'm living on borrowed time. By the way—" he grasped the older man's hand between both of his "—the name's Mitch Valetti. It's a pleasure to meet you."

"Funny, I knew you were in the business the minute you walked in. Maybe it's true that cops have a certain identifying swagger."

"If so, the academy ought to work on that problem for when we go undercover."

"Well, the chief asked if I'd teach after I recover. Right now, I can't say I'm considering it. Training is a big responsibility with the street punks getting rougher.

Speaking of streets…'' He turned his attention to Gillian. ''I wasn't sure you'd survive on the run. Where have you been keeping yourself?''

Gillian started to answer, but Mitch slid his arms around her from behind and set his chin on top of her head. ''She's been here and there.''

The man in the bed swung his eyes to Mitch. ''You don't trust me, do you?''

''Generally cautious, Malone. Nothing personal. I think we agree those men who want to get their hands on Gilly are bad news.''

''Gilly? Oh.'' The old man frowned. ''I remember you said Daryl gave you an alias. Conrad must not know that. When he phoned, he still called you Noelle.''

''You've heard from Conrad?''

''Who's that?'' Mitch asked.

''Daryl's older brother,'' she said absently. ''I left him with the mess of a funeral and the chore of notifying Daryl's clients. I'm sure he gave you an earful about me,'' she muttered to Malone.

''I've never been Conrad's favorite person,'' Malone returned. ''I figured he must've been in a real tizzy to call me. Twice. The first time, I was still in the hospital. The chief was having my incoming calls screened. I took Conrad's so I could offer my condolences and explain why I wouldn't be able to attend Daryl's service. Also, I wanted to see if he could shed any light on the two guys who tried to put me in the morgue.''

''Could he?'' Mitch and Gillian echoed as one voice.

Malone gave a snort. ''Typical Conrad. He didn't want to talk about anyone but himself. As you said, he's miffed at you for running off. He called you irresponsible and even hinted you might be dangerous.''

''What?'' Gillian sputtered. Then she waved a hand

airily. "I *knew* he'd blame me for Daryl's death. Conrad never wanted Daryl to marry me."

"So," Mitch interrupted, "did you tell the brother Gilly had been in touch?"

The man in the bed shifted, reaching both hands out to accept a steaming mug of coffee his sister had brought in on a rolling cart.

"I was there both times Patrick talked to Conrad," Noreen said. "The first call, Pat, you asked why Conrad blamed Noelle when you knew for a fact that Daryl had been involved with some shady customers. You said Conrad got huffy, defended Daryl vigorously, then hung up on you."

"That's right. He called again the day I was released. He asked if I'd heard from you. Said bills were piling up at the business and house, and he couldn't do anything about withdrawing money from Daryl's business because of your partnership. He said that according to the bank, Daryl had withdrawn a large amount of cash a week before his death. Conrad told me the police wanted to question you in connection with that and other things."

"That would be the cash Daryl placed in the envelope, along with my fake license and social security card," Gillian admitted with a guilty shrug.

Mitch dumped cream in his coffee. "Gillian said you were like a dad to her ex-husband, Patrick. Yet it doesn't sound as if you're on good terms with his brother."

"You've got that right." Malone made a face as he sipped from his cup. "Conrad was a seventeen-year-old know-it-all at the time their folks died. His dad and I were fraternity brothers and lifelong friends. I thought it was well understood that I'd take the boys if anything happened to their parents. Conrad said he should be man of the house. He contested the will. It really irked him that I held power over his inheritance until he was twenty-five. Actually, both boys' money was in trust.''

"Daryl's portion went toward starting his business—and buying my flower shop. Conrad warned Daryl against spending part of his inheritance on me.''

"You own a flower shop?'' Mitch sounded surprised. "I knew you'd worked for a florist. You never mentioned owning a shop.''

"After I lost the baby…'' She choked on the words. When she could talk again, she cleared her throat and continued. "I suffered severe postpartum depression. I was mentally and physically unable to carry on.'' She rose and went to stand at the window, gazing blankly on a beautifully green golf course. "Daryl couldn't run his firm and oversee my shop, as well. He asked me to sell before I was released from the hospital. My friends thought that when I got well, I'd want to work again. It took longer than anyone imagined.'' Her voice was raspy. "Anyway, I didn't argue about selling.''

Shifting his position, Mitch saw the tears that trickled down her pale face. He hurt for her, and couldn't begin to imagine the pain she'd suffered at losing her baby. Now it seemed she'd lost her career and her marriage, too. She was dead wrong about not being a strong woman. She was.

The old cop spoke to Gillian, jerking Mitch out of his stupor. "Daryl phoned a few days after you lost the baby. The only other time I heard him sound so torn up was the day we buried his parents. I had the impression he was terrified that you were going to die too, Noelle.''

"I did, in a way.''

Mitch set his cup back on the cart and joined her at the window. "It doesn't pay to focus on the past, Gilly.'' He used his thumbs to massage her backbone to her shoulders. She stood unmoving for several minutes, then finally relaxed against his hands.

"Thanks, Mitch. I know we didn't come here to reminisce."

"Which brings up a point," Patrick said. "I assume you came for reasons other than to inquire after my health."

"That was the primary reason," Gillian assured him.

"Well, if you're up to it, I'd hoped we could do a little trading of information," Mitch admitted.

"If you three are going to talk cop stuff, I'll go back to preparing my beef stew. I can't abide hearing about people in danger. That's why I quit keeping house for Patrick a few years ago and moved here. Later, he finagled a job in Flagstaff. You promised me you retired for good," she scolded her brother.

"I have. I have," he muttered. "Do I look like I'm trekking with them after bad guys? No. We're only talking, Noreen. Speculating."

"Humph. I know you, Pat Malone. If there's any feasible way, you'll get involved."

"There's no feasible way, ma'am," Mitch reiterated.

Noreen, like so many women, let herself be charmed by Mitch Valetti's brilliant smile. "I'll hold you to your word," she said. "No doubt this *speculating* will take time. You and Noelle are invited to stay for supper. Plain fare, but filling."

"I never turn down a home-cooked meal." Again Mitch flashed a winsome grin. He helped Noreen wheel the coffee cart out, then closed the door. "The fewer ears, the better."

"I'm not sure I can tell you anything Noelle... er...Gillian hasn't already filled you in on." Pat slapped at the pillow on which he rested his cast. Gillian plumped the ones behind his back.

"Thanks," he said, returning his attention to Mitch.

"I got a good look at the men who ran you down. If you can't fill in the names, I'll stop by my old precinct later to see if I can identify them. Guys like that always have records a mile long."

"They do. I'll save you a step. I know who they are."

"You know their names?"

"Lenny 'The Arm' Capputo, and Foss Turpin, sometimes known as The Turtle."

Mitch quickly dug a small notebook he'd taken from Regan's kitchen drawer out of his pocket. He removed a stubby pencil from the spiral binding, flipped open the cover and began to scribble.

Gillian rubbed at goose bumps rising along her arms. "Lenny 'The Arm' sounds like someone who should be one of Al Capone's gangsters."

"I wish all gangsters had died out with Capone." Patrick adjusted a set of pulleys and raised his leg an inch off the pillow.

Mitch turned to a clean page. "I would've nicknamed him Lenny 'The Mouth.' Your turtle couldn't shut his partner up."

Malone bent his arm behind his head and propped himself up. "He's not *my* turtle. They're a nasty duo. That's why the department had me under wraps as long as they did and screened my calls. It's why I'm recovering at Noreen's. Our snitches fingered them. Appearing talkative and bumbling is their trademark. Reportedly they only work for big money up-front. Well, don't take my word for it. Read their rap sheets. These boys are butt-deep in organized crime."

Mitch frowned. ''Then you think Gilly's ex stumbled onto something pretty big?''

''My sources say it takes a couple hundred G's each to hire Capputo and Turpin.''

''Holy shi—'' Mitch snapped his jaw shut on the invective.

''My sentiments exactly,'' Patrick murmured.

Gillian, who was leaning against the old man's bed, whipped her head around. ''Two-hundred-thousand dollars?'' she whispered.

''Two-hundred grand each,'' Mitch repeated, sounding grim.

''Yeah.'' Patrick looked more than a little worried. ''They earn two-hundred-thousand dollars apiece for their dirty work. Someone's paying them big bucks to find you. I presume they've been ordered to bring you to their boss. Otherwise, they'd have gunned us down the way they did Daryl. Him they wanted dead. Now the question I have—did they get paid for one job and this is a second? If so, we're talking a bundle of cash. That ups the ante considerably on what Daryl's information is worth.''

''Damn!'' Mitch exploded.

''That ought to give you a rough idea why I took myself out of the equation,'' Patrick said wryly.

''No wonder Daryl went to such lengths to get Gilly out of town. Is that why you advised her to hit the road?''

Patrick shook his head. ''I only had Daryl's sketchy e-mail and a gut hunch to go on. What concerned me most was how quickly those goons showed up. It takes a big man pulling strings to get fast action like that.''

''Yeah. I've had some experience fighting a well-entrenched crime boss.''

''A successful experience?'' Malone asked.

Mitch closed his eyes and pinched the bridge of his nose between thumb and forefinger. "They were out on bail before the ink on my booking paper was dry."

"That's what we ran into in Flagstaff, too." He took a deep breath. "So, how long can you keep Gillian hidden?"

"Not indefinitely," Mitch said. "And as you know, the statute of limitations never runs out if they wasted Daryl."

"I wasn't thinking of hiding her indefinitely." Patrick stared intently at Mitch. "My snitch on the street is pretty reliable. He said Capputo and Turpin get antsy if things don't break their way. They have patience up to a point, then they run back to their money source and make new demands. If you know where they are now and can afford to put a twenty-four-hour tail on them, they'll eventually lead you to the top dog."

"I don't have much money I can access," Gillian muttered, breaking into their conversation. "How much would a twenty-four-hour tail cost?"

"A down-and-out P.I. can be had cheap. Or a retired cop. In fact, those are the types of assignments I figured I'd take for a while until my ranch starts paying."

A slow smile blossomed on Malone's craggy face. "There you go, Noelle. I mean, Gillian. Can you afford a retired cop?"

"There's a problem with that," Mitch was quick to say. "I'm not exposing Gilly to a chase. Neither am I letting her out of my sight. I'll have to chew on your suggestion, Patrick. My first order of business is to find a safe spot for her to go underground. At least until we turn up hard evidence. Something other than he-said, she-said stuff."

Noreen opened the door and stuck her head inside in

time to hear Mitch. "I came to announce supper. Pat can't come to the table, so if it's all right with everyone, I'll serve trays in here. If you two would like to wash up, I'll point you to the bathrooms. I, um, there's a part of being laid up that Pat hates to deal with. He grumbles, but it must be done," she said, producing a bed pan from a cupboard in the room. "Feel free to stroll around the patio and watch the golfers. I'll call you when we're finished."

"Dammit, Noreen." The old man's face turned florid shades of purple. "It's bad enough you have to witness the loss of a man's dignity. No need to announce my incapacities to the world."

Mitch held up a hand. "Been there, done that, man. I swore about having to use that damned thing until one day the nurses were tied up and were very late getting around to help me. Can truthfully say I never complained again."

"You'd do well to listen to his advice, Patrick. Oh, and Mitch, I couldn't help overhearing the conversation as I walked in. The need you have for a hideaway," she added when a look of puzzlement crossed his face. "I may have a solution. We'll discuss it at supper."

Mitch was the first to make his way to the patio. He placed a booted foot on the low brick wall and scanned the deep green fanning out from the tenth tee. "Do you play golf?" he asked as Gillian exited the house.

"No. Soil this rich should be used for growing flowers, in my opinion. Do you play?"

"Nope. But I could stand having all this behind my house. It'd make a fantastic pasture."

"Noreen must golf. Why else would she pay the exorbitant association fees? I know that communities like this share in the greens upkeep."

"They're a pair, aren't they?"

"Do you trust Patrick now?"

"Don't see any reason not to. He didn't have to give me those names. I still want to swing by the precinct and match up their mug shots. I'll know in a flash if we've got the right guys."

"We could leave now." Gillian glanced toward the house. "I hate putting Noreen out by staying to eat."

"I'd say her feelings will be hurt if we leave. Besides, I want to hear her suggestion about a safe house. I'd also like to kick a few ideas around with Malone on where he suspects Daryl might have hidden a key."

"I don't think Patrick has any clue."

"He might if we brainstorm. Daryl lived with him as a kid. When it comes to putting stuff away for safekeeping, boys develop hard-to-break habits."

"Is that right?" She sent him a curious glance. "Where would you hide something?"

He gave a sheepish grin. "You've been in my house. I tend to leave things lying out in plain sight. So if it were me, I'd probably have tossed it in your purse."

"Well, we know Daryl didn't do that."

Noreen waved from the window.

Mitch stood aside and let Gillian precede him into the house. "I like your view from the patio," he told Noreen politely.

"So do I. Until I moved Pat in, I played golf at ten o'clock every day. And I will again after he's able to go home."

Gillian slowed her steps. "It's nice that you have each other. I'm an only child. I've always envied siblings. Especially large families."

"The Malones had one," the older woman said with a chuckle. "Twelve in all. We're scattered hither and yon. Patrick's the eldest son. I'm the eldest daughter. We spent a lot of time caring for the ten who came after us, and I think that's the biggest reason neither of us married.'' She shook her head. "Our siblings thought if we weren't going to marry, we should have dedicated our lives to the church. We both enjoy our freedom too much, I'm afraid.''

"I've never thought in terms of a dozen when I imagined a *large* family," Gillian exclaimed.

"That's good." Mitch stopped dead in his tracks, not having the vaguest idea why he'd felt compelled to make a remark like that.

The women simply laughed at his stunned expression.

"I'll help Noreen prepare the trays," Gillian informed Mitch. "Didn't you say you had something else you wanted to discuss with Sergeant Malone?"

"Yeah. Okay, I get the message. You ladies want to gossip." Mitch turned and disappeared into the den.

"Ah, Valetti. What happened to Noelle…uh, Gillian— Damned if I can remember her new name."

"Both names are hers. Noelle's her middle name."

"That a fact? I got their wedding invitation. I must've known it then. Daryl rang me up a couple of times a month. Noelle's all I ever heard him call her."

"Gilly said he liked that name better. From the time they met, he insisted she drop Gillian. I figure he must have been pretty scared to phony an ID for her the way he did."

Pain flashed in the old man's eyes. "I keep thinking if maybe I hadn't been so busy looking down the road at retirement, he might've opened up to me earlier."

"Sounds to me as if he came to you when he was ready. Gilly said Daryl didn't do anything on the spur of the moment."

"True. He was methodical as a kid. Used to drive me nuts. Noreen, too. That boy wasn't to be rushed."

"Since you knew him so well, do you have any thoughts on what he might have done with the all-important key?"

"I guess Noelle told you we searched the car and everything she owned. In fact, we'd finished a thorough shakedown of her car and suitcases a few minutes before Capputo and Turpin ran me down."

"She told me. She traded the car because she was afraid they'd track her through the one they'd been following."

"Smart gal, ain't she?"

"Very. Are you avoiding my question about the key?"

"Not at all. I'm blamed if I have any idea what the boy did with the damn thing. I spent some time thinking it over while I was flat on my back in the hospital. Especially as the days wore on and the department didn't bring me word of any Jane Does matching her description."

They sat for a moment, eyeing one another.

"Of course, I wasn't looking for a redhead with short hair," Malone admitted.

"There's always the possibility Daryl never had time to hide the documents, and then return to where he stored the automobile. Or maybe he died with the key on him."

"Could be. Only Daryl was precise. According to his e-mail, his wife had the key. I was left with the feeling that it wouldn't be easy to find unless we knew where to look. Daryl said he thought the client was on to him. He said he'd be in touch through a safer channel and that he'd give me all the information then. Next thing, Noelle shows up at the station, in a panic, saying people were after her and Daryl had been shot down on his porch."

Mitch continued to mull over the situation in his head. He usually tried to put himself in a victim's shoes. Now he wondered how Daryl McGrath would think, what steps he'd take. To do a credible job, Mitch needed to know a lot more about Gilly's ex.

At that moment, she appeared in the doorway carrying two trays of piping hot stew. Thick pieces of buttered bread sat on side plates next to frosty glasses of iced tea. She handed one tray to Mitch, then eased the hospital table across Patrick's bed. Gillian unwrapped his silverware and tucked the napkin securely under his chin.

"Aren't you going to tuck my napkin in?" Mitch teased.

Gillian danced across the floor on her toes, batting her eyes like a caricature of a ditzy waitress. "Certainly, sir. If you'd break your arm, I'd be happy to oblige."

Patrick guffawed. "Being in this contraption does have some advantages."

"What might those be?" Noreen asked her brother as she whisked through the room bearing her tray and Gillian's.

"Noelle spread out my napkin nice and neat, and placed my spoon right in my hand. You could take some lessons, wench."

"I'll wench you," his sister muttered. "If I start giving you the royal treatment you'll be wanting to move in permanently."

"Tell her, Mitch. A man would sooner be locked up in prison than spend his days lazing about in bed."

Mitch clapped a hand over his heart. "I try never to argue with a pretty woman. But," he drawled, letting Noreen preen a bit, "in this instance, I have to vouch for what Patrick says."

"Enough baloney," Noreen chided. "Eat."

Mitch noted that the banter had cheered the older couple, who were obviously getting weary of each other's constant company.

"This stew is excellent," Gillian praised when everyone had fallen silent. "It's even better than Bert's, isn't it, Mitch?"

"If you ever tell Bert I said so, you'll be toast. But, yes, it's great, and I'm a stew connoisseur."

Noreen snapped Mitch's leg with her napkin. "I know you're trying to get back in my good graces. It might work, young man, but you'll have to compliment my homemade bread, too."

"Yum," was all Mitch said.

"Well, that'll do. Now, about your situation… I'd like to offer you and Gilly the use of my condominium in Sedona as a hideout." She smiled fleetingly. "I suppose with all those words of flattery about my stew—which, I might add, one person in this room doesn't appreciate—I'll have to toss in my biweekly visits to the spa, as well. That, my dears, is pampering at its best."

Mitch's eyebrows shot straight up.

Leaning toward Patrick, Gillian whispered, "Where's Sedona?"

"Are you kidding?" Mitch yelped. "Sedona is the heart of the Red Rock Country. In other words, one step down from heaven."

Noreen had obviously decided earlier to make them the offer. She took a key out of her apron pocket, and a hand-drawn map. She passed both to Mitch.

He accepted them eagerly, and began at once to scan the map.

Gillian stiffened primly. "A few minutes ago, I made up my mind. I'm not running again," she said, setting her tray aside.

Mitch glanced up and saw she was serious. "Gilly, this condo is the answer to a prayer. Sedona teems with tourists. You'll be able to get lost in the crowd. It won't be for more than a couple of weeks. With the information Patrick supplied, Ethan will nab those bastards in short order."

"They're slippery," Patrick added. "The number-one question is, can your friend hold them for any length of time after he nabs them?"

"Long enough to place a bug in the ear of the New Orleans police. If there's even one solid bit of proof that they're involved in Daryl's murder—" Mitch snapped his fingers "—they'll be extradited like that."

In spite of the fact that everyone in the room seemed to agree, Gillian stubbornly dug in her heels. "A minute ago we were all laughing," she said wistfully. "I want to live like that again. I simply can't face spending the rest of my life looking over one shoulder. I want what I haven't had in a long time. A normal life. I won't get that hiding in a borrowed condominium. Not only that, if the leader in all this has the power you and Patrick say he has, what's to prevent him from sending another team of assassins after me? And then another?"

"She has a point," Patrick admitted hesitantly.

Mitch raked his fingers through his hair. "Your plan would be to do what, Gilly?"

"I haven't thought that far ahead." She shrugged. "Why put anyone else at risk? What if I sent word that I wanted to meet with them?"

"Oh, great. So they could blow you away in a park or something?"

"No." Gillian pursed her lips, and swung one foot rapidly, a sure sign she was irritated. "Surely they wouldn't shoot me in…say, a busy coffee house."

Patrick was already shaking his head. "Are you forgetting they gunned Daryl down in a residential district with neighbors looking on? And tried to run you down in a police parking lot, getting me by accident? I don't like it. Furthermore, where would that get you? You don't have what they want, so you have no bargaining chip."

"Amen." Mitch stood, looming over Gillian. "You aren't dealing with rational human beings, Gilly. These people have no ethics."

"Then I'll just have to find the key. Maybe I missed it in my old car. I'll explain to the man I sold it to. I'll buy it back. If need be, we can tear the whole automobile apart."

"Okay, I concede to that. We'll buy it back and drive it to Sedona. A week, Gilly, give me a week to make some headway cracking this case. If seven days go by and Ethan and I haven't made any progress, we talk about trying it your way."

She nibbled on a fingernail. Tension all but crackled in the room. Ultimately, Noreen injected the deciding factor.

"Take a good look at how Mitch limps. Stop and consider how long Patrick's been attached to those ropes and weights. And they're walking in clover compared to Daryl. Ask yourself if a week is too much time to invest in your health and well-being. Your *future*."

Gillian flipped a red curl out of her eyes. "Thank you. I wasn't thinking clearly. Mitch, I'm going to listen to you and Patrick. After all, you two are experts in these matters. I think I've just been on the run for so many weeks, I'm ready to disregard caution and take back my life. Since you're all sure that no one else will be injured on my account, I'll agree to hibernate for a week."

"A week." Mitch slowly let out the breath he'd been holding. Although he and the seasoned cop swapped looks of dismay, they both pasted on sunny smiles for Gillian's benefit.

"Noreen. Patrick." Mitch took first one wrinkled hand, then the other. "I hate to eat and run, but I've got a lot of holes to plug. I'd better get started."

"Noreen will see you out. If I think of anything else that'll be of help, I'll give you a jingle at the condo."

Mitch snapped his fingers. "Glad you reminded me." He pulled a card out of his wallet. "Ignore the title. The cell phone's a good number and less traceable."

Gillian kissed Patrick's forehead and Noreen's cheek. "You've been so kind. Daryl knew he was lucky to have you step in for his folks. I'm sorry we never managed to get together while he and I were married, and before…before…" Her voice broke.

"It's all right, Noelle. Lord willing, we'll all be around a week from now and we'll see each other then. You two take care, okay?"

"We will, sir, and thanks for everything." Mitch handed Gilly his handkerchief to blot her eyes as they walked out.

"Mitch," Gillian murmured in the dark confines of the car some time later. They were well on their way back to Desert City. "If anything happens, if this doesn't work out, I want you to know—"

"Everything's going to work out," he said fiercely to halt her morbid train of thought.

He sounded so confident, Gillian sank back and closed her eyes. She fell asleep at once and dreamed of endless, happy nights in the company of Mitch Valetti.

CHAPTER TWELVE

IN THE LOWER basement of the Desert City police station, Mitch, Gillian and Ethan clustered around a computer screen, reading the criminal records of Foss Turpin and Lenny Capputo. Ethan had pulled them from the national database.

Mitch leaned away from the screen first, rocked in his chair, and picked up a metal ruler, which he bent back and forth, trying to ignore the burning in his gut.

Gillian slid off her perch on the corner of Ethan's desk, and cleared her throat. "If those men have been arrested so many times and they've done all the terrible things listed there, how can they still be running around free?"

"That's the downside of police work," Ethan said, still flipping through screens. "If cops make one minor error in the arrest and booking process, the perp walks. There's a lot of money driving big crime syndicates. They hire the best, craftiest lawyers money can buy. An even uglier truth is that sometimes they use their dirty money to grease palms throughout a justice system that should be on our side."

"I hate to appear naive," Gillian murmured. "But those Lenny and Foss characters have been accused of heinous crimes. They associate with known drug lords, pimps and assassins."

"They aren't your average boys next door, that's for

sure," Ethan agreed, pausing to open a pack of gum and pass it around.

Mitch's brooding expression prompted Gillian to continue. "I've probably said this before, but I'll say it again. Daryl wasn't the type of person to get mixed up with anyone of that ilk."

Mitch flung the ruler down on the desk with a loud pop. "You *have* said it before, Gilly. So did Sergeant Malone. Tell us more about Daryl. Ethan and I need background details so we can ferret out what triggered your ex-husband's plunge into underworld activities."

"Be candid," Ethan urged.

"Candid? Of course," Gillian whispered. "It seems eons since Daryl and I met. Funny how a person you think you know so well becomes a total stranger."

Ethan crumpled his coffee cup and tossed it into an overflowing wastebasket. Mitch dragged a straight chair over, turned it around and straddled it. He patted the seat of the swivel chair he'd vacated, indicating Gillian should sit, too.

"How far back do you want me to go?"

Ethan sent a hard look toward Mitch. "If it's not too uncomfortable, start where you met and got married."

"In a Midwest college. We both worked to pay our fees and expenses, which excluded us from the in crowd. We didn't fall crazy in love, at least not in the way my girlfriends described." Gillian couldn't take her eyes off Mitch while she revisited her past. Did he understand that Daryl had never exhilarated her with a touch? Not like Mitch did.

"In the beginning, we met mostly in the library. If neither of us had to work, we'd go to a coffee house and talk. Back then, we talked openly about our feelings and dreams. I majored in horticulture, Daryl in accounting.

After our marriage fell apart, I realized we'd stopped communicating. Twenty hours a day, Daryl immersed himself in his numbers. I kept my nose in gardening magazines. In bed, where most couples communicate,'' she said, blushing brightly, ''Daryl stayed awake half the night playing number games. He was especially fond of those pattern analysis books available through Mensa. He kept stacks of them beside the bed. Neat stacks.''

''Yet you both achieved your goals,'' Mitch said thoughtfully.

''Our professional goals,'' Gillian corrected. ''We were so focused on career success, somewhere along the way our personal objectives got canceled out.''

A strange expression flickered over Ethan's face. ''Regan and I discussed that very problem recently. Work, family and community activities all conspire to steal a couple's time from each other.''

Gillian shook her head vigorously. ''It doesn't have to be like that.''

Mitch shifted a hip and rubbed at a stitch developing in his side. ''We're veering off track. What does any of this have to do with Daryl taking on a client tied to a crime syndicate?''

''You're the one who wanted to know everything about him,'' Gillian said defensively.

''Let her tell it her way, Mitch.''

Mitch had fallen hard for this woman, and he discovered belatedly that he didn't want to hear intimate details about her life with a former lover. Glowering at Ethan, Mitch crossed his arms over the chair back. Closing his eyes, he rested his forehead on his wrists and slowly counted to ten.

''To make a long story short,'' Gillian resumed in a less sure voice, ''we moved to New Orleans to be closer to Daryl's only sibling. Conrad owns and operates a successful antique import shop there. Daryl and I devoted our lives to making our businesses as profitable as Conrad's. It seemed to me that he was always challenging Daryl to do better. After a few years, money was less tight for us. I was able to hire part-time help at the flower shop. I thought it was time to start our family. To my dismay, Daryl didn't agree."

In the drawn-out silence following her statement, Mitch and Ethan both heard what Gillian didn't say: Daryl McGrath hadn't wanted baby Katie.

"I waited six months before taking a second stab at changing his mind. By then he was even more adamant. I take full blame for the decision I made to stop taking birth control pills. At the time, I convinced myself that if I got pregnant Daryl would really be happy. I was wrong. So very wrong. A husband and wife should reach agreement on such an important issue." Gillian's voice dropped to a stricken whisper.

Mitch catapulted to his feet. His chair fell over with a crash. "Let's go," he ordered, righting the chair, then tugging Gillian to her feet.

Ethan also scrambled up. "Mitch, for God's sake, what's gotten into you? We were finally getting to some possible reasons McGrath reversed character and went off the deep end."

"None of these details changes your job, partner. You have to track down Capputo and Turpin and bring them in for questioning. If a mob attorney shows up to bail them out, you phone New Orleans and request extradition. With Gilly safe in Sedona, I'll be free to follow them to Louisiana to see who intervenes. Or I'll hire Bob Wentzel to go."

"I don't need you telling me how to do my job."

Gillian placed herself between them. "Please! I won't have you trashing your friendship on my account."

No one moved for a heated moment. Then both men visibly cooled off.

Ethan was the one who finally set Gilly's mind at ease. "We've had worse fights. If our friendship isn't stronger than a few arguments, it deserves to die."

Mitch neither concurred nor disagreed. He unfolded the address Noreen Malone had given him and scribbled it in Ethan's notebook. "We're going to your house now. Odella should be back with Gilly's clothes. Then I'll run home and pack a bag. We'll swing by Dave's place and ask him to keep an eye on the ranch. It'll be late when we reach Sedona. First, we're going down south to try to buy back Gilly's car. I'll drop it off at Impound if you'll submit a request to have it shaken down for any sign of a key."

Ethan nodded. "Hey, what are your plans for Trooper while you're gone? You can't take him to some posh condo."

"Maybe Dave..."

"What about Jeremy? He's been bugging my folks for a dog. I promised him I'd do what I could to convince them. This will give him a chance to see if he can handle school and a dog. Plus, he'll continue Trooper's training."

"Who's Jeremy?" Gillian asked the question offhand-edly.

"My foster brother," Ethan replied. "He's still in high school. This month, he's sure he wants to be a dog han-dler. Next month, who knows." A smile wreathed Ethan's face.

"Or maybe he'll want to be a cop," Gillian suggested in a light voice.

Her remark didn't coax a comment or a smile from Mitch, however. He continued to look like a thundercloud waiting for a party to rain on.

She didn't have long to wait for the deluge once they'd fastened their seat belts and were driving in the direction of the Knights' house.

"You said you tricked your husband into having a baby." Mitch's blunt remark seemed to echo inside the cab of his pickup. "You went off the pill without telling him."

Gillian exhaled on a long hiss of air. "Wha-aa-at?"

It didn't seem possible, but the tension that existed between them wound even tighter. "Up on the mountain, you didn't seem too worried about birth control. Damn, I always take care of…well, I've never had an accident before," Mitch said, gripping the steering wheel so hard his knuckles turned white.

"I haven't needed to worry. I mean…there's been no reason to until…until…" Squeezing her eyes shut, she massaged her temples. "There's no reason to think—"

"How do you figure? We went at it hot and heavy. The damned rubber split."

"I know." She tried to hide her flaming cheeks by covering them with her hands. "My, ah, over the ten months, I lost a lot of weight. My periods have been really erratic," she blurted. "I told you that." Underneath her protests, Gillian suffered a mixture of fear along with an unreasonable ray of hope. While she was afraid of losing another baby, deep down, she'd love to be pregnant. She longed for a child.

Plainly, Mitch felt more like Daryl on the subject of starting a family. But plenty of women raised families alone. She could. She had skills and a college degree.

She also had criminals demanding she turn over something she didn't possess.

Mitch cast furtive glances in her direction. Mostly he had to pay attention to driving as the traffic on the freeway filled in. "What are you thinking about?"

"Ways to reassure you there's no cause for concern. I was sick, really nauseated, almost from the moment of conception last time. I feel fine, Mitch."

"Oh. Well, maybe after we settle into Noreen's condo, we can check the phone book and locate a doctor."

"What for?"

Mitch tripped over his tongue. "You know…a female doctor."

Gillian found herself growing irritated. "A female physician, huh? In what specialty, Mitch?"

His brows lowered into a straight line. "Are you having me on?"

"Yes." She was dangerously close to erupting. "Oh, Mitch. Tell me why men are so adept at initiating sex, and so abysmal when it comes to frank discussions about it?"

"Who initiated *this* conversation?"

"You did. In anger."

"More at myself than you, Gilly. I'm sorry," he said softly. "I shouldn't have said that about tricking Daryl. I understand how you felt, wanting to have a baby." He sighed. "But you're right. It should be a mutual decision. I know a lot of guys who feel their partner's solely responsible for making or not making babies. I consider it a fifty-fifty deal. So now I feel responsible. The other day, when I saw the condition of the condom, I should've called a halt. Instead, I lost all control."

She debated the wisdom of admitting she'd lost control, as well. It was just as well that she'd learned now, though, where they stood. Where Mitch stood. Gone were those seductive daydreams—in which her problems disappeared and she lived happily ever after in Desert City with Mitch Valetti.

Clearly, no such notion had popped into Mitch's head. "Quit worrying," she said firmly. "Find a new topic, Mitch. We've worn this one out."

"For now. We're almost at Ethan's. I see Odella's car in the drive. Remember, we can't stay long—we've got a lot to do. I hope we don't have to haggle to buy back your car. Once we drop it off at Impound, the staff will conduct a thorough sweep. That'll be one thing less to worry about. If there's a scrap of loose metal hidden anywhere, you can bet your boots they'll find it."

"When will they get to the car? If it's soon and they turn up a key, won't we have gone to Sedona for nothing? You said it was a four-hour drive from here."

"Believe me, you won't mind the drive. Not even at night. Up there, even the stars are bigger and brighter."

"If you're so crazy about Sedona, why live here?"

"I wish I'd invested in a piece of vacation property in Sedona when I first moved to the desert. These days the cost is prohibitive."

Gillian let the information sink in as Mitch parked, got out and came around the car to open her door. His courtliness was refreshing. It was a shame that he fit, in so many ways, her ideal vision of the perfect mate. When had Daryl fallen short? Or had her ideals changed after she'd lost Katie?

Regan met them at the door. "I'm glad to see you two. We expected you back much sooner. Odella's been waiting. Gillian, your apartment's been tossed."

"Tossed?" Gilly paused in the hall where she'd bent

to lift one of the boys. Mark, she thought, as she tried to recall if he had the darker hair or if that was Rick.

"Sorry, cop jargon rubs off on spouses. Searched. Your apartment's been searched."

"Tossed is more descriptive," Odella interjected. "Drawers were dumped. Your sofa cushions were slashed. And I'm afraid there are no pockets left on any of your jeans." She stepped over a spill of large, snap-together blocks to join the others in the hall.

"Did you let Ethan know?" Mitch hauled out his cell phone. "Were you careful not to disturb the mess, Odella?" As Odella nodded, he muttered, "We'll have our guys dead to rights if Ethan can match their prints to any in Gilly's apartment. Unless they wore gloves," he said more to himself. "Yeah, I think both of 'em had gloves yesterday."

Regan shut the door behind Mitch and moved everyone down the hall. "I left Ethan a message. Amy said he flew past her on his way to request a car examination."

"My car," Gillian announced. "The one I drove from New Orleans, not the one outside. Mitch, if you're afraid the man I sold the car to will give us a hard time, we could trade him the one I have now. It's newer and has fewer miles on the odometer. I don't mind absorbing the loss if it'll speed things along."

"Might. Odella, you say Gilly's clothes were ruined?"

"Yep. And your cosmetics and toiletries were a fright. Not that you had many to begin with."

Regan scooped Cara out of her walker and kissed away the baby's tears. She'd been howling over having gotten the device wedged into a corner behind Regan's office door. "Don't forget to tell Gilly they emptied out her bathroom wastebasket and probably know she's coloring her hair."

Odella laughed. "Seems to me you just told her."

"Not everything. I didn't say you stopped at the pharmacy on your way here and bought a sable rinse. Mitch, can you go trade for the car by yourself? Odella and I will be undertaking Gilly's next makeover in about half an hour. Those thugs won't be looking for someone with brown hair."

"At this rate," Mitch grumbled, "we'll never get to her hideout. But I learned months ago not to argue with Regan when she gets something in her head. Gilly, I'll need the name and address of the guy who bought your car."

"It's in my purse. Oh, wait. What about my purse?"

"Trashed," Odella supplied. "They dumped the contents, and cut up the lining. If you had any money, I'm afraid it's gone. Otherwise, I brought the stuff that spilled."

Tears speckled Gillian's eyelashes. "That was everything I'd saved from working at the café. How will I replace my clothes? I have funds in an account at home. But I've been afraid to use my debit card or access any Noelle McGrath credit cards."

Mitch gathered her and baby Mark into his arms. "God, Gilly, I'm sorry. Your life seems to go from bad to worse."

"Good thing she has you," Regan said staunchly.

"And us," Odella added. "Although I've gotta run. Roger phoned. One of our sons came by the house. He's taking us to dinner. I never turn down a free meal," she said, laughing. She squeezed Gillian's shoulder on her way out.

Gillian sniffed and snuggled tighter into the hollow of

Mitch's shoulder. "I can't believe I ever thought you were working with those men." She drew from his warmth and his strength. "Thank goodness they didn't get their hands on Katie's suitcase." Gilly lifted one of Mark's pudgy fingers and kissed the dimpled knuckle. She wished she could kiss Mitch, but didn't feel right doing so in front of Regan.

Regan's eyes filled with tears. "Ethan told me you were the mother Mitch has been trying to locate. I can't have children of my own, Gillian. So I identify with your loss. Although, with the babies and Ethan, my life is finally complete. This is as good a time as any to apologize for asking if you were pregnant the night Mitch brought you to dinner."

"You did *what?*" Mitch stiffened. "Jeez, Regan."

"So sue me. You said eating made her sick, and she denied having an eating disorder. Butt out, Valetti. It's Gilly I'm apologizing to."

"And I accept." Gillian said, emerging from the circle of Mitch's arms.

Mitch reluctantly let her go.

Regan pointed to the kitchen clock. "Hadn't you better get going after that car? Otherwise, it'll be too late to show up at anyone's house to dicker."

He automatically checked his watch and saw that time was getting away from them. He'd like to take Regan aside and subtly ask more about the signs and symptoms of pregnancy. Gilly had brushed his earlier concerns aside all too blithely. If, by some twist of fate, he'd created a baby with her, he wanted to know so he could do the right thing. He wasn't a man to use a woman for personal pleasure, then walk away, leaving her to deal with consequences. Not only that, this was *Gillian.* She'd already taken up residence in his fantasies. Though, Lord knew she hadn't given him any reason to hope she felt the same. On that sour note, he strode past Regan and slammed out of the house.

"I wonder what's bothering Mitch," Regan mused, as she and Gillian watched him stalk off without so much as a goodbye.

Gillian suspected she knew what troubled him. Inadvertently, she sneaked a hand to her flat belly. If by some miracle, she carried Mitch Valetti's baby, she would deem it a gift. Why couldn't men be happy about such joyous news? she wondered sadly, remembering the fights she'd had with Daryl. Mitch's reaction today had been only slightly milder. There was probably no reason for Mitch to worry—or for her to hope. Her chances of being pregnant weren't very great.

"I'm afraid I blew into town, Regan, and disrupted poor Mitch's entire life. I've told him time and again that he shouldn't involve himself in my troubles. He won't listen."

"Mitch puts his heart and soul into everything he does. It's not your fault...unless you're stringing him along."

Gillian's face underwent such a profound and deep softening that Regan hugged her impulsively. Flinging an arm around Gilly in sisterly fashion, Regan turned her toward the master bath, where she and Odella had already set out everything to transform Noelle McGrath, now Gillian Stevens, from a redhead into a brunette.

THEY DIDN'T lay eyes on Mitch again for almost two weeks. The car had been resold into Mexico. He went after it because Ethan thought it was of paramount importance. Gillian stayed with Regan and Ethan. She kept a low profile. Mitch, who worried constantly about her situation, drove them crazy with phone calls.

The men in the blue car managed to stay two steps ahead of Ethan. However, Ethan had several good leads to follow by the time Mitch slipped into town again under the cover of darkness and knocked at the Knights' door.

He was admitted by Gilly and stared at her in shock. Someone, Regan presumably, had cut Gilly's hair as short as a boy's. The fall of red bangs he'd found so attractive now kissed her forehead in feathery brown curls. There was no hair to speak of in back—at least, not enough to run his fingers through. Only wisps touched her cheeks; the rest had been clipped close to her head above her ears. Even the blue eyes he'd counted on to read her moods had turned brown as a doe's.

"Well," she said, pirouetting under his nose. "Say something, darn it. Regan worked hard to create this masterpiece."

Swallowing the curse he'd been about to utter, Mitch gained control of his roiling senses. She was still pretty, but in a different way. *Cute* was the word, he supposed. Pixie-ish. "I li-ike it," he stammered. "I understand why you ladies changed the hair from red to brown. But…I'm not hallucinating…your eyes were blue?"

"Designer contacts, silly," Regan sang out from the kitchen. "Nonprescription."

"She's feeding the kids," Gillian confided. "I know that when you phoned from the station, you said we needed to leave right away. But if we can spare a few minutes, I'd like to finish helping. The kids all have sniffles. And Regan's had a tough few days."

"Uh, we can leave whenever you want. You've been okay here for two weeks. I was about ready to say to heck with finding the car. When I finally tracked it down in Hermosillo, the owner was tickled to trade up. He didn't even question when I said you wanted it back out of sentimentality. I tell you, some people are too gullible for words.''

Gillian led the way down the hall. Mitch hung back to savor the sway of her hips. He flinched when she turned short of the door and smacked into the wall.

''For God's sake, Gilly, can't you see? A disguise is one thing, putting yourself at risk is something else entirely.''

''Odella bought plain glass lenses. I've experienced some distortion. Not much, but having a foreign object in your eye takes some getting used to.''

''So what do you think?'' Regan asked the minute Mitch entered her kitchen. ''Isn't she adorable?''

''She was adorable before.''

''You don't like the makeover?'' Regan frowned.

''Back off, Regan. Did I say I didn't like it? Sheesh. Women!'' He bent over and wiped green beans off Rick's chin. ''Take my word on this, guy. Don't venture any opinions on how a woman looks until you're a hundred and five. By then you'll both be farsighted enough that she can't argue your point.''

''Mitch, you're bad.'' Regan popped another spoonful of beans into Rick's mouth. ''Tell Uncle Mitch he'll never go wrong if he learns to say *Honey, you're beautiful.*''

''And get my face slapped? Forget it, kid. Listen to me.''

Gillian finished feeding Cara. She cleaned the baby's face and hands with a damp washcloth, then lifted her out of the high chair. ''You and Ethan are so lucky,'' Gillian declared, kissing Cara's silky hair. ''Even though they'll always have a special bond, all four kids will develop uniquely as you encourage them to form their own opinions.''

She blushed profusely when it became apparent that Regan and Mitch had stopped their banter to stare at her. "I—I read a lot of books on child-rearing when I was pregnant."

"A miracle in itself, what with old Daryl staying up nights to play with his numbers," Mitch breathed testily.

"Don't make me sorry I told you that, Mitch. We've already established I was at fault. Look, the kids are done eating. If we're going to Sedona tonight, hadn't we better head out?"

"Yes," Regan said. "Gillian, I put together some knock-around outfits, a nightie I've never worn and a package of new panties. And Mitch, Ethan brought over some of your long-sleeved shirts and two pairs of jeans. They're in a duffel I put in the hall. He thinks it's better if you don't go out to the ranch. So he had your pickup brought here, too."

Mitch nodded. "Yeah. He told me. I agree."

"Then you know his brothers are helping Dave look after your horses. Oh, and Jeremy's looking after Trooper. That dog will come back to you spoiled rotten."

"Thanks, Regan. Tell Ethan I'll be in touch as planned."

"Is that all?"

"One more thing. Inform Gilly that she can't take Cara."

"Wouldn't I love to." Gillian's voice sounded so full of longing, Mitch pursed his lips and did some yearning himself. Something seemed to shift inside him as he watched her bestow tender kisses on each of the four babies. He was dog tired, and he'd missed her a lot. He wondered what she'd say if he admitted it. Probably nothing. She seemed to have made herself right at home here.

"Do you want to shower and shave before taking off?" Regan asked Mitch.

He passed a hand over a stubbled jaw. "I drove all night. Since I was driving a car I didn't own, I wanted to get it back on U.S. soil as quickly as possible." He grimaced. "The motel I booked in Hermosillo boasted very few of the comforts of home. So, yeah, I'll grab a shower if Gilly doesn't mind waiting another half-hour."

"I don't mind. Frankly, after a two-week delay, I'm not sure we really need to go to Sedona."

"Ethan thinks you should," Regan said, casting a worried glance between them. They both nodded.

Stars had popped out overhead before Mitch and a very subdued Gillian ultimately drove onto the freeway. She seemed melancholy, lost in private thoughts. Mitch shoved a disc in the player and leaned back, prepared to enjoy a quiet drive.

"Is country music all you have?" she asked when the song ended and switched to another mournful tune.

"Uh-oh. We're in trouble if you hate country-and-western music."

"I don't *hate* it."

"Good, because up to now I've thought we were pretty compatible."

Gillian turned despite the seat belt, angling to face him. "A couple of weeks ago, when we were at the station, it didn't sound as if you thought that. When you sided with Daryl after I admitted I'd gone off the pill without telling him."

Mitch drummed his fingers in time to the background beat. "I can't judge you, Gilly. Not after seeing you with the babies. You love kids. It shows."

"So, you don't think I acted selfishly?"

He glanced at her quickly, then away again. "Are you

looking for someone to say unequivocally that you were wrong? Is this self-flagellation?''

She inspected her fingernails in the light that flashed inside the cab from passing cars. ''Maybe. It was the beginning of the end of my marriage. Yes, I feel guilty. Daryl might still be alive and we wouldn't be skulking through the night if I hadn't expressly gone against a wish he'd made quite clear.''

''The bad thing about playing *if only,* Gilly, is that you can play the blame game until hell freezes over and the outcome doesn't change. I know. I spent weeks after my surgery trying to figure out what would've happened if Tony DeSalvo hadn't heard me climbing in Ethan's front window. Maybe he wouldn't have shot up Ethan's house and knocked Regan around. Then again, if I hadn't drawn his fire, he might have killed us all. Things happen for a reason.''

''I guess.''

They sank again into silence until they'd traveled beyond the outskirts of Phoenix. Mitch stopped to gas the truck at a well-lit truck stop. Gillian went inside to find a ladies' room and buy him the peanut-butter crackers and bottled water he requested.

''Find everything okay?'' he asked when she crawled back into the cab.

''I never realized how many kinds of crackers there are on the market. I ended up buying three varieties,'' she said, dumping the sack between them. ''It's a good thing water is water,'' she added, unscrewing the lid on a bottle she handed Mitch.

''Well, no,'' he said, grinning. ''There's mineral water and soda water and spring water—ouch!''

She'd swatted his arm.

Their mood continued to lighten as they left the city

lights behind. Traffic thinned once they entered open country and entered the first switchback of a winding highway.

"Is it my imagination, or have you lost even more weight while I was off chasing your car?" Mitch asked her.

She looked surprised. "I haven't weighed myself, but I've been eating. In fact, this week I've been ravenous."

"Huh. Good. I've been worried about you."

"Mitch, will you tell me something honestly?" Gillian asked when she'd crumpled his snack wrappers and stowed them in the empty sack.

"If I can. I've found that whenever people start a question by asking that, they usually want an answer to the impossible."

She swallowed a big dose of guilty conscience along with her gulp of water.

"So, shoot. What were you going to ask?"

"The impossible," she admitted, her lips twitching.

They both laughed. "I'll bet I can guess what you were going to ask," Mitch teased. "You're wondering if Ethan will arrest Capputo and Turbin, and if they'll sing their rotten heads off so someone can nail the bastard at the top and you'll be free."

"How did you know?"

He reached across the empty space and stroked her trembling hand. "It's natural. I felt the same way until a jury handed down its verdict, putting DeSalvo behind bars for life."

Gillian drew comfort from his warm hand. "You and Pat Malone said it's almost impossible to pin anything substantial on men in the upper echelons of crime syndicates. How can I help being concerned?"

Mitch linked their fingers. "I wish you'd let me and

Ethan do the worrying. Ethan, mostly. If he builds a strong enough case to forward to New Orleans, that ought to ensure Lenny and Foss get hard time. When underlings are faced with taking the full rap, they start to squeal on the folks who hired them. More and more mobs are breaking up. Of course, it'd help if we found that key. Malone believes that whatever Daryl has hidden will be the final touch.''

''*If* is the biggest little word,'' Gillian lamented.

Bringing their joined hands to his lips, Mitch eased her fingers loose so he could press a kiss onto her palm.

Gillian shivered. Not in fear this time. She recognized the heat of desire spreading slowly through her body. She'd tried not to miss him—but she had.

Without stopping to think, she unfastened her seatbelt, slid closer to Mitch, and buckled herself into the center lap belt.

His eyes, caught in a sliver of moonlight, glittered with approval and something more. A sound of male satisfaction hummed in his throat as he placed his arm around her, urging her against the hollow of his shoulder.

''Are we climbing?'' She sat forward.

''Yep.'' Mitch tugged her back where he thought she belonged.

She sprang up again. ''I feel curves.''

''Hey, isn't that my line?'' he murmured in a sexy voice. Indeed his right hand was making a thorough exploration of Gillian's curves.

Taken by surprise, she felt her body flow against him, even as she batted at his arm. ''Watch the road.''

''Okay, but don't worry. There aren't any drop-offs,'' he murmured.

''I climbed a big mountain getting to Flagstaff. You know, I'd never imagined mountains in the desert.'' Sighing, she sank back against him. "I wish it was daylight. What I can see by the light of the moon seems beautiful. Almost unearthly."

"I told you it's a slice of heaven. I don't know exactly where Noreen's condo is, but from her map I think her terrace overlooks the red rocks. If so, we'll have coffee on the terrace. I promise you're in for a real treat."

"I'm looking forward to it."

After yawning repeatedly, Gilly dropped off to sleep about an hour from their destination. Exhausted himself, every chance he got, Mitch turned his head to watch her sleeping. Her new look took some getting used to. Yet long before he passed through the village of Oak Creek and turned at the bridge that led into Sedona, he'd fallen for her all over again.

He hated to wake her up, especially as it was nearly midnight. Even then, a few die-hard visitors still roamed the streets, window-shopping. Noreen had said her complex had off-street parking. That appealed to Mitch. He'd kept an eye on his rearview mirror throughout the drive— without Gilly's noticing. Mitch didn't believe they'd been followed, but with the curving road he couldn't be totally sure.

It was a good thing he'd waited until she fell asleep to phone Ethan, though. Mitch was mildly disturbed by what his former partner had to say. Her car was clean as a whistle. Even more bothersome, a reliable snitch of Ethan's attested to the fact that Capputo and Turpin had, just yesterday, flashed big bills around a local tavern. Then, as though someone had flipped a switch, today the men had vanished into thin air.

Apparently the engine's silence caused Gillian to stir. She sat up, blinked and gazed, eyes slightly unfocused at Mitch. "Are we there?"

"Yes. Are you awake enough to walk inside?"

She nodded, but fumbled with her seat belt.

He released it for her and helped her out. "I'll grab the bag Regan packed for you, and your little case with the, uh…Katie's things. We'll follow that cinder path around to those wooden stairs. Thank goodness the grounds are well-lit."

"You don't think we're in danger here, do you?" She was so close on his heels she almost tripped.

"Relax. We're fine." He unlocked the door to the condo, reached inside and switched on an interior light.

"Oh, isn't it beautiful?" Gillian turned around slowly, soaking in the simplicity of the furnishings. All light wood and Southwestern colors—perfect for this room with its huge windows and sand-colored walls.

"Small."

"But comfortable. Noreen obviously likes love seats," she remarked. "Remember, she had one in her living room at the house in Phoenix, as well."

Mitch said something indiscernible from an adjacent room.

"What?" Gilly called, slipping off her jacket. The minute she entered the bedroom she saw what had him concerned. This was a one-bedroom condo. With a large, comfortable-looking bed, but all the same, just one. And neither one of them would fit on those small love seats.

"Look, I didn't know," he said.

"The bed's as big as a football field. Can't we share?"

Their eyes met across the Southwest-print comforter. "I still haven't bought any protection, Gillian."

She rolled her eyes. "That wasn't an invitation to have sex."

"I consider what we did a few weeks ago *making love,*" he said. "That night at your place… Well, I don't know if I can ignore you like that again. And if we share, I don't want there to be any confusion. When I'm in bed with a woman, the only pattern analysis on my mind is how well two bodies merge into one.''

Gillian dropped her jacket on the floor and sank to the bed on one knee, trying not to think about long-term consequences of what she had in mind. Eyes steadily on his, she raised her arms. "I'm not planning to read gardening magazines tonight, Mitch.''

She might have wanted him to say something—a few endearments, maybe. The snick of the light switch plunging the room into darkness was all she got from Mitch Valetti.

His silence would have bothered her if he hadn't undressed her with such reverence and touched her so tenderly that a lack of words didn't matter. Tonight, it was enough to know they were safe. To know that Mitch was one of the good guys. To know she was powerless to change how she felt about him and equally powerless to change their circumstances.

Mitch represented the very best of the good guys in Gillian's estimation. If this short week was all the time she would be granted to love him, then so be it.

CHAPTER THIRTEEN

THE PLAY of light across his face woke Mitch the next morning. He stretched before fully opening his eyes. When he did pry them open, wearing little more than a satisfied grin, he expected to find Gillian curled beside him in a similar state.

Her side of the bed was empty, giving him a sense of déjà vu.

Throwing aside the covers, Mitch bounded out into the cool air, his heart thumping wildly because of her absence. He started toward the living room, then doubled back for his jeans. Hopping on one foot, he finally got them up over his hips.

His heart fell into a more normal rhythm when the scent of coffee swirled around him. Gillian had obviously found Noreen's supplies. Too bad she hadn't turned up the thermostat. Mitch shivered. He'd forgotten how chilly Arizona mountain air could be.

Cold though he was, he made his way barefoot and shirtless to the kitchen. His concern didn't fully abate until he saw a flash of red on the patio, and realized he was looking through the sliding glass door at Gilly. Wrapped in a quilt whose edges flapped in the breeze, she sat transfixed by the first rays of sun highlighting the reddish layers of Coffee Pot Rock.

She looked so adorable, he didn't take time to pour

himself coffee. Instead, he slid back the glass door and hauled her into his arms for a good-morning kiss.

Gillian returned his effusive welcome. When they finally broke apart, Mitch entertained visions of heading right back to bed...with her.

"Oh, my God. You were so right, Mitch!" Gilly threw her arms outward as if to embrace the view. "This is *heavenly*. Truly the most beautiful place I've ever seen. Watching the sun come up by inches and spill out all that glorious color was an incredible experience."

"Mmm," he said, swooping down to kiss her again. "Last night was a pretty incredible experience."

"It was," she said, tracing two fingertips around the laugh lines bracketing his lips. "Magnificent. Just not as spiritual as seeing the sun rise. Unless it's a combination of the two that's left me feeling so good."

"I'd like to take full credit. But more than likely you can attribute your mood to the Harmonic Convergence of Sedona."

"What's that?"

"The area boasts six vortexes. They're literally fields of concentrated energy. Magnetic, some say. Metaphysical, according to New Agers. If you're interested, we can go for a walk later today and pick up some literature."

"Then we aren't confined to the condo?"

He thought for a minute. In light of Gillian's enthusiasm, he deliberately turned a deaf ear to Ethan's last dispatch regarding Turpin and Capputo's disappearance. "We can go out within reason. Sedona is an experience I'd hate you to miss."

She threw her arms around him and pelted kisses over his eyes, nose and lips. "I want to go now and look around town. Do some shopping. Get your shoes on, Mitch.''

"Hey, hey," he said weakly, bowled over by her barrage of kisses. She didn't object too strenuously, however, when he carried her back to bed for another hour of unhurried lovemaking.

"Heading our list," Mitch murmured lazily, after they'd untangled their limbs. "A supply of condoms.''

"Is your philosophy better late than never?" Gillian tossed aside the covers and presented him with her naked back. She couldn't say exactly why, but a knot of disappointment tightened in her stomach. Last night and this morning had been utterly fantastic. So wonderful that she'd dropped her guard and begun to hope for a shared experience that might lead to...to something permanent.

Curled contentedly in his arms, listening to the steady beat of his pulse, Gillian had dared to dream again. She'd lost hope for the future when Katie died. Now, with Mitch, her heart had begun to thaw and make room for foolish possibilities.

"Gilly?"

"Hm?" She heard the rustle of sheets and assumed he'd seen her tense up. Gathering her clothing, which he'd ripped off in haste, she dashed into the bathroom before Mitch could question her further. She'd made one bad marriage. If Mitch had other ideas about this relationship, if he shied away from commitment because he'd once been burned, she wouldn't pressure him into anything. The sex was fabulous. Surely she was modern enough to enjoy a no-strings affair. And if it turned out to be too late to avoid the pregnancy he feared, then he need never know. Quite simple, really.

Only a tiny shred of concern connected with pregnancy itself remained on the fringes of her mind. After all, the

OB who delivered Katie told her nothing had been genetically wrong. He said the odds of having a second stillborn were one in two million.

Gillian stepped under a hot shower, fully prepared to accept any outcome that might be the result of their lovemaking.

FLOPPING BACK on the pillow, Mitch considered joining Gillian in the shower. It was tempting—but he hadn't misread her body language when he'd brought up the subject of buying condoms. Was she worried that she might already be pregnant? Last time that came up, she'd been quick to point out how highly unlikely such a result might be. She'd said nothing of the kind today.

He drummed his fingers on his bare chest while mulling over possible ways of getting her to see a doctor. Relaxed by the sound of the shower, he soon drifted off.

He surged up like a shot approximately an hour later, awakened by the slam of the outside door. He charged out of bed, naked again, only this time he didn't bother donning pants before tearing into the living room.

Midway across the floor, he collided with Gillian, who was marching toward the kitchen. The plastic sack she held flew up and out of her arms. Groceries rained around them, including a dozen eggs, one of which broke atop Mitch's bare foot.

"Where in hell have you been?" he demanded at the same time she shouted, "What do you mean racing out here like some demented fool?" Kneeling, she snatched at grocery items. Suddenly she went still and started to cry.

Mitch made a bad job of trying to scoop up the slimy egg intact, all the while trying to console her. "I'm sorry I yelled, Gilly. But dammit all, you scared me, slamming the door like that. Anyway, why would you go out alone?''

''To buy your stupid condoms,'' she returned, throwing the box at his head seconds before stomping into the kitchen, her chin raised to an angle that dared Mitch to say one more word.

He successfully ducked the flying box, waddling off the hardwood to the kitchen tile, trying to keep the runny egg white on his foot from dripping.

Gillian started to brush past him, going for a second load. Her gaze lit on the dark-red indentations where bullets had pierced his flesh. A network of scars fanned out where surgeons had repaired his shattered hip. ''Lord, Mitch.'' She reached out to touch him, then withdrew, struggling to find words to articulate her feelings of sorrow. ''I hadn't noticed how...how bad your scars are until now. Please, forgive me for carrying on like that.''

''Gilly, Gilly. It's all right.'' Mitch dumped the sloppy egg yolk down the sink, ripped off a paper towel and mopped his foot. ''Luckily, you have lousy aim,'' he said, in an attempt to divert her. When Mitch first moved into the Knights' house, Ethan and Regan had also tended to smother him with care and concern. Mitch wasn't used to it.

''I know I shouldn't have gone out by myself,'' she babbled. ''But you can look out the window and see the convenience store across the street. I wanted to surprise you with breakfast.''

He bundled her into his arms, loving the feel of her still-cool jacket and jeans against his naked skin. ''One of us is overdressed,'' he said in a husky whisper, raising his head after kissing her quiet.

''Me,'' she sighed against his mouth.

Turning together, they stepped over the scattered items

still on the floor, including the condoms, and tumbled back into bed.

The normal hours for both breakfast and lunch had passed when they eventually surfaced again. This time they did shower together. Gillian gently soaped Mitch's angry-looking scars, and knew he was telling only half the truth when he said they didn't bother him much. The area was tender to her softest touch. She left the shower loathing the cruelty one human being could inflict on another.

Late though it was, Gillian used the eggs she'd managed to salvage to make an omelette. They didn't rush their meal and smiled often, entwining their fingers across the table in the way of new lovers.

Nothing remained on their plates when Gillian rose and began to gather the crockery for washing.

"Leave those. We'll clean up later. Let's go see the town."

"Won't walking up and down hills be too hard on your hip?"

"Nope. I want you to see how beautiful it is here." What Mitch didn't say was that he wanted Gillian to fall in love with Arizona—and with him—enough to stay. Forever.

They walked hand in hand, poking into specialty shops tucked into narrow malls. At one adobe-front store, Mitch insisted on buying her a native Zuni fetish necklace she admired.

"Each animal is representative of a living power," he told her. "You've chosen wisely in the bear." He touched a rosy quartz carving that lay nestled between her breasts. "According to legend, the bear embodies strength, courage, power, good luck and healing."

"Well, those are all things I need. You shouldn't have

been so extravagant, but I love it, Mitch. Thank you.''
As they walked, she kept touching the piece.

Mitch openly wore a smile. He enjoyed seeing her eyes
sparkle, even if they'd changed color on him. ''There's
another special place I want you to see.''

Rather than walk all the way back to the condo to get
his pickup, Mitch rented a Jeep and drove them to an
impressive church that seemed to grow right out of the
red rocks. Taking her hand, he led her inside.

''Mitch, it's absolutely awesome,'' she whispered. ''I
felt at peace earlier today while I watched the sun come
up. Here, I— It's— How it affects me is beyond words.''

He turned her around and pointed. ''In the rock face
across the gulch, can you see the natural formation of the
Madonna and child?''

Her breath caught. With her eyes glued on the sight,
Gilly covered her stomach with both hands. Surely this
was a sign she would have Mitch's baby one day.

Eventually he nudged her. ''You can't spend the night,
Gilly,'' he teased. ''I suggest we end our outing at a
Mexican restaurant I've heard has great food and a spec-
tacular view of the sunset.''

She roused herself but gazed at him out of unfocused
eyes. ''Should we spend money on eating out? I've never
cooked Mexican food, but I make some pretty good Ca-
jun dishes.''

''We won't use money, we'll give them plastic. It's
the American way.''

Rallying, she punched his arm playfully.

He hooted. Suddenly lighthearted, he looped his arm
around her neck and nibbled on her earlobe before racing
her to the Jeep—letting her beat him, of course.

Back in town, after Mitch had turned in the Jeep, they
crossed the street and climbed a set of steps leading to a

noisy restaurant. The place was packed with snowbirds. When it came their turn, they were delighted to receive a table on the patio. During dinner they were treated to a kaleidoscope of colors cartwheeling across the red rock formations.

"Spectacular view aside, chile relleno is nothing like what I expected," Gillian exclaimed. She'd done a good job of devouring most of what had been on her plate. "All the same it was delicious." She leaned back with a sigh.

Mitch swallowed the last bite of his Sonoran-style tamales. "I guess you are ravenous as you claimed. That's the most I've seen you eat since we met." In the fading rays of the sun, his eyes glowed with golden warmth. "We'll have to order Mexican food more often."

She crossed her eyes and puffed out her cheeks. "If I stick with you, Valetti, you'll have me waddling away from Sedona."

"Fat chance." When she giggled, he said, "I still think you've lost weight. Ready to leave? I don't want to rush you, but I should check in with Ethan again."

Gillian stopped clowning, sat up straight and felt for her good-luck necklace. "Lead the way," she said in a sober voice.

"Mitch." She clasped his hand as he stood. "I want you to know this has been the most wonderful day I've had in months. Years, maybe."

He savored her compliment as they strolled toward Noreen Malone's condo, which suddenly seemed like home to Mitch. *Because Gilly was there with him.*

"Brr." Gilly hunted for the thermostat after they'd entered the apartment and turned on the lights. "My education about Arizona has been sadly lacking. I'd never have expected the temperature to drop so drastically."

Mitch inspected her lightweight jacket. "Is that the warmest thing Regan rounded up for you?"

"No. She sent two sweatshirts. I'll bring one if we go out tomorrow. Would you like me to make coffee? I think I'd like some to warm up."

Mitch nodded, the phone already at his ear. He was relieved when Gillian went into the kitchen; this way he could speak more freely. "Hiya, partner. Just checking in."

There was loud swearing at the other end. Mitch cringed as he lowered the phone for a moment. "We went out for a few hours. I didn't know I was supposed to keep her prisoner. Next time I'll bring the cell phone."

Gillian walked back into the living room. Mitch turned his back on her. She took the hint and disappeared into the bedroom. "You brought in Turpin and Capputo? Good job! What do you mean the chief called in the FBI? Why can't *you* hold them? Anyway, isn't our objective to follow them to their leader? At least we'll know who posts bail."

Gillian returned. She carried the small suitcase that had become so familiar to Mitch. He frowned when she sat on one of the love seats and unpacked the quilt, the tiny pink dress and then set aside the urn.

He clapped a hand over the mouthpiece. "What are you doing?"

"Hunting for the key again. I got to thinking... Daryl might've slit one of the quilt blocks and slipped a key inside. Is your phone call private? If so, I can do this in the bedroom."

Mitch debated whether he should have her stay or go. What Ethan had to say did, after all, involve her. He shook his head brusquely before he went back to listening. His call ended a moment later. Mitch slammed the phone down, and released a pent-up breath.

Gillian was distracted from her task by his actions, and her hands stilled. ''Bad news?''

He saw she'd removed her colored contacts in the bedroom, and her tragic blue eyes were wary and fixed on him.

''Ethan arrested the men who've been tailing you.''

''Isn't that good?''

''They were bailed out faster than Ethan could sneeze. Capputo and Turpin each called a different attorney. Standard practice when these guys are associated with crime bosses. It confuses local authorities.'' He paced nervously, all the while massaging the back of his neck. ''In the case of our boys, both lawyers have been under FBI surveillance. Now the Fibbies want to talk to you.''

''Me?'' She looked like a rabbit facing a predator, not knowing which way to run.

''It's fairly standard operating procedure,'' he said, dropping to his knees beside her. ''You already know what kind of men Turpin and Capputo are. It shouldn't come as any surprise to hear they've made someone's ten most wanted list.''

''But the FBI! Mitch, I can't help them. Will you talk to them, please? You know everything I know.''

''I'll be here, Gilly, but they'll want to hear the story directly from you. That's just how those guys are. So, you repeat exactly what you told Ethan and me.''

''They—they won't confiscate my suitcase, will they?''

''They'd better not. Come on, I'll help you look through it again.''

They each patted down every colorful quilt square. Mitch loosened the lining in the case itself and double-checked all the corners. Sitting back on his heels, he watched Gilly carefully restore the items to the case. "I'll swear there's no key in that bag," he said as she lightly touched the urn and then closed the lid on the case.

"I know. Yet it's so unlike the Daryl I knew. He simply wouldn't tell Patrick I'd have a key in my possession and then not make sure I did."

"I think we have to assume his plans went awry."

"That's the part I can't fathom. His plans *never* went awry. He was so methodical about everything. Believe it or not, the clothes in Daryl's closet were number-coded."

"He dressed by number?" Mitch asked, incredulous.

"Yes. He tried to organize me, too. I hated studying a chart every morning to try and decide if it was a 4, 3, 6 day or a 2, 7, 8 one."

Mitch couldn't help laughing. "I shouldn't make fun of someone who can't defend his position. Obviously, he took numbers seriously. I'm beginning to see why you and Malone were so sure you'd find the key. But you've heard that saying about the best-laid plans."

"Maybe you ought to tell that to Turpin and Capputo."

"Tomorrow we'll ask the FBI to pass it along, with our regards—once they track those bastards down again. Tonight, though, is still ours to enjoy. Let's put this out of our minds and go to bed."

A smile worked its way across Gillian's face. "Wait till you get a load of the nightgown Regan sent for me to wear."

Mitch edged closer and waggled his brows. "I thought you looked fine without one."

"Isn't a hint of mystery supposed to be sexier? You know, something to make you wonder what's under the red satin?"

He rocked his hand back and forth. "I'm willing to show I'm broad-minded. How much time do you need to slip into your red-hot number? Sorry, I didn't mean to use that word—*number*, I mean."

"A minute or two." Her voice was low and sultry.

"I was about to go sample the coffee. But if you talk like that again, all bets are off."

She teased him further with a drawn-out kiss. Then before he could put his hands on her, she slithered out of his reach and pirouetted off to the bedroom.

Mitch rubbed both hands over his face, as if that would stave off the fire rising through his veins. He needed caffeine like he needed a hole in the head, but Gilly deserved a chance to deck herself out. She'd left most of what she owned behind in New Orleans, and then those sleazebags had slashed the pitifully few things he'd seen hanging in her closet.

Decision made, Mitch pulled himself together and went to pour a mug of coffee. Trusting she'd had hers earlier, he switched off the coffeemaker.

He stood at the glass door, staring at the winking stars that studded the night sky. He sensed her presence behind him, seconds before catching the scent of her perfume. Mitch turned and felt the air leave his lungs. The mug slipped from his grasp and hit the floor tile. Luckily it bounced instead of breaking. Coffee splashed his legs, but the heat seeping through the cuff of his jeans was tame compared to the fire consuming the rest of him.

Gillian posed in the doorway, one arm raised, her right hip casually leaning against the casing. A wide band of red lace flirted with her upper thighs, leaving a mile of leg smooth and bare. The same kind of peek-a-boo lace plunged in a deep V between her breasts, offering him an enticing, shadowy cleft.

"You were right and I was wrong," he said when he managed to find his voice. "Red satin *is* sexy. Damn sexy." Mitch stepped over the puddled coffee and knew Gilly could feel the effect of her appearance in the swell behind his jeans zipper as he crushed her tight and swung her into his arms.

He wanted to take his time tonight for her sake. But in less than five minutes, the red satin confection lay tangled on the bedroom floor.

Gillian had toyed with the idea of teasing him, maybe playing hard to get. One look into his smoky eyes and she was lost. Though both of them were hot and ready, Gilly hung on to her control long enough to press him into the mattress and to slide a thigh up and down his injured hip. Her last coherent thought—she was darned well going to treat him to seduction, Southern-style, tonight.

Mitch might have been the one to start out fully charged, but she soon caught up. They fell into a natural rhythm as the heat and pressure built and built and built—until a thin layer of resolve stood between each of them and explosion.

Gilly knew she'd achieved her aim when Mitch swore and begged for mercy. But he was too far gone to feel her catlike smile form around his exploring tongue.

Her heart pounded hard, like rushing water through her ears.

His almost leaped out of his chest.

Sweat slicked their bodies, drenching the sheets. Mitch wondered how high a man's body heat could rise before he died.

He needn't have been concerned. They did explode then, virtually together. In the moments that followed, he was positive he'd landed on a new planet. Or in heaven.

Why else would he be drifting among soft, downy clouds?

"Are you all right?" Gilly murmured, stirring at last.

"No, but I'll help you prepare my eulogy in the morning." He held her in place, stretched along the length of him, when she tried to wriggle off. With one limp hand, he awkwardly pulled the bedspread over their still-heated bodies.

This time, her smile curved against his chest. "We were pretty perfect, weren't we?"

His answer was to grasp the back of her head while he leaned forward and fused their mouths in a kiss of gratitude...and just plain happiness.

Afterward they slept, arms and legs entwined. Somewhere in the back of Mitch's mind lay a fuzzy intent to try to top their performance....

The next thing he knew, he and Gilly were ejected from a sound sleep by a loud knocking at the front door.

"It's them," Gilly cried in fear, snapping on the bedside lamp as she scrambled to pull on her nothing nightgown.

"Who?" Mitch hopped around on one foot, attempting to turn the second leg of yesterday's jeans right-side out.

"The men! The Arm and The Turtle."

"I don't think so." Mitch had finally managed to calm his pounding heart. "Those guys tried to break down the door of your apartment. Whoever's out there now is slightly more civilized. Maybe the FBI? I'll go check. Just in case we need to make a fast break, why don't you wear something more...substantial?" Even as he said it, his eyes caressed her.

She pointed at the bedside clock. "Mitch, it's 2:00 a.m. Who calls on anyone at that hour?"

Then they heard a gravelly voice announce, "FBI, open up."

"Well, now we know—and it's not exactly a surprise." He sighed. "I'll go take a gander at their ID while you change into something…warmer."

She was already gathering clothes from the duffel Regan had packed. "Be careful," she warned seconds before disappearing into the bathroom.

Mitch took time to pull on a T-shirt and his boots. He even finger-combed his hair on his way to the door. "Hold your horses," he called out. "We're not all night owls just because you are." He peered through the peephole. "Okay, I'm here. Let's see a badge."

Two men in dark suits held shields close to the halogen light illuminating the condo door. Satisfied, Mitch threw the dead bolt and the night lock and opened the door a few inches.

"We're here to talk to Noelle McGrath. She may be calling herself Gillian Stevens. Get her," snapped the bossier of the two men, shoving his way inside.

"State your name," said the other, a man who wore horned-rimmed glasses.

Mitch narrowed his eyes. "You know my name. Chief Wellington, Desert City P.D., gave it to you. Or Detective Ethan Knight did. I'm Mitch Valetti, formerly with the Desert City force."

"Don't get smart with us, Valetti. Ex-cops have zero authority."

"You've got no right to speak to Mitch like that," Gillian said in a cool voice from the bedroom doorway. "I'm Gillian Noelle McGrath. Please keep your voices down, and everyone sit. Noreen Malone was kind enough to let us stay in her home. I'd hate to have neighbors complain and cause her trouble."

Mitch felt a burst of pride in the woman who'd scrubbed her face to a little-girl shine, but who'd clearly taken command of the room.

The agents lumbered all the way in and sat down, trying to be civil. "I'm Agent Bob Hall, and my partner's Agent Kevin Eloy."

"Got any coffee?" Eloy, the one blinking behind glasses, asked hopefully.

Gilly raised her eyebrows. "I'll be glad to make some, but I doubt many normal people have a pot going at this hour."

"I'll zap what's left from last night in the microwave," Mitch offered. "It'll still be better than the rotgut stuff these guys guzzle day in and day out."

Gillian nodded, but she wished he'd stay. When he walked out of the room, the small amount of bravado she had disappeared with him.

"Well, well, Mrs. McGrath," Hall began the minute she'd settled on the love seat. "You and your husband, Daryl, kept company with some A-1 assholes."

Gillian bristled. "First, Daryl and I were divorced before he was killed. Second, from the little I know, they were his clients. I gather he didn't like them any better than you do. Otherwise, he wouldn't have made a list of their names." As Mitch had suggested earlier, Gillian began to tell them what she knew.

He came back with coffee for everyone before she'd finished her story. He sat on the overstuffed arm of her love seat and curved a reassuring hand over her shoulder.

"Names," Hall spat when she ended. "We need those names and any other particulars you can give us. The lawyers who bailed out Capputo and Turpin are both tied to known mobsters who deal in drugs, prostitution and gambling. We also suspect they're in the illegal weapons business now.''

''I—I—'' she stammered, turning a stricken face to Mitch.

''She just told you about the key. No one's been able to find it. Take it easy, Hall, she's not the enemy here.''

''You have proof of that?'' Hall curled his lip. ''She's a player in a field where the stakes are enormous and everyone plays or dies. How can we know she's not using you and Knight to cover her tush while she holds on to the key, trying to shake down the head honchos?''

''What are you saying?'' Gillian demanded. ''What's he saying?'' She looked at Mitch with frightened eyes.

''He's accusing you of extortion,'' Mitch replied, tightening his grip on her shoulder. ''Listen,'' he said, glaring at the agents. ''I'm sure you checked my credentials and Ethan Knight's. We're prepared to vouch for her. So is Pat Malone, retired Flagstaff P.D.''

''You've seen what happened to that guy, and you still trust her?'' Eloy shook his head. ''Bad things happen when she's around. I hope you're watching your back, Valetti.''

''My back is fine. Why don't you and Hall quit spinning your wheels here and round up Turpin and Capputo? And this time, hang on to them long enough to get a few names out of them.''

The two agents looked disgruntled. Finally Hall muttered, ''They're guilty as sin. We've got a good man on their tail. I didn't want to tell you this, but they paid Malone a second visit. Worked him over good. Lucky for Ms. Malone, she'd gone out to the pharmacy.''

''Dammit! How…'' Mitch doubled a fist.

Gillian swayed, and grabbed Mitch's arms. ''My God, no! How did they find him? Is…Patrick badly injured?''

"He'll live. Don't ask to see him. We've got him stashed, and have a man on him around the clock. As to how they found him, we're not sure yet."

Mitch thrust out a pugnacious jaw. "Ethan said you'd arrive here tomorrow afternoon. I'm guessing the reason you're early is because they forced Malone to tell them where Gilly's staying. When were you planning to let us know?"

"We weren't. Damn, I hate dealing with know-it-all ex-cops. Eloy and I are going to stake this place out tight. If either or both of those bastards show up, they're goners, all right?"

"Yeah, all right—if they don't get past you," Mitch said with some sarcasm.

Gillian jumped to her feet and paced the room, wringing her hands. "Why are they doing this? If they have the connections we think they do, they must know the police stripped my car and didn't find a key. Mitch, you said one of them searched my large suitcase. They even went back and tore up my apartment. Mitch and I double-checked the small bag I have. And they shredded my purse. Maybe Daryl planned to put the key in my luggage. He didn't. I swear I don't know anything about his client or where he might have hidden...whatever he hid." Covering her face, she started to cry quietly.

"Get out," Mitch ordered. "There's a limit to how far you can go in grilling an innocent citizen."

"We'll leave after we've had a look at that bag she's talking about. Eloy and I agree the car was clean and also the apartment. Knight's wife didn't want to tell us anything. Reading between the lines, we figured out that Mrs. McGrath is pretty possessive of one suitcase."

"She's not Mrs. McGrath. You heard her say she's divorced." Mitch wheeled to face the two agents.

"Show them the case, Mitch." Gillian blotted her tear-streaked cheeks, but tried not to speak in a teary voice. "Lord knows, no one wants that key to turn up more than I do."

Mitch didn't like it, but he complied with Gilly's request. He went into the bedroom and returned a moment later, carrying the compact case. "Careful," he growled when Bob Hall jerked it out of his hands.

"My God," the older man exclaimed, springing back as the lid popped open. "If this is your idea of a joke, Valetti, it's not very funny."

Gillian elbowed her way into the circle of men. "Daryl and I lost a child," she told them solemnly. "He knew, I'm sure, that I'd never agree to leave my only memories behind. We went through a terrible period. He didn't handle my grief very well. Packing this case was good and decent of Daryl. Look as much as you need to, but don't sully his intentions."

"No, ma'am." Instead, Agent Hall asked Gillian to empty out the contents of the case. Then he and Kevin Eloy felt under the lining, as had she and Mitch. Hall also pried up the metal corners that held the suitcase binding in place.

The younger agent gingerly lifted the quilt and examined each square. The little dress escaped, since there wasn't so much as a hem wide enough to hide a key.

Bob Hall nudged the pewter urn with the tip of his index finger. Sounding uncomfortable, he muttered, "Any way McGrath might have dropped a key inside? Is this the original urn? It couldn't be a duplicate to throw us off, could it?"

Gillian snatched back the urn, reverently holding it against her breast. "Daryl was preoccupied with his business and he was a workaholic. But he wasn't a cold-blooded man. He'd never do something as horrid as that. Besides, I saw him take this from my closet shelf. It's only in B-grade movies that ashes are kept on the mantel," she said scathingly.

The agents—and Mitch, too—seemed thoroughly cowed. Mitch because he'd placed the container on his mantel, hoping it'd somehow help him connect with the owner. He half suspected that in some mysterious way it had ultimately brought him and Gilly together.

"Maybe they snuffed your ex before he had a chance to hide the key in your things, Mrs. McGrath—er, Gillian. The trick will be to convince the folks who are worried about it that the evidence Daryl gathered has ended up in our hands."

"How can I convince them of anything?" Gillian wondered aloud as she carefully replaced baby Katie's things and again closed the lid.

"That's our job," Hall assured her, hitching up his belt. "Eloy and I are going out in the parking lot to hunker down. If those bastards show up here and try to get away with a B and E like they did at your apartment in Desert City, we'll nail their scruffy hides. If you two leave the condo, Mitch, give us a high sign of some kind. We'll keep one man here and the other will shadow you."

Mitch agreed halfheartedly as he escorted the agents to the door. He wished his mind wasn't so fuzzy from lack of sleep. Something that had just happened here was nudging his cop's instincts. Like Ethan, he'd developed an internal method of mentally sifting through clues that weren't really clues. When his sixth sense kicked in, it rarely gave him peace until he'd ferreted out what troubled him. Sleep might interrupt the process—but then again, sometimes he woke up with answers. All he knew was that right now, it was three-thirty in the morning. This was the third night in a row he'd been short on shut-eye.

Still, he took care to lock the front door and check the glass patio door and kitchen windows before he wrapped his arms around Gilly again. "Sweetheart, I know you feel steamrollered by those jerks. But I'm beat and you must be, too. Let's go back to bed for a couple of hours. Then we can sit down and sort everything out over break-fast."

She slid her arms around Mitch's waist and hugged him fiercely. "What if Turpin and Capputo turn up? How can you sleep, Mitch?"

"You let Hall, Eloy and me see to stuff like that. Be-sides, you heard them say they have a tail on those guys." Mitch kissed her, soft and fast at first, but he kept it up and grew more serious until she went limp in his arms.

Feeling victorious, Mitch bundled her up and carried her to bed. "We'll stay dressed. Guarantees we'll sleep that way instead of...well, you know. Plus, we'll be pre-pared if we need to dash out for any reason. Not that we will," he hastened to add.

She agreed and curled tightly against his side, listening to his heartbeat. When his breathing changed to steady and slow, Gillian eased away and sat up.

Mitch believed in her. He'd given her nothing but love and support. He'd already been injured badly; he didn't deserve to end up like poor Patrick Malone.

Standing silent a moment, she gazed lovingly on his sleeping form. Even after she'd bent and dropped a last kiss on his lips, she hadn't fully decided what she was going to do. However, as she slipped out of the bedroom, ideas began to tumble inside her head.

What if she talked with Hall and Eloy and prevailed on them to let her contact Capputo and his sidekick? Then she could explain face-to-face that she wasn't privy to anything Daryl might have known. She'd be able to assure them their secrets would remain safe. In turn, she'd ask only to be left alone. The agents could swoop in and pick them up afterward if they thought they could hold them.

The plan seemed so logical her heart began to sing. She took time to scribble Mitch a note and she left it by the coffeepot. Taking her little case to give to the agents for safekeeping, Gillian unlatched the door and quietly stepped out.

Her breath locked in her throat as two burly figures rose out of the gloom and pounced on her. One grabbed her around the waist. The other wrenched the suitcase from her hand and clapped a gloved hand over her mouth to stifle her scream.

At first she thought it was Hall and Eloy. But Gilly soon realized these intruders were bulkier and dressed not in suits but black jackets and dark caps pulled low over their foreheads. Unless she missed her guess, she'd just met Turpin and Capputo.

She'd *wanted* to meet with them, but on her terms and with FBI backup. Fright pumped adrenaline into her veins. She bit the man covering her mouth and managed one piercing scream before he swore and regained the upper hand.

Gilly saw lights pop on in the condominium to the right of theirs. She did her level best to slump and make herself harder to drag as she heard feet pounding in the parking lot below.

When shots rang out and thudded into the door at her back, she was so scared Mitch would come barreling out and get hit, she stopped fighting and let the men pull her along the access landing and down a dark stairwell. In a way, this was the opportunity she sought, Gillian told herself desperately. Her chance to explain that she was no threat to their boss.

Apparently, she wouldn't get that chance soon. Cringing, Gilly prayed every time the thug holding her shot over her head. She wanted them far away from Mitch. That was why she let them shove her into the back seat of a car without resisting. She opened her mouth to speak as the engine roared and the car squealed out of the lot. There was a loud crack, followed by a burst of light and pain slicing through her head. Another shot shattered the side window of the car and that was the last thing Gillian heard.

CHAPTER FOURTEEN

GROGGY AND disoriented from having fallen so deeply asleep, Mitch roused from a pleasant dream. Pitching upright, he thought he'd heard gunfire. Damn! He had. Rolling off the bed, he stopped to see if the sound had disturbed Gillian. His blood chilled. Her side of the bed was empty. Shouting her name, he charged into the living room. Seeing the door standing ajar made his stomach drop. More awake now, he lunged and yanked it fully open in time to see Bob Hall kneel down at the railing. With two hands wrapped firmly around his nine millimeter, he shot at a big sedan speeding out of the lot. The left side window of the car exploded. Glass flew everywhere.

The agent was good with a weapon, Mitch had to give him that.

"Where the hell were you, Valetti?" Hall shouted, adding a few other choice words as he lumbered to his feet and his partner stepped into a pool of light below.

"Hold your fire, Bob," Eloy yelled. "The suckers got away."

"I'm gonna follow them." Bob slammed his flat palm down on the balustrade. "Get up here, Kevin. Knock on doors and flash your badge. Dean Lucas can stay in Sedona and deal with the local cops, since he's the idiot who lost Capputo and Turpin and let them sneak in here under our noses. Valetti, you come with me."

"Where?" Mitch demanded. "What the hell is going on? Where's—"

"Shut up and shake a leg if you want to help me track the bastards who walked off with Noelle McGrath."

"Walked off with...*what?*" Mitch loped after the heavyset agent. Grabbing his elbow, Mitch pulled the agent up short.

"Caputo and Turpin waltzed in and took your woman." Hall shrugged Mitch off. "The way it looked to me at first, I thought she met them at the door. But for a while she seemed to be fighting them off, so I'll reserve judgment as to whether it was a put-up job or the real McCoy."

Stunned and battling a suddenly queasy stomach, Mitch limped down the steps beside Hall. He jumped into the agent's car without a word. After they'd roared off in the direction taken by the sedan, he collected his reeling brain enough to say through clenched teeth, "Gilly did *not* cook up a deal with those SOBs. I'm willing to stake my life on it."

"Let's hope it won't come to that, Valetti." Bob Hall sounded grim. Neither man spoke thereafter. At least not to each other. Hall got on his radio and got in touch with other agents on the case. Mitch knew they were so far behind the dark sedan that only a visual sighting by another agent or one of a network of local cops would allow them to tail it. Closing his eyes, he massaged his forehead and asked for divine intervention. He begged whoever or whatever was out there to let him find Gillian. He had to tell her he'd fallen in love with her. He wished he'd done that already. So she wouldn't feel alone and afraid....

As the darkness turned pink in the early dawn, they got their first break. "Good news?" Mitch asked, sliding to the edge of his seat when Hall uttered into his cell phone, "About damn time."

"Just a minute, Valetti. Get somebody on it, Leroy. Find out if that plane filed a flight plan. If not, hand those call letters to the FAA so they can tell us what state registered the aircraft. We'll meet you at the Flagstaff airport in…say, fifteen minutes?"

"Flagstaff? You think they're flying her out of Flag?"

"Yeah. I may have to revise my report on Dean Lucas. He botched tailing Capputo, but he alerted agents in Flag and Bullhead City to be on the lookout for the sedan. Leroy Madison tailed 'em to the Flagstaff airport. They dumped the car and he saw them hustle McGrath into a light plane. One we know was used more than once for drug trafficking."

"I don't like the sound of this," Mitch said, slapping his right fist into his left hand. "Can you step on it, Hall?"

"Relax, Valetti. I can always feel when a net's closing in. My gut says we're inches from wrapping this baby up."

"That's it. The baby. Man, oh man, that's it." Mitch whirled to face Hall, straining his seat belt. "That's *it!*"

"What's it? What are you talking about, Valetti?"

"The key! We've been looking for a regular key. The truth's been in front of us all along."

"Spill it!"

"Baby Katie's urn. Well, not the urn exactly. The date carved on it. I'll bet my bottom dollar Daryl McGrath has a safe either at his home or his office programmed to open using the baby's date of birth. In this case, the code is also her date of death," he said, his voice dropping to a whisper.

"I don't know, Valetti…."

"Gilly said her ex made up number games all the time. Doesn't it stand to reason he'd do something clever like that? I mean, last night Gilly all but said it surprised her that Daryl was kind enough to pack that suitcase. He wasn't being kind at all. He was being cagy."

"You could be absolutely on target, Valetti," Hall said thoughtfully. "Okay…here's the deal. I'm willing to play your hunch. Say, do you remember the date? If so, I'll phone ahead and have the Bureau send a team of agents to check out McGrath's home and office."

Mitch hesitated.

"Oh, crap. Can't you remember the damned date?"

"I know what the numbers are. But I'll only give them to you if you make me a promise."

"Anything! We're running out of time here," Hall said, sounding impatient.

"I want your word, Bob. If I'm right, promise you'll let me use the information as a bargaining tool to get Gilly out of their clutches alive."

"I can't do that."

"Sorry, the numbers stay in my head." He paused. "You *can* do it. Question is, will you? Look, even if Capputo and Turpin ran me they'd only learn I'm an ex-Desert City cop. They won't have any idea I'm tied to the feds. Nor will Gilly guess we're working together."

"That's true. All right, I'll give my word. But if you blow this case, Valetti, your ass is grass."

Mitch only smiled. "The number is 11-18-00. Finding the safe is up to your men. I doubt it'll be sitting out in the open."

"If a safe exists, I guarantee we'll find it," Bob muttered fiercely.

THE CAR in which she'd been thrown sped along the country roads. Despite the jolting ride, Gillian didn't come around for some time. Feeling oozed into her body a little at a time. Her toes tingled, then she felt blood flow into her hands and arms. She expected to open her eyes and see Mitch lying beside her. When she raised her eyelids, pain slammed through her head, convincing her to shut them again. It was in that split second that memory returned. As nausea overtook her, she thought she'd be sick. She needed every ounce of concentration to keep the awful taste of bile confined to the back of her throat.

When her head finally stopped spinning and her breathing steadied, she cautiously opened her eyes. One of the ugliest men she'd ever seen stared back.

"She's wakin' up, Foss. Want me to bop her again?"

"Just if she tries to scream or pull any funny stuff."

"I won't." Gillian's voice sounded scratchy. "Wh-ere am I?" She realized the man peering down at her was seated, while she lay on a bumpy floor. The back of a car, she decided based on the rumble and sway beneath her.

"Never you mind, Mrs. McGrath. Our boss will ask the questions. You save your breath."

Gillian tried to move, but discovered her arms were bound in front of her and her legs had been taped at the ankles. "What happened to my suitcase?" Growing panicky, she tried to wiggle into a sitting position. The pain ripping through her head had her flopping back again with a groan.

"I said no questions." The man with the fat ugly face shoved her down with an equally fleshy hand.

Gillian's head struck the floor. Darkness rolled over her in waves, and she tasted blood where her teeth had clamped down and split her lip.

"Take it easy, Lenny. The boss said he wants her in one piece. Only way we're gonna find that key."

"We shouldn't't've put her suitcase in the trunk. The key's gotta be there. Why else would she and that crippled cop take it to their fancy mountain hideout?"

Gillian rallied again. "Daryl did *not* give me a key. In fact, I was going to leave the suitcase with the FBI agents in the parking lot. I intended to have them pass the word that I wanted to speak to your boss. I'm no threat to his operation. I don't know anything about it, and I have *no key.*"

Although she shook throughout her speech, Gillian enunciated the last words loudly and clearly.

She heard the man in the front seat, the one driving the car—Foss Turpin, she assumed—turn swiftly.

"Whadidshesay, Lenny? Those weren't local fuzz taking pot shots at us back there?"

Capputo reached down with stubby fingers and yanked Gillian up by the front of her jacket. Regan's jacket, she thought hysterically, hearing the material rip. She found herself worrying about the most trivial things—like replacing Regan's clothing once these men freed her. Because she couldn't, *wouldn't,* think about the alternative: not getting out of this predicament alive.

"Foss asked you a question. How many Fibbies? Who called the feds? That cop you shacked up with?"

Terrified, Gillian wondered how much to tell them. When Lenny shook her hard and she felt a button pop off Regan's jacket, she decided to give them the truth. She reasoned that if they had the connections Patrick Malone thought they had, it'd be a simple matter for them to check out everything she knew, anyway.

"There were two agents keeping watch in the parking lot. Apparently another one followed you from Desert

City. The FBI showed up when your lawyers bailed you out. They'd been watching the dealings of your attorneys."

The man in the front seat swore roundly. "Those birdbrains don't give up easy. Now we gotta change our plan. Lenny, get on the horn and call Jimmy up in Flagstaff. Tell him to warm up a plane."

"You know I hate flying," Lenny whined.

"Tough shit. I'm not too happy about losing my best car, either. Look at it this way, the sooner we dump her in the boss's lap, the faster we get our dough."

Gillian saw Lenny Capputo brighten at the prospect of collecting money for dumping her. She shivered involuntarily. These men were the dregs of society. She could only imagine the ruthlessness of the person or persons at the top.

They dropped one bit of information she found somewhat cheering. Turpin insinuated that the agents would probably follow them. Which might or might not mean Mitch would, too. If all the shooting had roused him from sleep, she knew in her heart that he'd try to rescue her. Cold spread in her stomach. This entire debacle had come about through her efforts to spare him. God, she was already to blame for Patrick Malone's beating. Now the blood of any agent injured in the recent shooting would also be on her conscience. She slumped back into her uncomfortable position the minute Lenny Capputo let go of her.

There she lay in a shaking, miserable heap until they stopped and roughly transferred her like so much freight into the cabin of a small airplane. Feeling the framework of the craft jiggle and bounce during engine warmup, Gillian was inclined to agree with Lenny on one point.

She'd never flown in a light plane, but she was pretty sure she wasn't going to like it.

AGENT HALL roared right onto the tarmac of the Flagstaff airport. He'd heeded Mitch's urge to step on the gas. Luckily other agents had paved the way and men dressed in dark suits were stationed at intervals, waving him on toward a hangar where Mitch saw a border patrol plane warming up.

He and Hall catapulted from both sides of the car. A dark-skinned man whose suit jacket and tie flapped wildly in a wind whipped up by the plane's turbo engines stabbed an index finger toward the sky.

Shielding his eyes against the rising sun, Mitch saw a small plane winging its way toward the eastern horizon.

"What in hell happened?" Bob shouted at the man.

"It took time to check all the newly filed flight plans. This is a busy airport, Bob."

"I know. Sorry for taking your head off, Bayless. It's damn frustrating to be this close and still lose the SOBs. Mitch, this is Cal Bayless. He works out of our Northern Arizona office. Cal, Mitch Valetti, formerly Desert City P.D. Mitch is a friend of the kidnapped woman."

Mitch shook hands. "Did you get their flight plan?" he asked Cal.

"Headed for Louisiana, but these guys are no dummies. They reserved the right to change their minds on where they might land to refuel—any one of three airports. Their final destination is also questionable. Shreveport, Baton Rouge or New Orleans were named as possible termination points."

"That's a no-brainer," Mitch said. "Gilly's from New Orleans. That's where her ex had his CPA firm."

"Speaking of his firm," Bob interjected, "any news,

Cal, from our men in the field? I shipped them some coded data en route. I said I was headed here, and they should let you know if they got lucky.''

"No reports so far, Bob. We heard from Kevin Eloy. He's settled with the condo owners on an amount for property damage from your fire fight. The local police are giving us their full cooperation.''

"That's something," Bob grumbled. "I hate citizen uprisings. Especially when all we're trying to do is rid the world of scum. When will our flight be checked out and ready to roll?'' he asked abruptly.

"You can board. Elerson's piloting. He's into the countdown now. He told me we have priority clearance with the tower to take off whenever you're set.''

"Your plane is larger than theirs," Mitch noted. "Can we beat them to New Orleans?''

"You'll have to ask the pilot," Cal said with a shrug.

"Let's go, Valetti. I don't like using civilians, but your game plan sounds workable. I'd deal with the devil himself to shut this operation down.''

Forcing his bad leg to cooperate, Mitch jogged toward the plane.

"Damn," Bob wheezed, struggling to keep abreast. "I didn't ask Cal to tell us who that plane's registered to.''

"Too late now," Mitch informed him. He'd already bounded into the craft. Glancing back, he'd seen Cal Bayless wave and climb into the automobile Bob had left running.

"Doesn't matter. We'll find out before they land somewhere. I hope you're right about them going to New Orleans. Hell, I hope you're right about a lot of things, Valetti.''

"Not half as much as I do," he murmured. "When I

think of Gilly in the hands of a clown who has more to gain by killing her than letting her walk free..."

"He could off her if he finds out she really *doesn't* know where the key is—or where to find McGrath's list. Now *that* guy was a dummy. Why didn't he contact us from the get-go? Or ship his information to the nearest agency?"

"That is curious," Mitch agreed. "Especially when he had the wherewithal to contact Patrick Malone."

Hall shrugged. "Folks in trouble often spill their guts to someone they trust. Maybe McGrath still had feelings for his ex. He might've figured if Malone couldn't take care of her, he'd put her in touch with someone who could."

Mitch looked bleak. "Yeah. We'll never know what course of action Gilly's ex might've taken if he'd given her the code outright—or hadn't been struck down so quickly."

"For all of Daryl McGrath's cleverness, this organization has the resources to outsmart him every step of the way. Except for actually laying their hands on Daryl's key."

"So, you think it's bigger than a money-laundering scheme? Gilly said that's what Daryl told Malone he'd uncovered. Ethan and I thought it might be someone channeling local gambling funds. I've only been to New Orleans once, but I noticed a lot of cash changing hands in clubs down on Bourbon Street."

"Son, there's not a big city in the U.S. of A. that doesn't have its own illegal crap going on."

"I've policed big and small towns. You don't have to tell me about the amount of sleaze in the world." He frowned and raised his hand in a helpless gesture. "I'm worried about Gillian. I just wish to hell I could be sure that she realizes there's no honor among thieves," he said as they buckled in for the flight.

"Thieves and worse," Bob lamented.

The men drifted into silence as the six-seater plane taxied down the runway and lifted off. Once they were airborne and cleared to use electronic devices, Hall flipped open a laptop computer he'd grabbed before they left the car.

"What are you doing?" Mitch asked with mild curiosity.

"Trying to get someone at headquarters to complete a trace on ownership of that Cessna. I'm not holding my breath, mind you. Guys like we're dealing with are too clever to own anything easily traceable. Sometimes we get lucky, though, and manage to track something back through a chain of phony corporations."

"Won't that take a long time?"

Bob smiled genuinely for the first time in their association. "The more powerful our computer programs become, the less clever these criminals seem. Dirty money buys a lot of muscle, but so far the white hats are still ahead. We have honor and integrity on our side," he said smugly, "not to mention a higher level of education."

Mitch made a sound in his throat. "The longer I worked the streets as a cop, the harder I found that is to believe. Look how fast those slick lawyers sprung Turpin and Capputo. If the good guys are so smart, why does evil like that still walk?"

"I didn't say our system was perfect. But you gotta keep believing we'll win more times than we fail."

Mitch linked his hands between his knees and brooded. "I'll tell you right now, Hall, I'm not giving up until I get Gilly back. Anything I can do to accomplish that, I will. Even if it means sinking to their level."

"Bingo!" Hall shouted excitedly, grinning from ear to ear.

Mitch caught his excitement. "You figured out who owns the plane? That was fast."

"Better, Valetti. One of our men uncovered Daryl McGrath's safe. At his house. It turned up when an agent sat on the raised hearth and felt the slab of flagstone move. The safe was there all along. Right under the slab. And your idea paid off, so I owe you one. Bunch of notebooks inside."

"What do they say? Who are these bastards?"

"Whoa. We're good, but his notebooks are coded and deciphering them will take time. Duffy, my contact, says it looks as if Daryl detailed every move the organization made since the sailing of the *Mayflower*. But he's written it all in number codes. Even worse, each page seems to have a different formula."

"Good old Daryl," Mitch groaned. "Gilly told me he was obsessive. How long will it take to get answers, does Duffy think? Soon enough to round up these guys before that plane lands?" Mitch chewed worriedly on his bottom lip.

"You're wanting miracles, boy."

"Damn right. I want Gilly back in one piece, and I don't want her falling into the hands of anyone who'll use her as a bargaining chip."

"Huh. I'd like to promise you that, Valetti. Only I quit believing in Santa Claus and the Tooth Fairy a long time ago."

Mitch slumped in his seat. He'd hate to be the one who'd handed the authorities the key, only to find out he'd put Gilly in greater danger.

"Hold on," Bob mumbled. "My office is forwarding some tracking information on that airplane."

Again Mitch sat on pins and needles as he anxiously awaited the new facts.

"Like I thought. A web of dummy companies. A non-existent law firm leases the plane from a flight school that isn't recorded as legit in any state. The flight school supposedly has the craft on loan from an East Indian rug dealer. He's a real person, at least. He has a passport."

"So, you're saying this ring is international?"

"Not necessarily. Shoot, the rug dealer's another blind. He's in Attica doing ten to twenty for bringing more than rugs into the country."

"Jeez, Hall. I can see I've never appreciated the FBI nearly enough. Pretty impressive how you've filtered through all those facts. Layer after layer of 'em."

"Ah, another convert. Wait, hold the presses, I'm getting more data. The rug dealer fronted for a consortium headquartered in Turkey."

Mitch snorted disgustedly. "Don't tell me anymore. The mud only gets deeper. Somehow it all flows back to New Orleans. We know that because Daryl McGrath did the books dealing with huge sums of money being washed through a phony carpet company. Hmm. Maybe it's not phony. Did anyone look into that?"

"It's phony all right. We may finally have scraped off enough layers. The money for the plane originated with a bank draft drawn on a Swiss bank. An account set up by an American firm. Supposedly, the funds are used for the purpose of facilitating faster trading in antiques. The firm's officers aren't listed with the bank in Switzerland. It's called Antiques and More. I'll just bet if we can run that business to ground, we'll be knocking at the door of our wheeler-dealers."

"Antiques," Mitch murmured. "Antiques. Damn, there's something Gilly said about antiques. I can't remember. It's there, but out of reach." He doubled his fists, then ran both hands over a jaw in need of a shave. "Give me a minute to collect my thoughts, Hall, and I'll try to come up with what she said."

"Hurry up, okay? So far, it appears that our source has dried up."

"Oh man, oh man, oh man. I've *got* it." Mitch nearly vaulted from his seat. "I'll hand it to you on a platter, Hall. Only if I'm right this time, Gilly's in more danger than my worst nightmare. So, I want a second deal up-front. I want your word that you'll hold off picking up this guy until you give me one clear shot at rescuing her."

"I can force you to tell me, Valetti. You can't withhold information from the FBI. I'll toss your sorry ass in the slammer until you cooperate."

Mitch's eyes were cold and serious. "Yeah, you can do that."

"Dammit, Valetti! Give me what you have."

"So we have a deal? Your word?" Mitch held out his hand to the agent.

Hall took it, reluctance showing. But he did shake.

ONCE THE INITIAL queasiness associated with the small plane's liftoff had passed, Gillian forced herself to relax. If she was quiet and listened to as much as possible, maybe she'd overhear something useful.

Her nerves were jumpy again. And her stomach, which had been on the verge of embarrassing her since the outset of this ordeal. Was it possible that she might be in the early stages of pregnancy? The joyous thought gave her something beyond her immediate plight to concentrate on.

Through no fault of her own, she'd lost one baby.

Surely God wouldn't be so cruel as to take another from her.

Turpin and Capputo didn't talk much. They seemed edgy, staring out the windows on either side of the small craft. No one paid attention to Gillian, who lay on the floor, bound hand and foot.

After what felt like hours, Gillian felt her stomach reacting adversely to another shift in atmospheric pressure. She moaned and gagged, blinking morosely up at Lenny Capputo. "Are we there?" she asked weakly.

"None of your business."

"I think I'm going to throw up," Gillian said, sliding up against the bulkhead.

Turpin started to unwind the tape from her ankles. "Can you hold off puking for five minutes? We're landing to take on fuel. An old melon farmer in Brady—one of us—owns this airstrip. If you keep your trap shut, I'll ask if you can use his john."

"Yes," Gilly murmured, fighting off the waves of nausea. "I won't say a word if Mr. Brady lets me use his facilities."

"His name isn't Brady. That's the town. Brady, Texas, you stupid broad," Lenny Capputo snapped.

Foss Turpin cut him off with a glare.

"What do we care if she knows where we stop to refuel, Foss? Like she's going to whisper our secret to a cantaloupe? Give me a break. We'll have her delivered safe and sound and we'll be hoisting a brew *years* before the feds figure out where we've gone."

"Shut up, Lenny. This is the last job I'm doing with you. One of these days your mouth will get you sent upriver. I ain't about to be on the raft with you."

"Screw you. Think you're so smart? Well, brains won't get you jackshit without me. Because you're too squeamish to ice anyone.'' He pulled a glinting steel weapon from the back of his belt and ran the tip of the barrel along Gillian's cheek. "If the boss wants the chick done like her old man, I say you don't have the guts."

Gilly struggled to keep from fainting. She'd suspected these men had killed Daryl. Until now, she hadn't known for sure.

"I do my share," Turpin argued. "All I ask is that you zip your lip until this is over and we have our cash in hand. I got a bad feeling, Lenny, about those feds getting on our tail so fast. I'll take the woman to the house to use the *facilities*," he mimicked Gillian. "You see about refueling."

"As long as you keep an eye on her. She shouldn't've taken so long to find. Her cop boyfriend's to blame. I hope he *is* on our tail. I'd like to pay him back for the night we spent in that jerkwater jail."

As Gilly stumbled off the plane, she grasped at one hope. That Mitch was following, and by some miracle, he'd find a way to save her.

Then in the next breath, she prayed he wouldn't come within a country mile of the boss. Whoever he was, he had to be even worse than these men. Maybe a *lot* worse.

Barely lasting until they entered the run-down house, and the gnarled old farmer showed Foss where to take her, Gilly emptied the contents of her stomach into the toilet. She felt immediately better. The faint hope that she might truly be pregnant with Mitch's baby jump-started her heart again.

After splashing water on her hands and face and patting herself dry with a towel the old fellow offered, Gillian thanked him for his kindness.

"Airsick?" he inquired sympathetically.

She glanced up and discovered that Foss had gone inside the bathroom to use it himself. He'd momentarily closed the door. "I think I'm pregnant," she whispered to the farmer, drawing his attention to her bound hands. It struck Gillian that this man might be her last link to anyone—to Mitch, in particular. "I know Mr. Turpin said you were one of them. But I suspect the baby's father might be following us. If a dark-haired cowboy-type shows up here asking questions, would you please tell him I may be carrying his child?"

The old man didn't agree or decline. Foss burst out of the privy, halting any conversation. Gillian didn't think she'd misread the empathy in the old man's rheumy eyes. She mustered a smile for the farmer as Turpin shoved her outside and across the field, pushing her roughly into the plane.

"What were you and the old geezer talking about?" he demanded as the plane soared aloft.

"Melons," Gillian said, gritting her teeth against Turpin's fetid breath. "You know how men are when you ask about their work."

Capputo laughed. "If it wasn't for our boss, that old fart would be rotting in an old folks home. See? The boss grants favors from time to time. He's got a wife, but I hear he's not averse to entertaining pretty women like you at his apartment in town. That's where we're going. Give him what he wants, maybe he'll keep you around for a while."

Gillian's eyes blazed. "I'd rather die than give a man like that one ounce of pleasure."

Lenny's demeanor changed. "Nothing I hate more than an uppity broad." He tightened her bonds.

Gillian clamped her teeth shut on her anger. She'd show them, though. She had fight left in her.

The remainder of the flight dragged, at this stage, Gillian just wanted it over and done with. She hadn't slept much in two days. She wore borrowed clothes and desperately wanted a bath. Yet when they exited the plane in a spot she knew was rural Louisiana from the swampy odor, her heart almost thrashed out of her chest. It didn't help that one of the men blindfolded her for a car ride.

Over her pounding heart, Gilly started to identify familiar city noises about an hour later. Cars honking, street vendors hawking wares. The smell of flowers floated in the open windows along with heavy, humid air. Gillian knew instinctively that they were headed for the Quarter.

The car slowed to a crawl. Gates creaked open on rusty-sounding hinges. They closed after the car passed through. Soon, she was dragged out of the back seat. Car doors banged shut, and she stumbled up concrete steps.

Another door, a residence, she assumed, also scraped as it opened to whichever man knocked. Now the steps they ascended were carpeted. Thick and opulent carpeting, unless she missed her guess.

They entered yet another door at the top of the stairs. Cigar smoke curdled her stomach. A den? A library? Maybe this was truly her final destination, Gilly thought, her knees beginning to knock.

She was slammed into a chair and ordered to sit. Something hard was dropped into her lap. She recoiled at first. Until she realized it was her suitcase of precious cargo. An odd feeling of peace descended on Gillian.

Time passed. Gillian grew tired of sitting in one place and shifted slightly to give her aching back relief. That was when she heard the door open and a heavy tread on the carpet. Suddenly her blindfold was whisked off. She blinked once, twice. The low light filtering through iron-grated, mullioned windows spilled over a mahogany desk.

Someone stepped out from behind her.

Gilly lifted her eyes. Then her mouth curved into a smile. "Conrad! Thank God." Tears sprang to her eyes. "How—? Where—? Oh, please, unwrap this tape." She lifted her arms, which had been resting on the suitcase.

Her ex-brother-in-law reached out a hand and slapped her so hard, Gilly's already aching head almost spun off her shoulders. Surprise and an iron will kept her from falling out of the velvet chair. *"You,"* she whispered through the coppery taste of her own blood. "No," she said, her voice rising hysterically. "I don't believe you'd have Daryl killed. Conrad, for God's sake! Not your own brother. Daryl *worshiped* you."

"Not me. You. And the head of this outfit will kill us both unless you give me that key," McGrath snarled. "I brought Daryl onboard. I really thought after he got smart and divorced you, he'd be a valuable asset. But between you and that damned interfering Patrick Malone, my little brother developed a conscience. Well, make no mistake. I have no such compunction. I want the key and the address where Daryl hid all that information. I'm not letting either of you ruin what I've spent twenty years developing. I've got twenty-four hours to hand over that list to my bosses. I want it *now*, Noelle."

"I don't have it, Conrad. Daryl never gave me a key."

"I know what's in that suitcase, Noelle. I'm pulling off the tape around your wrists, and you'll open it and get me the key, or I'll incinerate everything in there while you watch."

"I don't *have* any key! God in heaven, you've got to believe me. I've searched this case over and over. Also the car Daryl provided, and the other bag he packed for me. You had him killed before he could finish," she accused.

Conrad hit her again. This time, Gillian did fly off the chair and lay sprawled on the floor. She huddled there, mentally preparing for death. But the outer door opened and a small man with downcast eyes called to Conrad. "Sir?"

"What, dammit? Get out. Can't you see I'm busy?"

"Sorry, but there's a man at the front door asking to see you. A man with a limp. He's quite insistent that I interrupt whatever you're doing to say he has something you want. A key, he said. Uh…of course I'll send him away. Sorry to bother you."

"Wait!" McGrath roared.

Gillian curled into a tighter ball. It could only be Mitch at the door. Her heart burst with love and relief. And yet a saner part of her wanted to scream at him to run. The madness glowing deep in Conrad's eyes sent pinpricks of fear up her spine. Not for her. For Mitch.

The warning died in her throat as her former brother-in-law jerked her up by the nape of her neck, breaking the fetish bear necklace Mitch had bought her in Sedona. Tiny turquoise-and-shell heishi beads rained over her suitcase, which had sprung open to spill its contents over Conrad's expensive Oriental rug.

Soundless tears ran down Gilly's cheeks as she landed hard in the chair where he threw her.

"Show him in, Ainsley. And set the Dobermans loose in case he brought backup," Conrad instructed in a cold voice, striking terror in Gillian's heart.

CHAPTER FIFTEEN

THE MOMENT Mitch entered the room and saw Gillian's swollen, tear-streaked face, fury more immediate than he'd ever felt raged through him. The handprint marring one side of her face torched a deep, white-hot rage in his belly.

Yet one wrong move could blow apart Bob Hall's only chance at taking down this slimy bastard.

Mitch clenched his hands tight against his sides and ground his back teeth. The man he guessed to be Conrad McGrath stepped calmly behind Gilly and pressed the nose of a Sauer P38 to her temple.

Slow and easy, Mitch spread his hands and lifted them away from his sides to indicate he was unarmed. A rush of blood pumped furiously in his chest.

McGrath backed toward his desk, and pushed a button on his phone. As Mitch had assumed, two musclemen appeared to frisk him none too gently. Not Capputo and Turpin—because Hall had picked them up leaving the residence. But these men looked equally nasty.

"Hey, take it easy," he growled. "I'm not packin'. I came to deal. Mitch Valetti's the name." He didn't extend his hand; if he did, he wouldn't be able to keep himself from punching McGrath's lights out or wringing the SOB's neck.

McGrath smirked. "We've had reports on you, Valetti. Turn him upside down and inside out, Beau. The minute a key falls out, you have my permission to dispose of all this trash.'' He tapped Gilly's head with his gun, sending Mitch's temper soaring higher.

He dared not look at her face or he'd lose it for sure. ''You're not bargaining with a fool, McGrath.''

''No, I'm parlaying with a pig.''

A muscle jumped in Mitch's jaw. He made himself laugh. ''Don't hold your breath waiting for me to disagree. I'm the one trying to make ends meet on the state's paltry retirement pay.''

Conrad's eyes glittered with a new light as he weighed what Mitch had implied—that money mattered more than principal.

Gillian stared at Mitch, and she almost hyperventilated in disbelief. How could she have read him so wrong? He was one of those cops on the take.

Her heart dropped end over end. The scene in the room grew fuzzy around the edges, as once again nausea threatened.

Mitch absorbed her reaction because he needed to play a game more intricate than chess. There must be no missteps that some slick lawyer could pounce on and use against them later in court. He wanted this scum put away. For good.

''How much, Valetti? And what makes you think the people I work for will let you walk after we get the key?''

Mitch shook his head. ''The key isn't any piece of metal, McGrath. Surely you knew your brother better. His key's in the form of a numerical code.'' *So,* he thought as he spoke, *Conrad's not the ringleader of this organization.*

''Damn it to hell.'' Conrad faltered for the first time since Mitch had come into the room. ''I could have Beau and Sal beat the information out of you.''

"You could try." Mitch spread his legs and crossed his arms. "On the other hand, why not work together? The FBI's breathing down our necks. I had a devil of a time shaking them after the truth hit me. I can take you where Daryl hid his list, and you'll be able to appease your boss. I can do that now—after I see half a mil in cash. Once you burn Daryl's list, the FBI's got nothing on you."

"Don't do it, Mitch." Gillian strained away from Conrad as she pleaded.

Before the words were out he clipped the side of her head with the butt of his revolver. "Shut up! I'm trying to think this through."

Beau spoke up. "You want me to call and ask Mr. Calofonzo what we should do?"

"Hit her again," Mitch warned in a low, deadly voice, "and the deal's off."

"No," Conrad snapped at both men. Facing Mitch, he added, "My brother's slut isn't part of any deal. Daryl's reason for turning on us was to impress Noelle and get her back. He actually told me that! If he'd stuck with me, he would've been set for life. Daryl didn't need her. *She's* to blame for all this. I intend to see her dead."

Mitch felt his gut churn. Again, he couldn't glance her way. "Then kill us both right now and take your chances with the FBI."

Beau, clearly muscle for someone above McGrath, stepped forward. "Sal and me can do 'em anyway. What's to stop us once we get Daryl's stuff? The boss wants that list."

"Don't you understand, Beau? The feds know Valetti's here," Conrad screeched, obviously starting to come apart.

Mitch knew he didn't have much time. There was dissension in the ranks. And Bob Hall had given him only half an hour in which to negotiate. Then agents would drop out of helicopters onto the roof. Obviously McGrath was feeling squeezed from both sides. He couldn't decide which way to jump. Mitch knew the slightest provocation could touch off a gun battle that might leave Gilly and him dead.

"The list is waiting," Mitch said, prodding Conrad to decide. "One thing I'll tell you—it's always been in Daryl's house."

"You lie," Beau fumed. "We tore his house apart."

"Without me," Mitch said directly to Conrad, "you'll never find Daryl's hiding place. Agent Hall might figure it out, though. I was with him when I guessed the code."

"All right. Everybody shut up! Valetti, you, me and Sal will go to Daryl's to see if you're telling the truth. Noelle stays here with Beau. You'll get your money when I have the list in hand."

"Try again. I checked you out, McGrath. Half a mil is chump change to your organization. I say you put the money together while I help my woman pick up her beads. Then we'll all go to Daryl's. One big happy family." Mitch's smile matched Conrad's earlier one for icy shrewdness.

"I won't go a step with either of you," Gillian declared stoutly, although it was awkward to talk with a swollen jaw.

Mitch dealt her a glance that shut her up as he went down on one knee and began placing necklace pieces in her suitcase. When a bead pinged off Katie's urn, Mitch touched the vase, letting one finger softly trace the child's name.

Gillian saw the look on Mitch's face. Conrad didn't. His expression gave her new hope—maybe Mitch *wasn't* a cop gone bad. Maybe things weren't what they seemed....

· Conrad tucked the revolver in his belt, watching Mitch rise, leaving Gilly to finish and close her case.

McGrath gave Mitch a light punch on the arm. "Calofonzo can use a man like you. All the big man has to do is snap his fingers, and he can get you a chick younger and prettier than Noelle. Whadaya say, Valetti?"

"It's a tempting offer." Mitch rocked back on his boot heels, pretending to consider. "Except I own a sweet little horse ranch in Arizona. And the difference between us, Conrad...I'm not greedy. I have a hankering to keep this woman barefoot, pregnant and down on the farm." Mitch winked, guffawing raucously enough, he hoped, to cover Gilly's look of revulsion.

McGrath began to sweat. "I don't know. The boss already has people in your state. But...once you sign a receipt for the half mil, you're in our pocket."

Like hell. Mitch smiled to hide the thought he was afraid might show in is eyes.

A lock of rust-colored hair flopped over Conrad's forehead giving him the look of a crazed bantam rooster.

Mitch tipped forward on the balls of his feet. He wasn't foolish enough to trust Conrad, under any circumstances. Mitch had never heard of Calofonzo, but he knew the type. It didn't matter how high up Conrad had been. In recruiting Daryl, he'd made a mistake. The net was closing at both ends, and McGrath had to realize his livelihood—and his life—were in jeopardy.

"Sal. Bring the Lincoln Town Car around." Spinning, Conrad leveled a warning at Mitch. "Anything goes wrong, here or at Daryl's, Beau will kill Noelle first and you second."

Keeping his eyes cold, Mitch inclined his head minimally. Inside he shouted *yes, yes, yes.* "Gilly, if you've found all your beads, get ready to leave."

"Gilly?" Conrad turned from an open wall safe.

"I like her first name better than her middle one, which Daryl preferred," he explained, countering Conrad's uneasy regard.

Gillian obeyed without question, although her fingers shook so hard she had difficulty snapping the locks on the case. She hated them all. Her only hope now was the absent FBI. *Where were they?*

Within minutes, Conrad produced a duffel bag filled with stacks of cash. Mitch made himself concentrate on the haul Bob would make once he and Gilly were in the clear. His main fear continued to be that she'd talk to him on the ride and risk spoiling the impression he'd carefully created for the benefit of Conrad and his henchmen. The impression of a collaborator, a man as corrupt as they were.

Fortunately, the car was big and Conrad split them up. He was no one's fool, either. Otherwise, he wouldn't have climbed this high in the organization. Mitch found it interesting that Daryl was his brother's weak link. Daryl McGrath might well turn out to be Gillian's hero in all of this.

However much Mitch longed to press his face to the darkened windows and make sure Hall's agents were stationed along the route as planned, he forced himself to relax. Luckily it was a short drive to Daryl's more modest home. Mitch tried to forget that the man had lived here with Gillian. To forget they'd made baby Katie here.

Without being told, Sal drove down a back alley. He stopped at the rear of the house. Mitch hadn't counted on that. He had to trust that Bob's men saw them and would adjust their strike accordingly.

He held his breath when Beau suggested taking a look around the property. Down the street should be a crew of three putting out traffic cones. The workmen, really agents, would block the street at both ends, sealing off traffic from gunfire they had to anticipate.

Mitch's stomach felt jumpy.

Across the street, another agent should be posing as a roofer. His truck would appear to be filled with supplies, but under the tarp were four additional agents from the New Orleans office. As well, if all went according to plan, in a field nearby sat a DEA helicopter carrying Bob himself.

Beau stuck his shaggy head in Conrad's lowered window. "A few dudes working down the street. One's in the manhole, and a couple more are unloading red cones."

McGrath stiffened. Mitch felt him and remained as loose as he was before.

"They look real. They're wearing city coveralls and they're sweaty."

"This is normally a quiet street. Okay. Let's do this and do it quick. Sal, you stay in the car and keep the engine running."

Watching McGrath yank Gilly out of the car made Mitch ram his fists in his front jeans pockets. *We're so close,* he kept telling himself. *Don't fly off the handle and wreck it now.*

Mitch shouldn't have been shocked by how fast Beau picked the lock on Daryl's back door. But criminals' abilities never ceased to amaze him.

"Okay, Valetti," Beau muttered. "Which room?"

"Living room," Mitch said, moving unerringly into the room with the flagstone fireplace.

"Find the safe and make it fast. This place gives me the creeps."

"It ought to, you bastard," Gillian hissed over top of the suitcase she had wrapped tightly in both arms. "Your own brother bled to death on the front porch, thanks to you."

Too fast for Mitch to react, Conrad cuffed her hard upside the head. She sank like a rock, the suitcase breaking her fall.

Conrad stepped over her prostrate form, training the gun on Mitch. "Daryl should've listened to me about her. In a way, his blood *is* on my hands. But if you're smart, Valetti, you'll realize two dead bodies more or less won't matter. Tell Beau where to find the stash or watch Noelle die. If the list is there, I'll be nice and kill you first."

His laughter unleashed Mitch's fury, which had been held in check too long. To hell with the plans. Mitch sprang, catching Conrad off guard and around the neck in a choke hold. The Sauer spun out of the man's limp hand. Using Conrad as a shield, Mitch placed himself between Gilly and Beau, who had belatedly managed to yank his weapon from his shoulder holster.

Although Conrad cursed and kicked and fought, Mitch—who'd kept his upper body strong working horses and digging fence-post holes—didn't give him any room to maneuver. Mitch battled an urge to snap the bastard's neck for what he'd done to Gillian. It would be so easy and it'd save the state the time and expense of a trial.

Reason swept over him, cooling his hatred. Reason was what separated him from lowlife like Conrad McGrath and the man who ran this dirty organization. The reward would be in watching them caged forever like the rats they were.

Calofonzo's empire had imploded. Unwittingly, Gillian had wrenched the confession from Conrad that Bob needed to bring down the whole bunch.

During Mitch's initial visit here, he'd seen Bob's agents wire the room. Bob already had Daryl's notebook. Although Mitch had tried to talk Hall into replacing the book with a fake, Bob had refused. Daryl's safe was empty.

Now Mitch had only one thought—*where the hell was the FBI?*

Mitch heard Gillian groan behind him as his muscles began to feel the strain of keeping a grip on McGrath. At last—the front door burst open and the first of the agents poured inside.

"Took your damned time," Mitch grunted, his words drowned by the pop of bullets flying between them and Beau, overlaid by the whup-whup of helicopter rotors.

"You're a dirty-dealing double-crosser," Conrad screamed, veins standing out on his forehead.

"He is, isn't he?" Gillian said, sounding woozy. Mitch realized she'd climbed to her feet and now held McGrath's Sauer unsteadily in her hand. Mitch thought she was trying to train it on Conrad, but he couldn't be a hundred-percent positive she wasn't aiming at his head. Not until she whispered, "Thank God, Mitch," and gave him a trembling smile.

Bob Hall relieved Mitch of his burden by handcuffing Conrad's wrists behind his back. Other agents did the same with Beau, who hadn't given up easily. He and Sal, who'd waited in the car, both needed an ambulance. An agent phoned for one.

Only after McGrath was subdued did Gilly drop the gun. Mitch beckoned her with his own shaky arms. She sank into them, burying her face in the pulsing warmth of his neck. "Mitch, I thought you'd been sucked in by the promise of money. I thought you'd joined Conrad...." Great, gulping sobs shook her slender body.

Mitch pressed reassuring kisses along her tear-damp eyelids, and even softer kisses on her poor injured jaw. "I'm sorry you couldn't tell how badly I wanted to kill him with my bare hands."

"Lucky for all of us you didn't," Bob exclaimed. "Daryl's book alone won't stand up in court. I need live witnesses. Otherwise, some of this bunch might've slipped through our hands again."

"But not now?" Gillian asked anxiously. "A man named Calofonzo is the real leader. You'll get him, too, won't you?"

Bob Hall's grin lit up his craggy face. "You bet. With luck we'll have the motley crew sitting on death row in time for me to dance at your wedding."

Gillian still clutched Mitch's waist. She stepped back now and gaped at Hall.

"What? You *are* gonna marry the guy, aren't you? Fussing about you being pregnant is all he's done since Kevin Eloy landed in Brady, Texas, and had an enlightening chat with an old melon farmer."

Gillian went white and gasped.

"Wait," Hall said, frowning. "Was the part about the pregnancy a lie?"

Mitch looked so staggered by the possibility, Gilly felt even guiltier. "I—I'm not sure," she admitted. "My nausea could've come from nerves. I—I thought they were going to kill me. The farmer was one of them, Mitch. I knew he wouldn't pass on a message if I just said I loved you."

Mitch framed her swollen jaw between palms that still

stung from subduing Gilly's captor. "Do you? Love me?"

Feeling exposed and vulnerable in a room filled with strangers, Gilly's troubled gaze made a circuit of the agents staring at her. What if Mitch was hoping against hope that she wasn't pregnant—and that she wouldn't foolishly admit in front of all these men that she was crazy in love with him?

Her hesitation lasted just long enough for Mitch to feel her rejection. He unwound her arms from around his waist and put distance between them.

Gillian blinked furiously to block threatening tears. So much had happened in the last forty-eight hours. In the last two months, really. Her head ached, her jaw felt stiff and her body begged to sleep for a week.

There was no guarantee that she and Mitch hadn't been reacting to all the emotions surrounding her circumstances. After all, they'd met in the midst of intrigue. What did either of them know about the other? Did love happen that fast? Or had she simply fallen for him because her life with Daryl had been so devoid of passion? Were her feelings confused by grief for Katie—and for Daryl? Maybe they should back off and take a hard look at their lives. Mustering her courage, she faced Mitch. "New Orleans is my home. Yours is Arizona. Mitch—I..."

His dark regard silenced her. "You've decided to stay here?"

"I have a town house. And Daryl's business affairs must be in shambles."

"I need her here for the grand jury investigation," Bob quickly added. "You, too, Mitch. I'll have to have your testimony."

Mitch closed off every shred of feeling. He was good

at it. He'd done it many times over the years. "You and I both know it's not necessary for me to be here in person, Bob. I'll give you a sworn deposition before I leave town. Which will be soon, I hope. If one of your men will see that Gil...er, Mrs. McGrath gets home, I'll either hitch a ride to the airport with you or grab a cab. I can also have Ethan witness my deposition and overnight it to you all neatly stamped by Desert City P.D.'s notary."

Gillian didn't know why it felt as though her world had just split apart, since her life had been in chaos since she'd learned of her pregnancy with Katie. She prayed she could manage to hold on to her control long enough to leave with some pride. Swiftly, she gathered up her battered suitcase, along with the tattered emotions that made her Gillian Noelle McGrath. She hurried out, never once turning her eyes toward Mitch. If she did, she'd embarrass them all.

He watched her go in turmoil, not even attempting to remain dispassionate. He felt as if his living, breathing soul had been ripped out.

A voice broke through the foggy haze. "Don't tell me you're just going to walk away from Gillian after everything you went through to find her?" The pugnacious angle of Bob Hall's square jaw shouted his disbelief.

Mitch gave himself a mental shake. "For the record, Bob. She's the one doing the walking."

"Yeah, but—" the older man scratched his chin "—I'm not sure I know what happened here."

"Come on, Hall. You don't strike me as the cupid type. What's not to understand? The lady took a powder. We had an affair. It was good while it lasted. She's moving on."

"I'll tell you what boggles my mind. How a nice guy who knocked himself out trying to save this woman—

the same man who acted giddy as a kid over the prospect of becoming a dad—hell, I don't understand how someone like that can clam up, shut down and say *so long, it's been good to know ya.*"

"Will you run me to the airport or shall I call a cab?"

"Sure, I'll drive you. Why not? But I'm changing my opinion. You aren't a nice guy, after all."

AT HOME AGAIN, Mitch holed up alone at his ranch. He concentrated on expanding his herd. For six months, he avoided efforts by his friends to get through to him, and he avoided going into town. He refused Ethan and Regan's phone calls.

And he acted so surly whenever Ethan dropped by, that his closest friend stopped coming to see him.

Ethan Knight pieced together what information he could from reading the final FBI report submitted to his chief. It looked to him as if Mitch had left New Orleans a hero. And Gillian, the woman they all assumed he'd been nuts about, had been absolved of any wrongdoing. It should've ended happily for everyone involved. But it hadn't.

"Have you seen Mitch in town at all since he left here that night with Gillian?" Regan demanded of Ethan one night at dinner.

"You know I haven't. The fool's turned himself into a recluse. Last time I stopped by his ranch, Mitch looked really ragged. What made you ask now?" Ethan opened a package of baby biscuits and handed one to each of the four toddlers. Three had finally gotten the requisite number of teeth, and were caught up to other kids their age. Only Cara lagged behind, but she improved daily.

"I received a box from Gilly today. The clothes I lent her, plus a new jacket. She said mine got ripped by the men who kidnapped her. She apologized for taking so long, but she's had a lot on her plate. Her ex-husband's business was a legal mess.''

"So what's that got to do with Mitch?''

"Read her note, Ethan. She seems starved for information about him. From the way Flo and Bert talked, I had the impression Gillian dumped Mitch. Now I'm not so sure.''

Ethan scanned the note and frowned. "She asks one simple question here. *How's Mitch?*''

"Yeah. So?''

"So from that you gather she's pining away in New Orleans for my ex-friend. Ex because the dodo's quit calling, quit shaving and has become a damned hermit.''

"Really? He's quit shaving? There you go. They're both pining away. Ethan, it's up to us to get them together.''

"Oh, no.'' Ethan held up his hands. "Aren't we being tortured enough having three kids potty training and one cutting molars all at the same time?''

"Mmm. Oh, thank you, sweetheart. You just gave me the perfect reason to invite Gillian for a visit. Look at me. I can't handle potty-training three kiddies on my own. Woe is me,'' she drawled dramatically.

Ethan smiled and leaned over to kiss her lips. Angela gurgled something that sounded like "Dadee,'' and landed a spoonful of mashed potatoes smack in Ethan's eye. He wiped the mess away with his napkin. "Don't wait for letters to go back and forth,'' he muttered. "Wire her a ticket tomorrow.''

"I'm ahead of you—I already did. Or rather, Odella took care of those arrangements today. Gilly arrives on Friday at five o'clock. Can you pick her up at the airport on your way home from work?''

Ethan nodded dumbly while Regan flung her arms around him and delivered a smacking kiss on his nose. "I'll give you a better thank you tonight after we get the kids to bed," she promised without coyness, making his acceptance over being outmaneuvered a *lot* easier to accept.

ON FRIDAY, Ethan dashed into the local airport in time to hear a droning voice announce the arrival of Gilly's plane. He paced anxiously, wondering if Regan had done the wrong thing by inviting Gillian to visit. Maybe it was a dirty trick to play on Mitch.

Two things floored Ethan Knight about the woman who approached him. He would have let her pass without a glance had she not grabbed his arm and said his name. Last time he'd seen her she wasn't a blonde, nor had she been wearing a maternity smock that failed to conceal a rounded belly.

"I'm sorry to shock you, Ethan, and I see I have." Gilly's face flamed. "I expected Regan to meet me. My, er, uh…condition might have been easier to explain to a woman."

"You don't owe me any explanation." Ethan snatched up the overnight case she'd set atop a compact case on wheels. "Is this the extent of your luggage?"

"Yes. I know Regan doesn't really need my help with the quadruplets. And I'll be returning her ticket, of course. I don't need money, Ethan, not after settling Daryl's estate. What Regan's invitation did was light a fire under me. I realized I couldn't put off talking face-to-face with Mitch any longer." She chewed on her upper lip.

"In fact, I'd count it as a great favor, Ethan, if you'd

run me by his ranch and wait while I deliver a message. I shouldn't be long saying what needs to be said.''

Ethan's eyes settled on her expanding waistline. ''I wouldn't be too sure.'' As they walked out to his SUV, Ethan indulged in a bit of meddling—the very thing he accused Mitch of doing early on in his own relationship with Regan.

Stowing her bags in the back seat with Taz, Ethan casually brought up Mitch's unhappy childhood. ''He's always lacked a family to lean on, so to speak. Since he got back from New Orleans, he's cut himself off from all his friends. From everyone. He's hiding out, Gillian. And he's hurting,'' Ethan said, his tone bordering on accusatory.

Gilly listened. She didn't say anything.

Ethan chose the shortcut he and Mitch had used the day they caught her in Mitch's living room. Once again he drove as fast as the limit allowed.

Turning into Valetti's lane, Ethan slowed before he neared the end and stopped outside the fence. He and Gilly saw Mitch and Trooper leave the barn.

''He looks terrible,'' Gilly whispered. Her breath caught, and she quickly skimmed away tears.

''Sure you want me to wait?'' Ethan asked softly.

''Yes.'' Even as she whispered it, Gillian climbed from the vehicle.

Mitch saw her at once. While Trooper bounded forward to greet their visitor, Mitch hung back. His gaze swept over her a second time. His eyes left her beautiful face and skidded back to her belly. To the smock fluttering in the cold east wind.

His heart rate went up twenty points as joy and hope warred with a terrible fear that she'd come to ask him to sign release papers giving up all rights to his child.

Mitch knew the baby was his. He'd known back in Sedona the day she denied the possibility. He'd known when Eloy phoned in from Brady, Texas. He'd known in New Orleans, the day Gillian claimed her nausea was due to nerves. What he hadn't known was what in hell to do about it.

They met at the corner of his repaired fence. Trooper yipped at first one, and then the other, butting them playfully with his head.

Gilly patted the dog's silky ears. "Mitch..." She had a neat laundry list of things she'd prepared to say. Instead, she choked on a sob and said brokenly, "Oh, God, Mitch. I've—I've—missed you."

Her admission didn't sink in right away. The instant it did, Mitch tossed aside the argument he'd begun to compose, demanding a spot in his baby's life. "Same goes for me. Oh, Gilly... We need to talk."

"Noreen Malone came to New Orleans," Gilly blurted. "She helped me finalize Daryl's business holdings. Patrick is recovering. Slowly but steadily. We weren't to blame for the second attack on him. He telephoned Conrad, just to chat about Daryl's funeral and how things were going...."

"I know. He called me. So did Bob Hall. Everyone has, but you."

"I'm sorry. It's been hectic. I sold Daryl's house and furniture, and my town house. I put all my things in storage."

"Really? What are you going to do?" He didn't want to sound hopeful.

"Uh...Flo said my old job's there any time I want it. They hired someone but she's planning to go back to college and would like to work fewer hours."

"Wait tables all day in your condition? I don't think so."

"Then what?" A world of possibility hung on those two small words.

"Enough talk. It's time for action, Gilly." Closing the gap, Mitch gathered her against him and lifted her off her feet, all the while fusing their lips in a kiss that went on so long, Ethan tooted his car horn.

The longer they ignored him, the less sure he was about how to proceed. Digging out his cell phone, he called Regan.

"She's pregnant? That's exactly what I thought. For heavens sake, Ethan, leave her bags on Mitch's porch and come home. You can watch the kids while I round up some people to start planning Mitch and Gilly's wedding."

"Aren't you rushing things? They're not even engaged."

"Ah, my love. Soon. Odella and I have the most romantic wedding in mind. All we need is for Mitch and Gilly to give us the go-ahead."

IT WASN'T UNTIL late the next afternoon that anyone saw or heard from the couple. Phone messages between Mitch's friends and former co-workers ran hot and heavy.

Shortly after four o'clock, Regan saw them drive up and climb out of Mitch's Corvette. Not an easy feat for Gillian in her very pregnant state.

Calling to Odella, Regan hurried down the hall and threw open the door. She met them both with tears and outstretched arms. "Those sappy smiles you two are wearing can only be good news." She kept crying and patting Mitch's clean-shaven face.

Odella grinned over Regan's shoulder as she gripped

the hands of two toddlers staring shyly at the new arrivals.

"We're getting married," Mitch announced, turning to filter his fingers lovingly through Gillian's longer, silkier hair.

"This is the real me," Gilly exclaimed as she noticed Odella eying her from head to toe.

"It suits you," Regan exclaimed, tugging the couple inside. "And your coloring is perfect for a winter wedding." She and Odella alternately rattled off possibilities for flowers and dress colors. "Ethan's mom volunteered her home for the reception. They have a covered patio. If the weather holds, people can easily spill over onto it." She stopped in midsentence on seeing Mitch and Gilly exchange looks of dismay.

"Am I getting ahead of myself?"

"Would you and Ethan mind driving to Sedona to stand up with us?" Gilly asked. "We'd like to include Odella and Roger, as well. Also Bert and Flo. Bob Hall and some of the other agents. Noreen Malone's promised to bring Patrick. Mitch's sisters and their families are coming. Not his parents but that's no big surprise. And my mom and stepfather said they'd fly in. I can't believe it, but my mother said they'd look at buying a winter home here, what with the prospect of spending time with their grandchild." Gilly's fingers sought and found the bear fetish she wore—the necklace Mitch had bought her. The same one Conrad had broken when he threw her across the room. Having it repaired was the first thing she did when she thought she'd lost Mitch forever. Wearing it daily connected them in a way she couldn't begin to explain.

"Sedona is where we really fell hopelessly in love," she added. "This morning, Mitch phoned up there and found a church able to accommodate a small wedding next weekend.''

"How absolutely perfect," Odella said, hoisting two wide-eyed toddlers to her hips as she nudged Regan aside to make room for two more who teetered into the room wearing brand-new shoes. "I can't think of a better place in Arizona to pledge your love and cast aside old grief than among those ancient towering rocks," she said quietly.

"Exactly," Mitch and Gilly exclaimed. "You tell them the rest," she urged Mitch, rising on tiptoes to brush his lips with a feather-soft kiss.

He did so with difficulty, his attention lingering on Gilly's kissable mouth. "After our wedding service, I've arranged for a ceremony to inter Katie's ashes to a crypt. Bob Hall put me in touch with a stained-glass artist in Sedona. Today, I…we…commissioned her to design a window for the chapel. It's going to be patterned after Katie's baby quilt.''

"As a sort of memorial where we can go anytime and always know she's safe," Gillian said. "Safe and never forgotten."

Regan and Odella began to cry openly.

"No tears," Mitch remonstrated. "We intend Katie's window to be a place of celebration. After all, she brought Gilly and me together." The two gazed into each other's eyes and began to lean closer.

Regan and Odella tiptoed away, leaving the couple engrossed in a not-so-chaste kiss that boded well for the long-term outcome of their love.

"I'm such a sucker for happy endings," Odella sighed.

"Me, too." Regan stole one last look at her husband's best friend. Mitch's lips were on Gillian's, while his right hand lightly cradled their unborn child.

Watch out for exciting new covers on your favourite books!

Every month we bring you romantic fiction that you love!
Now it will be even easier to find your favourite book with our **fabulous new covers!**

We've listened to you – our loyal readers, and as of **August publications** you'll find that...

We've improved:

☑ *Variety between the books*
☑ *Ease of selection*
☑ *Flashes or symbols to highlight mini-series and themes*

We've kept:

☑ *The familiar cover colours*
☑ *The series names you know*
☑ *The style and quality of the stories you love*

Be sure to look out for next months titles so that you can preview our exciting new look.

❤ SILHOUETTE® SUPERROMANCE™

AVAILABLE FROM 21ST MAY 2004

A BABY OF HER OWN Brenda Novak

Nine Months Later

Delaney Lawson wants a baby…and it might just be that handsome stranger Connor Armstrong will be the man to provide one. Afterwards she wonders if she's done the right thing, but now it's too late. Because she's pregnant— and Connor is her neighbour!

THE FARMER'S WIFE Lori Handeland

When Kim Luchetti left home, she didn't think she'd ever be back to stay. But her father is ill, and Brian Riley, her ex-boyfriend, has had an accident. Her guilt over their complicated past stops her from abandoning him again, and she agrees to stay—temporarily…or so she thinks!

THE PERFECT MUM Janice Kay Johnson

Under One Roof

Everyone thinks Kathleen is perfect—and she's beginning to wonder if that's a good thing. After all, it didn't help her marriage and it might have something to do with her daughter's illness. And now she's met Logan Carr…and he's making her doubt her priorities.

MAGGIE'S GUARDIAN Anna Adams

Count on a Cop

Tessa Gabriel is the prime suspect in her best friend David's murder. Her ex-husband Noah is a homicide cop, and he's determined to find the real killer. But if he's going to succeed, he and Tessa will have to learn how to work together—and how to *be* together.

AVAILABLE FROM 21ST MAY 2004

Sensation™

Passionate and thrilling romantic adventures

SHOOTING STARR Kathleen Creighton
LAST MAN STANDING Wendy Rosnau
ON DEAN'S WATCH Linda Winstead Jones
SAVING DR RYAN Karen Templeton
THE LAST HONOURABLE MAN Vickie Taylor
NORTHERN EXPOSURE Debra Lee Brown

Special Edition™

Life, love and family

SHOWDOWN! Laurie Paige
THE SUMMER HOUSE Susan Mallery & Teresa Southwick
HER BABY SECRET Victoria Pade
BALANCING ACT Lilian Darcy
EXPECTING THE CEO'S BABY Karen Rose Smith
MAN BEHIND THE BADGE Pamela Toth

Intrigue™

Breathtaking romantic suspense

ROCKY MOUNTAIN MAVERICK Gayle Wilson
HER SECRET ALIBI Debra Webb
CLAIMING HIS FAMILY Ann Voss Peterson
ATTEMPTED MATRIMONY Joanna Wayne

Desire™ 2-in-1

Passionate, dramatic love stories

SCENES OF PASSION Suzanne Brockmann
A BACHELOR AND A BABY Marie Ferrarella

HER CONVENIENT MILLIONAIRE Gail Dayton
THE GENTRYS: CAL Linda Conrad

WARRIOR IN HER BED Cathleen Galitz
COWBOY BOSS Kathie DeNosky

Spence Harrison has to solve the mystery of his past so that he can be free to love the woman who has infiltrated his heart.

The Country Club

FE)219

FREE!
2 Books
and a surprise gift!

We would like to take this opportunity to thank you for reading this Silhouette® book by offering you the chance to take TWO more specially selected titles from the Superromance™ series absolutely FREE! We're also making this offer to introduce you to the benefits of the Reader Service™—

★ FREE home delivery
★ FREE gifts and competitions
★ FREE monthly Newsletter
★ Books available before they're in the shops
★ Exclusive Reader Service discount

Accepting these FREE books and gift places you under no obligation to buy; you may cancel at any time, even after receiving your free shipment. Simply complete your details below and return the entire page to the address below. *You don't even need a stamp!*

YES! Please send me 2 free Superromance books and a surprise gift. I understand that unless you hear from me, I will receive 4 superb new titles every month for just £3.59 each, postage and packing free. I am under no obligation to purchase any books and may cancel my subscription at any time. The free books and gift will be mine to keep in any case.

U4ZEE

Ms/Mrs/Miss/Mr ....Initials...
BLOCK CAPITALS PLEASE

Surname..

Address..

....

....Postcode ....

Send this whole page to:
UK: The Reader Service, FREEPOST CN81, Croydon, CR9 3WZ
EIRE: The Reader Service, PO Box 4546, Kilcock, County Kildare (stamp required)